"Have  other than ⎯⎯⎯⎯⎯... She shrugged. "Different? *More?*"

He stretched his free hand across the table and held both of hers.

"I have what's called eidetic memory," she said. "I can recall memories, dates, full books of information after reading or seeing them one time. I can tell you what day of the week a certain date fell in any year, and I know where I've been every single day of my life."

"I have to think that's a blessing because of your occupation, but I'm sensing you feel it's also, what? A curse? A burden?"

"An inconvenience more than anything." She shook her head and dropped her gaze to their joined hands. "Being the smart girl in class was fun in middle school. My home life wasn't exactly normal, and there were so many times I was made fun of because my clothes came from secondhand stores, or my shoes were a little too big when I walked. Being smart made me"—she shrugged again—"special. Not so much in high school and college. Guys don't routinely like a girl who's smarter than they are. Their egos can't take it."

"Not true," he said immediately. "At least, not in my case or in any of my brothers. My sister-in-law and her own sisters are all wickedly smart, much smarter than my brothers about certain things."

"But I'm sure they're all gorgeous, as well."

"I can't deny that because they are. But so are you, Lexi."

Praise for Peggy Jaeger

Review for A PRIDE OF BROTHERS: RICK
"Readers had better have a fan or the air-conditioner on while reading this book because it gets HOT! The chemistry between Abby and Rick is absolutely off the charts."

~*InD'Tale Magazine*

"The romance is HOT HOT HOT! By the time I finished, I was hyperventilating with an erratic pulse. Such a great reading experience, I can't wait for the next book in the series."

~*N.N. Light's Book Heaven*

A Pride of Brothers: Aiden

by

Peggy Jaeger

A Pride of Brothers, Book 2

This is a work of fiction. Names, characters, places, and incidents are either the product of the author's imagination or are used fictitiously, and any resemblance to actual persons living or dead, business establishments, events, or locales, is entirely coincidental.

A Pride of Brothers: Aiden

COPYRIGHT © 2021 by Margaret-Mary Jaeger

All rights reserved. No part of this book may be used or reproduced in any manner whatsoever without written permission of the author or The Wild Rose Press, Inc. except in the case of brief quotations embodied in critical articles or reviews.
Contact Information: info@thewildrosepress.com

Cover Art by *Kristian Norris*

The Wild Rose Press, Inc.
PO Box 708
Adams Basin, NY 14410-0708
Visit us at www.thewildrosepress.com

Publishing History
First Edition, 2021
Trade Paperback ISBN 978-1-5092-3827-9
Digital ISBN 978-1-5092-3828-6

Published in the United States of America

Dedication

To the Public Library Ladies who fostered my love of reading and writing all during my childhood…I wouldn't be a writer if it weren't for all your love, support, and kindness. You are my heroes.

Chapter 1

"Here you go, sir." The waitress dropped Aiden's order next to his beer and placed the billfold alongside it. "I'll take this when you're ready." With a distracted smile, she moved to the next customer along the busy airport bar.

Tired, hungry, and itching to get home, Aiden bit into his preflight meal and all but sighed. A greasy burger, an ice-cold beer, and thoughts of his own bed were the only things keeping him sane right now. Less than three hours ago, he'd given his report to the client, then managed to book a last-minute flight home.

Home.

One of his two favorite four-letter words, both of which he'd been missing of late.

What his brother Josh had billed as a quick turnaround job had turned into a dumpster fire straight out of the gate. Unable to get to the root of the problem from his New York office, Aiden had flown to Atlanta to work directly from the client's home turf. The promised quick resolution morphed into two weeks, then eight, until Aiden finally caught a break and identified who'd been bilking the company's corporate funds.

After he'd handed over his detailed report, naming the CFO's much younger wife and her computer-hacker lover as the culprits, and providing irrefutable proof,

Aiden walked out of the owner's office and cabbed it straight to the airport.

With the prospect of a few days off before heading back to the private investigations firm he co-owned with his brothers, Aiden ate and flipped through his mental Rolodex for who could help him satisfy the other four-letter word occupying his mind. It had been a while since he'd enjoyed a woman's company, since he never mixed business with pleasure.

A long while.

He took a generous pull on his beer, let his gaze drift around the crowded bar, and indulged in one of his favorite pastimes, people watching.

Or as his older brother Dylan referred to it, asshole surveillance.

Since he was in an airport bar where happy hour occurred twenty-four seven, Dylan's description was the more accurate one.

The three middle-aged women sitting across from him, passing a cell phone back and forth, all the while laughing like they'd had more than a few cosmos, told him they were heading home from a fun-filled girls' getaway and reliving their antics through selfie scrolling.

The thirtyish guy a few stools down from them, a half-finished beer in front of him and a cell phone propped next to his laptop, screamed *workaholic businessman* trying to get a little more accomplished before heading off to his next meeting. The guy's attention flicked back and forth from the computer screen to the phone, as if willing it to ring.

Two flight attendants in uniform huddled in a corner booth sipping from coffee cups, a guy in a pilot's uniform seated with them. Since they all looked awake and fresh, Aiden figured they were waiting to head to their first flight of the day.

Overhead, the arrival and departure announcements were white noise in the already cacophonous terminal. Babies crying, kids whining, their harried parents arguing as they sped between connecting flights, were all a subtle hum. Aiden had the unique ability to shut it all out, quiet the racket, and concentrate his attention on whatever he needed, or wanted, to.

Right now, it was the smiling redhead on the other side of the bar and her drinking companion, who behaved like a man who'd recently returned from being lost in the Sahara for days. The moment he banged one empty glass down on the counter, he signaled to the bartender to pour him another. With each refill, the redhead got a little closer until she was a sigh away from sitting in the guy's lap. They'd already been seated when Aiden took his stool and ordered so he didn't know if they'd arrived together or had become fast and furious drinking buddies. Well, the guy was drinking. The redhead appeared to be enjoying sparkling water from what he could see.

From fifteen feet away, Aiden noted the concentrated way she pressed against her *friend*, talking close to his ear, one hand flirtatiously snaking up and down his expensive suit sleeve, the other hidden from view under the bar top.

That hand was either rubbing the guy's thigh, or trying to find its way into his pocket to lift his wallet. The latter notion got tossed when he spotted the wallet sitting next to the half-empty beer glass.

So, the thigh it was.

Lucky bastard.

Long lashes framed eyes tilting up a bit in the corners. Cheekbones modeled from ripe apples pulled up when she smiled, showing perfect white teeth. A cascade of shiny red curls drifted below her shoulder blades. When she dragged one finger behind her ear, tucking a tendril, and then gave the lobe a quick squeeze, Aiden's fingers tightened around his beer glass. The move, innately sensual, had the tips of his fingers itching to follow her lead and run them through her hair, down the slim column of her throat, across the swell of her breasts.

She leaned in and whispered something that had the guy's eyes widening and an expectant smirk slashing his face. A seductive grin crossed her lush mouth, and for a hot second Aiden's gut tightened, imagining what those full lips would feel like pressed against his.

Damn. He really needed to get…home.

Drunk Guy tugged a card from his open wallet and a quick movement from the redhead's hidden hand had Aiden squinting. She patted the guy's forearm and placed a swift peck to his cheek, leaving a crimson imprint in her wake. Lifting her purse from the bar, she hopped from the stool, then sauntered away while he motioned for the bartender to settle the tab.

Aiden tracked her as she sashayed away, tugging a small sky-blue roll-along suitcase behind her. Her short, formfitting dress showed off half her thighs and the length of her toned calves, made even longer by the three-inch icepick heels on her feet. As a man who appreciated many things in life, one of which was the way a woman walked, Aiden would bet his year-end partner bonus the redhead's sensual, smooth gait was ingrained in her DNA like her eye color.

The attention of every male in the place followed her. If she was aware of the effect she had, she gave no indication. All too soon she was swallowed up in the moving crowd.

Drunk Guy signed a receipt, a smarmy leer on his face, one Aiden recognized well.

Somebody's planning on getting lucky.

Unfortunately, it wasn't him.

While the other guy finished his beer, Aiden did the same, polished off his burger, then put two twenties in the folder for a twenty-three-dollar tab. With his duffle slung over his shoulder, he proceeded to his departure gate.

With forty-five minutes left before boarding, he stopped by the airport newsstand to grab a packet of gum, a bottle of overpriced water, and the current edition of his favorite sports magazine.

The newsstand was situated directly opposite the toilets, so Aiden made his way to the men's restroom, took care of business, then strolled toward his gate.

Drunk Guy stood outside the bar, his forehead a mass of grooves and trenches, his mouth pressed into a thin line filled with annoyance as he clutched his phone and turned his head right and left a number of times.

Aiden didn't think he was waiting for a break in the walking crowd to move forward.

Stood you up, didn't she?

With a silent chuckle, he shifted his bag and kept moving.

Eschewing the people mover for the added exercise he needed to offset the immobility of the next two hours in the air, Aiden's gaze roamed the terminal while he ambled along. He made it his business to always know the layout around him in order to stay alert for potential dangers or for situations that could escalate out of control in a heartbeat. More times than he gave himself credit for, he'd been able to stop an event from turning ugly by sizing up the mood of a room and acting with swift efficiency to counteract a negative outcome.

While panning the crowd, his attention was drawn to a person walking a few yards ahead of him.

Something was familiar about the way the smooth glide of the walker eating up the space in front of her tickled his memory. She moved like the redhead from the bar, one hip gently rolling with a step, then the other doing the same. But it wasn't the redhead with the flowing curls in front of him. This woman had a short cap of blonde hair that didn't come anywhere near her neck and stood stick straight. She wasn't dressed in a second-skin dress either, but a plain white short-sleeved shirt and a pair of straight-legged jeans. Shiny loafers shod her feet, not do-me stilettos.

The redhead had been tall, the woman in front of him, a pixie. She couldn't be more than five-two.

But that walk...

Aiden's gaze tracked downward and, as the woman turned right and moved into a gate seating area, he saw the suitcase she tugged behind her.

A small sky-blue roll-along.

Well, now.

He glanced up at the gate number she'd turned into, and *surprise, surprise*, it was the same as his. She claimed a seat at the end of a row, then tucked her suitcase under the chair, her boarding pass clutched in her hand.

Curiosity flowed through him. Could it be the same woman? The outward appearance said no, but the walk said…hell, yeah.

The waiting area was packed. He'd been lucky to grab the last available seat and hadn't balked at the first-class price in his zeal to get home. He'd have Josh tack the cost onto the client's final bill. Aiden weaved his way through his co-travelers until he stood a whisper behind the woman. Enough so he could observe her without her being aware he was.

The cut of those cheeks and the angle of her jaw convinced him she was the woman from the bar. Or if it wasn't, she had a twin.

The notion died when she lifted her hand and dragged it around and behind an ear, the hair grazing her cheek now tucked, and gave the lobe a gentle pinch.

Intrigued, Aiden glanced down at her boarding pass, then made his way over to the check-in agent. With all the added security checks and balances now making air travel so stringent, he wasn't sure his plan would work.

Five minutes later, courtesy of a subtle stretch of the truth, a quick flash of his investigator's license, and a smile he knew how to use to be charming, he had a new seat assignment. As he leaned a shoulder against a column and waited to board the plane, he grinned when the elderly woman who'd been summoned up to the counter found herself in possession of a first-class seat at an economy price. Her stunned expression had been worth the deception.

When it came time for him to board, he tossed his duffle over his shoulder again, waited until the fake redhead queued up, and then took a place in line a few travelers behind her.

This promised to be an interesting flight home.

****

Once she'd stowed her suitcase and secured her safety belt, Lexi let out the breath she'd been holding for hours and allowed her body to relax for the first time in days.

Everything, thankfully, had gone as planned. Now all she needed to do was get home and plug the information she'd pilfered from Peter Smith into a search engine.

A shudder of disgust slipped down her spine at the memory of his sweaty, sticky hands caressing her bare arm in the airport bar. She'd endured his repulsive touch, swallowing her repugnance and keeping her smile in place, because it got her one step closer to her objective.

The moment she'd walked away from him with the excuse to freshen up, she'd run to the airport bathroom and scrubbed her hands and forearms with scalding water and disinfecting soap until her pale skin glowed cherry-red.

A quick stop in a stall to remove her seduction-wear and wig, she then stuffed them into her carry-on and changed into her comfortable, everyday clothes and shoes. After she swiped at her face with a disposable makeup-remover cloth, she glanced at herself in the mirror, finger combed her short hair, and headed for her gate.

When she happened to walk right past her quarry as he stood outside the bar, furtively glancing right and left, she held back a self-satisfied smile. It wasn't until right then, when Smith looked straight at her and not one iota of recognition crossed his face, she'd known her disguise had truly worked.

If asked, he would only be able to describe what she'd shown him: a busty *femme fatale* looking for a little fast action.

Finally allowing a small smile of triumph free, Lexi settled into her seat and glanced out the cabin window.

When movement from the adjoining seat jostled her, she turned her attention from watching the bags being loaded onto the plane to find ridiculously long legs folding into the seat, and then two hundred well-packed pounds of male settled in next to her.

While he fastened his safety buckle, Lexi snuck a quick side-eye his way. He looked…familiar. It hit her a millisecond later.

The guy from the bar.

He'd been seated across from them, quietly nursing a beer and eating while she'd been seducing Smith. In all honesty, he was impossible to miss. From those piercing, crystal-blue eyes to the pelt of sable hair in desperate need of a trim, Lexi would need to be clinically visually impaired not to have noticed him. Defined cheeks cut from marble sloped into a square clean-shaven jaw, then tapered down to shoulders spanning a yard and then some. From the waist down he'd been hidden, but if his height could be measured using his torso as a guide stick, he was at least six foot, maybe more.

She'd caught a glimpse of him when she'd pulled her phone from her bag and hesitated at the thought he'd caught what she was doing. When his gaze shifted and trailed around the rest of the bar, she took the opportunity to do what she'd come to do.

Had he seen her take the pictures? The phone had been hidden under the bar rail and clasped in her hand close to her thighs. She'd practiced the move dozens of times, holding the phone in such a way she didn't have to look at it to know where to press to snap a photo, until she was satisfied she could do it without being detected. Smith, she felt certain, hadn't realized what she'd done.

Had this man?

After a final tug on his belt, he glanced her way, caught her staring at him, and smiled.

Oh...*my*.

His eyes were even more blue and enticing than she recalled. From across a bar, their true power hadn't been this apparent. Nor had the subtle laugh lines fanning from the corners of those spectacular eyes. A full and perfect mouth called to mind the busts of Greek and Roman gods she'd researched for a paper in graduate school. Proud warriors with the power to enchant a woman into supplication with just a look.

As he stared over at her through those dreamy eyes with his lips tugged into a disarming grin, heat flowed across her face and shot downward, warming the inside and outside of every inch of her body. Lexi reminded herself spontaneous combustion wasn't a real *thing*, despite the fact her internal temperature was inching up.

"Everything okay?"

And of course he had a voice that went hand in hand with the rest of him. Deep and seductive, warm and tantalizing.

After a few seconds, the embarrassing realization

she hadn't responded made her customary nerves skyrocket, and her trivia-laced brain shot out the first thing that came to it. "Did you know roughly a third of all people have some form of aviophobia?"

His eyes crinkled in the corners as his smile broadened. "Are you part of the minority or the majority of fliers?"

Lexi blinked, surprised he knew the meaning of the word. "I'm not afraid to fly."

"Me, either. I'm Aiden." He offered his hand.

After a quick glance down at it, she extended her own. Telling herself again self-immolation wasn't real, she was, nonetheless, thrilled when she didn't burst into flames from the warmth seeping from his hand into hers. Like slipping into a bubbling hot spring, her entire body was engulfed in a delicious liquid heat.

She swallowed, then said, "Lex."

His head tilted to one side, and his eyebrows slammed together. "You don't look like a super villain."

Charmed despite her nerves, she shook her head. "Short for Alexis. And no, my surname isn't Luther."

"Ah, well that explains it. Alexis is much prettier than Lex."

Heat rushed to her cheeks. "Most people call me Lexi," she said before she could stop herself.

Aiden nodded. "Pretty, too."

Their gazes dropped to their still joined hands. With another of those tantalizing grins, Aiden released his hold but not before giving hers a tiny squeeze.

The plane was filling fast, most of the seats now occupied, a few stragglers still in the central aisle, the flight crew ushering them along.

"Is New York your final destination?" Aiden asked. "Or are you connecting?"

"Final," she said, surprising herself. She never divulged information to strangers. Nerves beat within her again, and before she could stop the words from spewing, she said, "Did you know one point six three million people reside in Manhattan alone?"

"Well, I'm one of them, and I can't wait to get home."

When he sighed, something in Lexi responded to his wistfulness. "Have you been away long?"

"Too long."

Before she could ask why, the overhead announcements started. Because knowledge was the key to everything, Lexi gave all her attention to the flight attendants as they went through the safety precautions, even though she had them memorized.

Trying to be covert, she snaked her hand under the seat when told the cushion could be used as a floatation device during a water landing, just to make sure it was there and at the ready. She pulled the inflight instruction card from the pouch in front of her and took special notice of where the other exit doors were situated.

"You've flown before, right?" Aiden asked when the crew finished.

"Many times." She turned and found the ghost of a grin tripping across his mouth.

"Do you always listen so intently to the safety speech?"

"Of course. Don't you?"

He shook his head. "The narrative never changes. I could repeat it in my sleep."

She could too, but it didn't prevent her from actively listening to it each time.

A flight attendant, who'd been walking down the aisle assuring the overhead compartments were closed, stopped at their row.

"Hi." Her smile broadened when she lit on Aiden. "You two are seated next to the emergency exit door, and I want to make sure you know what to do in the event we need to access it."

She prattled on with the expectations, then asked, "Are you comfortable assuming that responsibility?"

Lexi said yes immediately.

"Thank you, and enjoy your flight." The last part was directed at her seatmate before the attendant turned to the couple across the aisle and started her spiel again.

Aiden's smile stayed in place when he turned back to her. With an eyebrow raised and the corners of his eyes narrowed, he said, "I get the feeling you requested this seat."

"I did."

"Should I be worried?"

It took her a moment to see past the humor lacing his words to the steely caution in his eyes.

"No, no. God, no. It's not *that.*"

The other eyebrow joined its mate. "Then...?"

Lexi swallowed and felt like she'd been pulled into the principal's office to explain an adolescent prank.

"Research shows the safest place to be in the event of"—she lowered her voice and shifted closer so her words wouldn't carry—"an inflight emergency, is sitting by this door. I can stay calm in an emergency, so I figure I'd rather leave my chances of surviving up to me than to a total stranger who might crack under pressure."

He stared at her a few beats, and she'd give the last chocolate candy she had in her secret stash in her office to know what he was thinking.

He leaned in closer, as she had to him. Her gaze dropped to his mouth when he asked, "Do you always like to be in control?"

For the first time in her adult life, Lexi couldn't speak. All the statistics she had running rampant in her brain about the psychological impacts of OCD and control issues stayed locked inside her. Her mouth fell open, but nothing came out. When Aiden's gaze flicked down to her parted lips, lingered for a moment, then dragged back up in time for her to catch his pupils dilate, she slammed her mouth shut and took a deep breath.

The thought he was flirting drifted into her mind and was quickly shooed away. Men didn't flirt with Alexis Buckley. The question came because he assumed she had some nefarious reason for wanting the emergency seat. In this day and age, who could blame him? Crazies came in all shapes and forms. And genders.

Lexi took another breath and then called forth her most professional voice, the one she used with recalcitrant students, annoying professors, and anyone who needed a firm hand.

"I've found," she said, happy her voice was controlled and modulated, just the way she liked it, "it's easier, and best, to rely on myself when situations arise that call for some kind of definitive action. If that's what you mean by being in control, then, yes."

She met his appraising stare with calm and cool

eyes and hoped that would be the end of it.

"Good to know," he said, just as the captain came over the loud speaker.

The next few minutes were spent in preparing for takeoff. Her row mate pulled a bottle of water and a magazine from the bag he'd stowed under the seat in front of him, then shoved the bag back in place before the final call for departure came.

As the plane's engines gunned and came up to speed for lift off, Lexi closed her eyes and calmed herself by mentally repeating the theories and principles of aerodynamics. Lift, gravitational force, thrust, and drag all combined to lend credence to the fact this multi-ton aircraft could climb into the sky and…fly. Right as they achieved coasting height and speed, Bernoulli's principle crossed her mind.

"I thought you weren't afraid to fly."

"I'm not." She opened her eyes and turned to him.

How was it possible for a grin to look patronizing and yet so damn sexy at the same time?

His gaze flicked down to her hands. When she followed suit, she found them grasping the armrest, her knuckles blanched of all color, her nails digging into the plastic.

Embarrassment heated her cheeks while she relaxed her grip, then moved her hands to her lap, where she folded them.

The sexy quotient on his face increased.

"Flying is the easy part, right?" he asked, conversationally. "It's the taking off that's stressful."

"The landing, too," she admitted.

"So," he said, crossing his arms over his substantial chest. The fabric pulled across his shoulders and gave her a view of the definition of his covered biceps. "What brought you to Atlanta, business or pleasure?"

"Business."

He nodded. "Did it go well?"

Exactly as planned.

"Yes."

Another nod. "Good for you. I bet it feels good to be going home. I know it does for me."

"You said you were away for a while?"

"Two months. Felt like two years. You?"

"Oh, not long. Just a few days."

"Quick turnaround, then?"

"Yes."

Careful. You don't want to be giving too much info away. It's a sure bet he doesn't recognize you from the bar.

Aiden pulled his water bottle from the holder and took a long pull. It reminded her she had her own drink stowed above them in her roll-along she'd forgotten to take out prior to being seated.

"I wish they'd turn the seat belt sign off," she said, glancing up at the still illuminated warning light, then out over the headrests of the seats in front of them. "I want to get my water from my carry-on. I can't believe I forgot to take it out before we took off. Did you know the humidity levels on a plane are sometimes less than 20 percent? You can get on at your departure site, and by the time you land, your skin can be dry and flaky and your mouth parched. Dehydration is one of the leading causes of headaches."

Aiden reached into his shirt pocket, extracted a packet of gum, then held it out to her. With a lopsided smirk she thought could charm the pants off the grumpiest female members of humanity, he said, "Have a couple of these until you can get to it. It'll keep your mouth…moist."

Why did everything he say sound as if it had a sexy, double meaning? And that he knew it did and said it anyway?

She took the package, willing herself to stop blushing like some virginal maiden in an old-fashioned historical romance novel. After popping two pieces of the mint gum into her mouth, she handed the package back to him. "Thanks."

"Any time." He placed the pack into his shirt pocket, never taking a piece for himself, and pulled out his magazine.

While he was engrossed in it, Lexi folded her hands into her lap again and categorized everything she needed to do once she got back to her apartment.

What she wouldn't give to have help with it all. But in asking for aid, from anyone, she was potentially putting them at risk for arrest or, at the very least, professional suicide.

No, better she do everything herself, try to find out as much as she could on her own rather than subject anyone she knew to censure. She'd just need to use all her skills in ways she'd never needed to before.

The Atlanta police had been no help and had dismissed her concerns outright. Without tangible proof, something she could present to them to confirm her suspicions and get them to investigate, they'd regarded her as if her imagination had run off the rails. The detective she'd spoken to had come right out and told her she should accept the evidence in front of her.

Moron.

Zoe's employer had been equally as useless, claiming they had no knowledge of anything she'd been doing, or involved in, on her own time.

Oh, Zoe.

With a mental wooden spoon, Lexi beat the sadness away that sprang up every time she pictured her sister's face. She shoved down her emotions and with a determined nod, snapped out of her gloominess.

Think. Research. Plan. Execute. That quartet had gotten her through all the horrible events of her life and had given her the wherewithal to succeed when failure had been the only foreseeable option.

First things first. She had to upload the picture of Smith's credit card and his driver's license to her computer and then try to download his current billing statements. It shouldn't be too hard to access now that she had the information.

Then she needed to find a connection, a link, *something*, to prove his involvement with Zoe.

The memory of Smith's fingers trailing down her bare arm had her shuddering again. The man was a pig. The desire to notify his wife and let her know exactly what a disgusting waste of a husband she had, moved through her brain, then quickly exited. To do so she'd have to explain her role in discovering how she knew he was a cheater.

Better to keep herself out of the conversation and let the poor woman remain ignorant.

"Cold?" Aiden asked.

"What?" She turned and blinked a few times.

"I asked if you're cold. You're shivering."

"I am?" She glanced down and noted goose pimples on her bared forearms. Her nipples had turned to pebbles and were visible through her bra and blouse. Mortified, she shielded them by crossing her arms over her chest.

"Want me to turn off the blower?" Aiden pointed to the panel above them. "It's on full blast. I'm taller than you and can reach it easier."

Lexi wasn't cold, but there was no way she could admit what had caused her visceral reaction, not without embarrassing herself by relating the truth of what she'd done. She bit down on a corner of her lip and nodded. Aiden stretched an arm up and over her to rotate the blower to the off position. To reach it he leaned over into her personal space, and the shoulder closest to hers bumped against her arm.

The goose bumps intensified tenfold from the exquisite—albeit brief—sensation of his shirt sliding along her arm.

The task completed, Aiden sat back and gifted her a smile. "Better?"

Lexi nodded again, swallowed, then in typical nervous fashion, said, "The *arrectoris pili* muscles in our bodies control our hair follicles. Whenever adrenaline is stimulated in our systems, the muscles contract and cause the hairs to stand erect, giving us goose bumps."

"You don't say?"

His eyes widened a hair, and when his gaze settled on hers, she couldn't discern if he was secretly attempting not to laugh or if he was truly interested.

Her palms turned sweaty under his perusal. No man had ever looked at her with such an all-consuming curiosity before.

Nodding again, she licked her desert-dry lips and

added, "They're called goose bumps because they resemble a goose or a turkey's skin after their feathers are plucked. The tiny bumps are where the feathers were situated."

After digesting the info for a moment, he asked, "Why aren't they called turkey bumps, then?"

She stared at him, unable to find an answer in the encyclopedia of knowledge stored insider her brain.

His grin broadened across his handsome face, and the humor dancing in his eyes had her breath catching. Leaning in a little closer he said, "Sorry. I couldn't resist."

"Resist what?"

Aiden shifted so his body was turned toward her, not only his head. "Teasing you."

Dammit, he *had* been laughing at her.

"I think I've learned more stuff about"—he lifted a hand and swiped it gently in the air—"*stuff* since I've been sitting here with you than I've learned in the entire past year. You must clean up at trivia night."

The blush running up her neck settled on her cheeks, scorching her. How could she admit the last time she'd been in a bar she'd been fifteen? And the reason was because she needed to haul her drunken mother off a stool before the woman did something she'd regret—like bring the wrong man home. Again.

"Sorry," she said. "I tend to spew out arcane things when I'm nervous."

Her blush intensified. Why had she revealed the one trait about herself she disliked the most?

"Don't be sorry. I think it's great. There's nothing sexier than a smart woman."

Yeah, right. You look like the kind of guy who

goes for a woman with brains. She averted her eyes so he wouldn't see her roll them.

"What do you for a living?" he asked. "You've got to be some kind of teacher or researcher. Anyone who knows so much about so much has to be. Smarts like yours shouldn't be wasted."

The compliment should have pleased her, but didn't. Just once in her life she'd like to be seen as something more than a brain full of knowledge and facts.

"I'm a librarian," she told him. "Actually, I've got a doctorate in library science."

Aiden whistled. "All the librarians I ever knew wore glasses and were in their eighties."

Charmed again, she tried not to smile but found it difficult. "Spent a lot of time in a library, did you? What for? Detention?"

His laugh sent her pili muscles contracting again.

"Sometimes, can't deny it. But mostly for pleasure. I would have spent a lot more time there, gladly, if the librarians looked like you."

Where was a mirror when you needed one? She imagined her face was the color of ripe strawberries about now from the amount of heat blazing them.

She was saved from further embarrassment when the seat belt sign finally turned off.

"You want to get your stuff?" he asked, already unbuckling his safety belt.

"If you don't mind." A quick glance down the aisle showed the flight crew already nearing with the drinks and snacks cart. "I don't want to hold them up."

While he stood in the aisle, she shimmied from her seat to his, then stood. Toe to toe, her assessment of his height was proven. He had to be over a foot taller than her.

"Which bin?" he asked.

She pointed and he opened it.

"The blue one," she told him.

Once she had everything from it she wanted, he hefted it back in place, secured the bin, then they both sat again.

"Thank you." She took a long sip from the bottle, a sigh breaking from deep within her at the cool, fresh taste of the lemon water she'd filled it with before leaving the hotel.

"Wetter now?" he asked.

Lexi choked and coughed the last sip. Gasping, she glared at him, suspicious the innocent expression on his face was anything but. It quickly morphed to concern.

"You okay?" he asked.

"Fine." She recapped the water, then pulled the seat table down to stow it.

After the flight attendants had wheeled the cart passed their row, dropping off minuscule bags of pretzels, Aiden asked her, "So what library do you work in?"

"Not so much work, as oversee," she said, then named the university library she was attached to.

That low whistle shot from him again. "Impressive. One of my brothers went to college there." He popped a few pretzels in his mouth. After swallowing he added, "And I can tell he didn't spend any time in the library."

"How do you know that?"

"Because if he had he would have mentioned the hot librarian running it."

When her skin began to heat again, she diverted the

conversation away from herself. "You have just the one brother?"

"Two others, and one, well, pseudo-adopted one. He was never legally adopted by my parents, but they took him in when he was eight and he lived with us until he went out on his own. He's my older brother's best friend and one of my partners."

"Partners?"

Aiden nodded. "My brothers, my brother-in-law, and Rick, my almost-adopted brother, all run our own company."

"That's a lot of testosterone in one place," she said, then blushed scarlet. "Sorry. That was rude."

"It really wasn't, and you're right." His sigh reached all the way across their seats and touched her. "Working with family is great. It can also be a pain in the ass. You can never get away from one another. Always up in each other's business. Personal privacy goes out the window, which is ridiculous considering what we do."

It sounded wonderful. She'd have given anything to have had that kind of relationship with her sister.

"What about you? Got any sibs?"

A swift stab of sorrow sliced through her heart. You'd think by now the pain would start to ebb. But it hadn't.

"Hey." Aiden touched her arm. "You okay? I lost you there for a second."

Concern danced across his grooved brow and lowered voice.

"Yes, sorry. I'm fine." A small throat clear, then she blinked back the tears she refused to let go. She took a breath. "A sister. I…had. A sister. She died. A few weeks ago."

"Saying I'm sorry never seems enough."

She nodded.

"Was she…sick?"

Healthy as a horse.

"It was sudden." *Gone in a heartbeat.* "It's why I was in Atlanta. She lives—lived—there. I had to clean out her apartment, settle her affairs."

"What about your parents? Did they help?"

Lexi almost laughed. She'd been more Zoe's parent than sister for the past fifteen years.

"My mother died several years ago, and my sister and I didn't share the same father." *I don't even know who he is. Or was, for that matter.*

The sympathy in Aiden's eyes was almost her undoing. There was something so kind, so…trustworthy about him. She never divulged anything about her life, and here she was telling him things even the people she worked with didn't know. What was that old saw? The intimacy of strangers? Maybe that was why she felt it easy to open up to him. She'd never see him again after they landed.

"I can never decide," he said, interrupting her thoughts, "which is tougher. A quick death where the person doesn't suffer, or a lingering one where you get a chance to say goodbye."

"In all honesty both are horrible."

"Truth." Aiden nodded. "Were you close with your sister?"

Not the way we should have been. Not at the end.

"We had a sizable age difference between us. Almost ten years. I was the big sis. The oldest." Her lips trembled when she pulled them into a sad line.

Rolling her eyes she added, "The bossy one, according to her. She was the baby and took full advantage of her status from the moment she realized it."

"And rightly so." The corners of his eyes crinkled. "I'm the youngest of my brothers, and I'll can tell you with 100 percent honesty, my oldest brother is the bossiest one of us. I think it comes with birth order, although he takes his so-called right uber-seriously. Especially at work."

This time her grin was steadier. "What kind of business do you all own together?"

"We a run a private security company."

"Security?"

"Personal bodyguards if a client needs protection from something or someone. Background checks for employers. Mostly we do investigations."

"What, like private eyes? Like on television?"

He laughed. "Nothing so glamorous. The fast cars and hot babes are all fantasy. It's a lot of boring research, computer work, and surveillance, but yeah, you could say I'm a private eye."

Lexi's entire mood turned on his words. The sorrow flew, the hurt dissolved. Even her nervous trivia-speak went dormant. She sat bolt upright, her knees bumping against the tabletop when she shifted. Excitement shot from her system as she turned her body, placed a hand across his forearm, and declared, "Oh, my God. You're the answer to my prayers."

Chapter 2

He'd been many things to many people in his life, some good, some, not so much. But he could truthfully admit no one had ever called him an answer to a prayer before. The statement was ego inflating and, at the same time, terrifying in its unspoken expectations.

The excitement shining from Lexi's eyes had turned the attractive hazel color to a vibrant and glittering green. For the first time she smiled fully at him, reminiscent of how she had with Drunk Guy in the airport. Aiden had been intrigued by those lips, with the swatch of crimson slashed over them, from across the bar. But now, devoid of all artifice, her smile was even more alluring and downright captivating than it had been before.

"If I believed in fate," she said, giving his arm a little squeeze before she removed her hand, "I would think sitting next to you had been arranged by some higher power."

In reality, not so high.

Aiden gave himself a mental pat on the back for being the master of his own fate and deciding to change his seat assignment. He'd done it out of idle curiosity to elicit any information he could to explain her wardrobe and character change. She was a mystery—a cute one—he wanted to solve to pass the time on the flight.

From the moment he'd taken his seat and she'd

turned to face him, though, his natural nosiness turned from mild to overpowering. She was such a mixture of sexy and sweet, of raw nerves and inner calm. When she related the reason she'd wanted the emergency-door seat, he believed her. Despite the trivia-speak babble he chalked up to nervous energy, he could see her taking command of a situation and acting accordingly if need be.

Why? He didn't have a clue. Sometimes a gut feeling was the only thing required to understand someone's motivation, and Aiden's gut had yet to steer him wrong.

"You must be thinking, who is this wacko I got stuck sitting next to," she said shaking her head.

"I can assure you I wasn't thinking that," he said. "At all."

The tops of her cheeks pinked, and when she bit down on a corner of her bottom lip, he felt a swift jab to his midsection.

She lifted her gaze to his. With her lip still caught between her teeth, she cocked her head. "You really are a private investigator?"

For an answer he lifted a hip, slid his wallet out of his pants pocket, then passed her one of his business cards.

"Brothers, Inc." She ran her index finger over the embossed firm name. "Aiden Keane, Security and Cyber Analyst. Analyst? For what?"

"Fraud investigations, mostly."

"I always imagined a private eye as someone a spouse would hire if they suspected their partner of cheating."

"Most of my brother's work was comprised of stuff

like that when he first opened the business. Working for divorce lawyers and such. Now we've got a more broad-based list of things we look into for clients."

"Is that what you were doing in Atlanta?"

"Sorry. I can't share any of the particulars with you. Professional confidentiality."

"No, of course not. Confidentiality. I understand. Who would trust an investigator who gossiped?"

Aiden nodded.

"Can anyone hire you, or do you only work for corporations and big businesses?"

"We're a private firm, but we take on all manner of clients."

It was her turn to nod. "I would imagine you're very expensive."

He took the question to mean she had limited funds. "Why don't you tell me why I'm—to quote you—an answer to your prayers, and we can go from there."

He watched the internal debate as her lovely face shot through several expressions. Her grooved and thoughtful brow went smooth, but then she bit down on the bottom corner of her mouth again. She swiped her finger over and around her ear, tucking the hair in front of it behind, and, as she'd done before, squeezed the lobe before letting go.

All the reasons she would need a private investigator ran through his head. Was she trying to find someone from her past? Worried a lover was cheating on her? Could she be embroiled in a blackmail scheme? Although the reasons to blackmail a librarian eluded him. Was she being stalked? Harassed?

A sigh thick with resignation flowed from her after

a moment lost in thought. At the same time, the seatbelt signal sounded and the captain came back over the loud speaker announcing they were starting their descent.

Lexi cast a quick look over the seats in front of them, then back to him.

"My sister died a few weeks ago," she began.

"So you said, and again, I'm sorry for your loss."

"Thank you." She took another breath. "Her name was Zoe, and she lived and worked in Atlanta. She'd just turned twenty-five."

"Young."

Lexi shook her head. "Only chronologically. Zoe was an old soul wrapped in a young woman's body. Mature beyond her years. She went through a rough patch as a teenager. Got in with a bad crowd. Did things she shouldn't have. But she turned her life around, graduated from college with a degree in journalism, and was working at a local Atlanta-based magazine. The last time we spoke she sounded…happy, for the first time in a while. Really happy."

Her voice lowered, grew soft, and for a moment she stopped.

Aiden's gaze flicked down to her lap where she held her hands folded together, her knuckles turning skeletal white under her grasp. He knew if he took her hand it would be ice cold. His fingers itched to share some of his warmth. He held back, though, sensing this woman wasn't the sort to accept comfort, to be seen as weak or needy. So he simply let her take the time she needed before going on.

"You asked if we were close," she said, lifting her gaze to his again. "We weren't. Not really. Part of it was the age difference. But the major reason had to do with our personalities. Zoe was the outgoing, up-for-anything girl, evidenced by the issues she had as a teen. I was—am—the serious one. I'd rather curl up with a book for the night than go clubbing. Because of those differences, we didn't share much of our lives."

Aiden shrugged. "It happens. Age gaps make it tough to relate sometimes."

"In truth I think Zoe had some stored resentment."

"About what?"

With another deep breath, she finally unlaced her fingers and folded her arms across her chest. "Our mother…died, when I was eighteen, Zoe nine. I became her legal guardian because we had no other family and I refused to allow my sister to be put in foster care."

Aiden whistled. "You were no more than a kid yourself."

The harsh sound that barked from her was so incongruous with her demeanor he almost laughed.

"Believe me, I was never a kid. Not a normal one, anyway. Zoe resented all the rules I placed on her while she was growing up and under my care. She could never understand why she needed them if we didn't have a parent around to enforce them." She shook her head. "Anyway, I received a call from the Atlanta police that she'd…died."

"Had she been sick? Or in an accident?"

"Neither. I was told she'd killed herself."

The news didn't shock him. Lexi could probably quote him a series of statistics about how people in their twenties died suddenly, and he'd bet suicide soared near the top of causes.

"Of course I didn't believe it. Zoe had so much to live for and was doing well with her job, and like I said, the last time we spoke she seemed happy." She rolled her eyes and added, "And I know people who've had a loved one kill themselves say that all the time. They had everything to live for, and there's no way they took their own lives. Then they discover all wasn't as rosy as they believed."

The flight crew made their final pass through the cabin as the captain once again announced the routine tables-upright-fasten-seatbelts spiel.

"Did she leave a note?"

Her slight hesitation before answering had his curiosity jumping. "A typewritten one left at her bedside. But I know in my heart my sister didn't kill herself. She wouldn't."

"At the risk of sounding insensitive, why are you so certain?"

She nailed him with a gaze so filled with suppressed anger and torment, once again the desire to pull her on to his lap and wipe those emotions clean barreled through him.

"Because our mother took her own life. Zoe was old enough to understand what happened and because of it, was always filled with anger about the selfishness of the act. She never would have done the same thing. I'm certain of it."

Aiden regarded her for a moment. Grief could make even the most logical and unemotional of people refuse to accept the fact of a loved one's suicide.

"What did the note say?"

She gave a dismissive wave of one of her hands. " 'Forgive me.' "

"That's all?"

"Yes. And again, that's not like my sister. She

never used one word if she could use twenty. There's no indication of what to forgive her for, or even who the note was addressed to. That all leads me to know she didn't write it."

"It sounds like you think someone else did."

Fury bounded in her eyes "That's exactly what I believe. My sister didn't take her own life. I'm certain she was murdered."

Aiden whistled again.

"If you think that, do you have any idea who would, or could have, done it? A jealous boyfriend, maybe?"

"No."

"Did you tell the police your suspicions?"

"I did, but they brushed me off."

"I'm gonna bet it's because you had no physical proof."

She nodded. "While I was packing up her belongings, I discovered her laptop and phone were missing. I told the police, and they said she was probably just robbed. I asked how she could have typed and then printed her supposed suicide note if she had been, but they brushed me off. They wrote up a report but told me recovering anything was a low priority and I'd probably never get them back."

"Unfortunately, that's true." He studied her again. "You think they were stolen for a reason related to her death, don't you?"

"Yes. It's too much of a coincidence, and I don't believe in coincidences. While in Atlanta, I met with the editor of her magazine, hoping she was working on something that might have been dangerous."

"Was she?"

She shook her head. "He told me Zoe was assigned the social fluff stuff. Wedding announcements, engagements, Rotary meetings. Events like that. She never worked on anything hardcore or newsworthy."

Something dinged in the back of Aiden's mind. "Have you been in Atlanta since your sister died?"

"No." She bit down on her lip again. "I flew out initially for a few days, but had to get back to work soon after. I packed up her stuff quickly, had most of it shipped back to me. It was only when I started going through it all I found the computer and phone missing. That's when I called the Atlanta police."

"So why were you back in Atlanta?"

He watched her closely, searching for another tell. She didn't know he recognized her as the redhead from the bar and wanted to keep her in the dark for the moment to see her reaction. Would she lie to him?

When she tucked her hair behind her ear again, he knew the question made her nervous.

"Following up on a lead."

"What kind of lead?"

The captain interrupted with the landing announcement.

Lexi said, "It's complicated and will take more time than we have now for me to explain. I need to get home and…see to some things first."

Aiden nodded. She hadn't outright lied to him, but she hadn't told him what she'd done, either. Looked like he was going to have to wait to hear what she had to say. As she had on takeoff, Lexi closed her eyes, grasped the armrests and, from the looks of her knuckles blanching again, held on tight. He didn't need to stifle his amusement because she couldn't see it spread across his face.

He took the opportunity to study her in repose. She certainly didn't seem like the type to make up a story like the one she'd told him. No, if he were a betting man he'd make book she truly believed her sister hadn't taken her own life.

Lexi had a gut reaction that told her the sister wouldn't—couldn't—have killed herself. Well, he'd relied on his gut instincts a time or two—or more—so he understood the feeling.

When they touched down in a perfectly smooth glide, Lexi let out an audible sigh and opened her eyes.

Aiden grinned. "Like I said, the flying is the easy part." When the tops of her cheeks went pink, it was like a stab to his gut again.

Since when did a woman blushing make him so…hot and bothered?

Yeah, it was a really long time since his second favorite word got any play; that had to be the explanation.

It appeared she wasn't going to tell him any more of her story, evidenced by the way she busied herself with silently gathering the things she'd removed from her bag. While he wanted to continue the conversation, he sensed she was conflicted. It was one thing to talk while you were virtual prisoners ten thousand feet up in the sky, quite another when back on the ground.

"Look," he said while they stood in the center aisle, waiting to exit the plane. She finally made eye contact again with him. "You've got my card. Why don't you go home, sleep on it tonight, and then if you want to talk to me some more about your sister's situation or have me dig around a little to see what I can find out, give me a call. I'm gonna be off for a few days and I have no pressing plans. Okay?"

As he stared down at her and waited for her reply, he hoped she took him up on his offer. If he wasn't so dog-tired and missing his own bed, he'd suggest they go somewhere for a drink or get something to eat so she could tell him more of the story now.

"I will," she said, then shuffled along with the other passengers as they deplaned.

Once they were through the jetway and heading toward the exits, she turned to him and said, shyly, "Thank you. For listening."

"It's what I do."

A moment later, she was swallowed up in the moving hoard just as she'd been in the Atlanta airport once she'd left the bar. Because of his height he was able to keep her in his line of sight.

At the bottom of the escalator, she hopped off and then went in the direction of the cab line, while he spotted his older brother, Dylan, waiting and holding a sign reading *Welcome Home, Brain.*

Dylan tossed him the cocky, shit-eating smirk he reserved for his baby brother. The one that, when he'd been a scrawny, shy, sickly kid, filled Aiden with insecurity. Not any longer. Now that he matched his brothers for height and strength, Aiden's insecurity was a thing of the past.

"Hey, baby bro," Dylan said, tugging his brother close and banging him on the back a few times.

"You're an asshole," Aiden said, "with that sign."

"Yeah, but ya love me anyway."

Aiden shook his head, while his brother tossed an arm over his shoulder and tugged him along.

"Car's right outside. And I brought a little lady along with me."

Aiden's mood lifted considerably. "You been taking good care of her for me? I better not find out she gained ten pounds and got lazy from lying around all day."

"Cool your jets. She's as fit as always. But I think she's forgotten all about you. Absence doesn't always make the heart grow fonder, and she now knows, firsthand, I'm the better brother in every way. She's grown quite used to being with me."

"Don't bet on it. She's as loyal as they come."

He'd parked the Jeep outside the loading zone barrier, its flashers on, the motor running.

"As least you kept the air conditioning on," Aiden said when he spotted the vehicle.

The moment he opened the passenger back door he was set upon by one hundred and twenty pounds of pure muscle and love.

Laughing, Aiden allowed himself to be licked and pawed, while he rubbed and loved on the dog that meant more to him than most people he knew.

"I missed you, too, girl. Did Uncle Dylan take good care of you?"

The dog answered by jumping and placing her paws on his shoulders, her tail swishing like a windshield wiper, and gracing his face with another slobbery lick.

"Dog's more spoiled than you were as a kid," Dylan said as he slid into the driver's seat. "Come on. I don't want to get ticketed."

Once the brothers and the excited chocolate Labrador were settled in, Dylan pulled out into traffic.

"She give you any trouble?" Aiden asked as he continued to rub the dog's neck where she peeked in between the front seats.

"Not an ounce. I don't think she even barked once while you were gone." He glanced at his younger brother, a sly grin gracing his face. "I never knew a dog was such a babe magnet. Whenever I took her for a run in the park, chicks flocked around her, and by extension, me. I got more numbers tossed my way than I could deal with."

Aiden frowned at him. "I don't like the idea of you using my dog to score with women."

"I didn't use Brontë for anything unseemly, but I couldn't help how many women thought she was quote, the most beautiful dog they'd ever seen, unquote, and just had to pet her and ask me all about her."

"I'm gonna bet you sang your own praises more than my dog's."

"I'm not taking any part of that bet." Dylan's smug grin pulled a headshake and a wry smile from Aiden.

"So, the trophy wife and her hacker boy-toy?" Dylan asked, referencing the case Aiden had closed in Atlanta. "No way you coulda seen that coming."

"Pissed me off, royally, when I finally realized it." Aiden continued rubbing his dog's neck as she tried to shove onto his lap. He kept her in place with a firm, loving hand. "The guy was good."

"Had to be if it took you so long to figure it out."

"Too bad he went to the dark side, cuz we could use someone with his skills. Each time I broke through a firewall, I hit another, more elaborate one. I had more headaches with this job than I've had in a while."

Aiden let out a deep sigh and rested his head

against the dog's snout. A love-filled lick wet his cheek.

"You feeling...okay?"

It was impossible not to miss the concern etched in his voice. "I'm fine. Don't worry."

Dylan nodded. "Well, you're home now, so that's good. Josh called me right after you told him you were done and said Kandy filled your fridge. You won't be hurting for grub for a while."

Aiden smiled. His brother's wife, chef-lebrity Kandy Laine, had a heart as big as the outdoors when it came to family and strived to ensure everyone in her realm ate well. The thought of all the delicious and comforting foods she'd made, which were now stocked in his apartment, sent a warm rush through him. Josh had lucked out in the married-for-life department. From the first time they'd been introduced, Aiden had felt as if he'd finally gotten the sister he'd always prayed for as a kid. The fact she was gorgeous, cooked like no one's business, and had the most welcoming smile he'd ever come across, didn't hurt either.

"You gonna get right back to work, or you taking some time?" Dylan asked.

"A few days. I need to get back on schedule, regroup, and see to a few things." He sighed again, suddenly tired. "Plus, I want my own bed."

With a nod, Dylan snuck a side-glance at him before concentrating back on the road. While he meandered them through the city traffic, Dylan clued him in on a few of the cases the firm was working on.

After pulling up to the front of Aiden's apartment building and double parking, Dylan clapped his brother on the back and said, "Let me know when you're ready to come back in. I could use your insights on a couple of the jobs."

"Will do. Thanks for getting me and for taking care of my girl."

Dylan bent and rubbed the dog's neck. "She can come hang with me anytime." He stood and told his brother, "Get some rest, cuz you look tired, baby bro."

That was the plan.

The moment Aiden opened his apartment door the sweet aroma of fresh flowers caught his attention. Brontë bolted past him and while she ran from room to room, getting reacquainted with her home's smells, Aiden dropped his keys on the kitchen counter and spied the bouquet with the note next to it.

~Welcome home. We missed you. Food in the fridge, sheets are freshly changed, and your niece and nephew want to see you when you're free~

Kandy's characteristic feminine signature with a smiley face drawn next to her name covered the bottom of the note.

Aiden reached into the refrigerator, navigating around shelves of plastic containers and casserole dishes, and pulled out a beer he knew his oldest brother had included with the food delivery.

"Bless you, bro," he murmured.

When he popped the bottle open, the dog shot back into the kitchen.

Her tail hadn't stopped wagging from the moment she'd met him at the airport. The breeze from all the movement felt like an airplane propeller spinning at take-off speed.

Responding to Aiden's hand signal, Brontë sat at his feet. Aiden knelt, the beer in one hand, and hugged the dog to him with the other.

"It's good to be home, isn't it, girl?"

For an answer, she licked his cheek, sniffed his beer, then flicked her tongue across his chin. Aiden swore she smiled at him when he asked if she was hungry.

He heated Kandy's chicken and rice casserole, filled Brontë's bowl with her own food, and then they ate together in the kitchen.

After examining the snail mail that had piled up for the eight weeks he'd been gone, he leashed Brontë and took her for a quick walk around the neighborhood before fatigue burned through all his energy. That done, he slid on his computer reading glasses, did a quick sweep of his email, then opened a secured browser he used only for work and typed in Alexis Buckley's name. She'd never told him her surname, but he'd seen it written across her boarding pass.

He opened the backdoor DMV site he used for investigations and found her listing. An address in Queens showed him she lived within walking distance from the college where she worked. Her age was listed as thirty-three, and he'd already guessed she was about one hundred and ten pounds.

In the college online directory, he found her picture and bio when he clicked on the campus's faculty listings.

Dr. Alexis E. Buckley, Dean of Libraries, complete with a full-faced color photo and a curriculum vitae. On the plane he'd thought the color of her eyes green until he noticed they shifted with her mood, giving credence to the hazel description on her driver's license. From the professional headshot staring back at him, they looked more blue-ish.

He read through her bio, making note of the young age she'd been when she'd received her doctorate.

Not bad for a girl who lost her mother and raised a sister when she was practically a kid herself. That kind of utter devotion and focus was rare. There were no marriages listed, nor children.

An all-too-familiar sense of fatigue barreled through him, and when Brontë nudged her snout against his leg and whined, he knew it was time to shut down.

"Okay, girl. I hear ya." He patted her head and allowed his hand to be summarily licked while he exited out of all the programs he'd opened and rebooted the computer before shutting it down. He dropped his glasses on his desk.

A hot, steamy shower later and he fell into bed, naked, the dog nestled at his feet.

Damn, he'd missed this bed.

Before falling asleep, Lexi's face crossed his mind. First, as the confident, hot, and seductive siren in the airport bar, complete with crimson mouth and stilettoes, then as the fresh-faced, nervous, and concerned sister sitting next to him in the plane.

He preferred the intelligent, trivia-spewing woman of the two. A quick mind had always intrigued him more than any other trait. He'd admitted it on the plane, even though her skeptical expression said she hadn't believed him. But add quiet beauty, a quirky personality, and vulnerability wrapped in steel, and his level of curiosity quadrupled.

Would she call him?

Just before he fell asleep to the dog's subtle snores, he hoped she would.

Chapter 3

After the best sleep he'd had in weeks, Aiden woke refreshed, recharged, and starving. A quick protein shake and he was out the door, his dog on his heels.

Brontë was in rare form as he ran her in the park on the beautiful June morning. He knew Dylan ran between five and seven miles every day, and it seemed he'd gotten Brontë up to his level. The dog, who typically started to slow down at about mile three of Aiden's runs, was still going strong at the five-mile marker.

"I should leave you with Dylan more often," he told the dog when he stopped and found a bench to sit and rest for a bit. "He pushes you a lot more than I do."

The dog gave him one of her serene *smiles,* stretched out on the ground next to the bench and yawned before dropping her head over her paws.

When he pulled his beeping phone from his running shorts, an unfamiliar number crossed the screen.

"This is Aiden."

"Oh, hi...I wasn't sure if I'd get you or an answering machine. This is Alexis. Um, Lexi. We met. Yesterday. On the plane?"

Aiden smiled at how nervous—and cute—she sounded. How could she possibly think he'd forgotten her?

He stretched his legs out and dropped his free hand to scratch Brontë behind her ear. "You get home okay after we landed?"

"Um, yes. No problems."

"Well, what can I do for you on this beautiful day, Lexi?"

"Oh, is it? I haven't been out yet. I, um, had a lot to do when I got home."

He chuckled to himself, thinking he wouldn't be surprised if she hit him up with some statistic about how much of a vacation a person who just got home from a vacation needed.

A deep breath came through the phone, and the idea she was trying to gear herself up to ask for help drifted through him. Should he take pity on her and offer his services again, or wait for her to ask?

He had nowhere to be, nothing to do, so he slouched down even more on the bench and waited her out.

"Well. I, um…" She cleared her throat. "I'm calling because, after everything we talked about yesterday, and because you're a, you know, private investigator, I, well, I want to ask for your help. Hire you. I want to hire you to help me find out what happened to my sister."

His grin grew.

"I don't know how much you charge," she continued. "But I need help—your kind of help and expertise. I can't do more than I've already done, and I'm at a standstill. So, like I said, I'd like to hire you to look into it. I don't have much available cash now, but I can give you a retainer to start."

"Don't worry about the money. I've got a few days

free, so how about I take a look at what you've got first, no charge."

"Oh, I can't *not* pay you. It seems…wrong, somehow."

"Like I said, let's not worry about it right now. Wait to see if I even have anything to offer. You may have already exhausted every avenue."

"I seriously doubt that."

He could hear the gears in her mind turning. "When would you like to start?"

"The Reverend John Trusler is credited with saying, 'There's no time like the present,' so how about now?"

The tiny breath he heard her pull in charmed him into another smile. In truth, he'd been hoping she'd say now.

"I'm sorry. That was rude. You're probably busy after just returning home. Got a thousand things to do. We can make it another time at your convenience."

"Give me an hour and text me your address," he said, pushing to a stand. Brontë lifted her head, and when Aiden gave her the signal to rise, she did and positioned herself by his side.

"Really? Oh, thank you. I can't tell you how much I appreciate this. I'll text you my address right now. And I'll see you shortly. Thanks, again."

"Lexi? One thing before we hang up."

"Yes?"

Aiden rubbed his dog's head, rewarded with a lolling tongue and a doggie-grin.

"How do you feel about dogs?"

****

Why in the name of all that's horrible and holy had

she responded like she had, asking if he knew dogs sweat from the bottoms of their feet?

You'd think by this age she'd be able to control her trivia-Tourette's.

Nope.

Nerves got to her every time.

Oh, who am I kidding?

It wasn't just simple nerves making her verbally vomit unimportant pieces of information at the drop of a hat. No, her reaction had more to do with the man who'd offered to help her than anything else.

It had taken her almost an hour to screw up her courage to call him. Every reason she could dream up not to had floated through her brain, been dissected, then tossed. In the end, she knew she had to ask *someone* for help. She'd been truthful when she'd admitted she couldn't go any further in her investigation. For all her knowledge and talents as a researcher, there were some things no amount of book learning could help with. She needed an expert in the field, someone who knew the ins and outs of cyber information gathering, and Aiden Keane fit the bill to perfection. The fact he was packed into six foot plus of delicious man-candy she couldn't help making a fool of herself in front of, was something she'd need to suck up and deal with.

A quick shower later, dressed and with her apartment clean and presentable, she heard the downstairs doorbell chime.

"Hey, it's Aiden," he said into the intercom. She buzzed him into the building, then stood by her opened apartment door and waited for the elevator to arrive. Instead of the mechanical motor indicating it rising to her fourth floor apartment, footfalls on the staircase echoed through the silent hallway.

When a long, brown snout peeked around the bannister, the mouth under it open and the long, pink tongue lolling out, Lexi slammed her hands together and began wringing them, only to stop once she realized they were sweating. She quickly rubbed them dry over the material of her jeans.

The dog was tethered to a leash held by the man she hadn't stopped thinking about all morning.

All night, too.

"I was expecting you to take the elevator," she said by way of greeting man and dog.

"Elevators can be confining," he said as he stopped in front of her, the sexy grin she'd memorized planted across his face. He made a motion with his hand, and the dog plopped down into a sitting position next to him. "We never pass up the chance to get in a little extra exercise." He scratched the dog behind an ear. "Plus, stairs have way better smells. Don't they, girl?" He glanced down at the dog, who lifted her head and cocked an ear.

"Oh, my goodness, is she…smiling?"

Both dog and man turned their attention to her.

"I like to think she is," he said. "This is Brontë. She's very gentle and loves to be petted. Especially by lovely ladies."

Lexi dropped her chin so he wouldn't see her blush as she reached out a hand and, with some trepidation, rubbed it along the dog's head. When the animal remained calm, she reached around to pet her.

"She really is gentle," Lexi said, charmed again when the dog's eyes fluttered at her touch. "Brontë?

Like in Charlotte and Emily?"

Aiden nodded.

"Read during your misspent time in the library?"

His grin took a slow stroll over his cheeks until his smile brightened the dim hallway.

Oh, my.

"That," he said, slipping his free hand into his pants pocket, "and I had a crush on a girl who was a huge fan of *Wuthering Heights* and *Jane Eyre."*

What did it say about her that she felt a tiny stab of envy for the girl? "That had to be a powerful crush," she said, peering up at him, "to make you name your dog after the author."

A shadow of sadness flickered across his eyes, but his expression remained unchanged as he asked, "Can we come in?"

When they were inside her apartment, he asked, "Mind if I take her off the leash? She won't get into any mischief, I promise."

"Of course."

Once the dog was freed, Aiden lifted his hand with his palm down, and patted the air. Brontë ambled over to the window, then settled down in front of it.

"You have her trained with hand signals?"

He nodded. When it appeared he wasn't going to say anything more on the matter, she said, "I read a research paper a few years ago about dogs in the military. Their handlers use nonverbal communication to train them in the event they find themselves in circumstances where a spoken command could be dangerous if heard by an enemy combatant."

"In some situations, staying silent can mean the difference between life and death."

Lexi glanced at the dog who had her head resting on top of her paws, her attention focused on the two humans in the room.

"She'll be fine," Aiden said. "Don't worry. Now, show me your stuff."

Her head whipped around to face him. He stood in front of her, hands casually resting in his pockets, head tilted to the left, and a look of utter calm on his face as he regarded her.

Wildfire engulfed her cheeks. He meant what she had concerning Zoe and not something…else.

Didn't he?

What am I thinking? Of course he didn't mean anything but that? It's why he's here, after all. To help me look into Zoe's death.

Lexi swallowed and willed her skin to return to its normal hue. "I have everything ready for you to go through."

With a tiny shake of her head to clear it, she led him into the room the superintendent had labeled a study when he'd originally shown her the place. A little bigger than the apartment's bathroom, the room was windowless, something that pleased her because it gave her the freedom to use the walls for whatever she wanted. Two of them were lined almost to the ceiling with filled bookshelves. A small desk she'd purchased from an online discount store sat against the largest wall, her desktop computer on top of it. On the wall above it hung a huge bulletin board, covered with the fruits of her investigation.

Copies of bills including Zoe's cellphone, electricity, and credit cards were lined up according to month on one side. Lexi had yellow-markered several line items. Receipts from restaurants, parking stubs, even movie ticket stubs covered another, again, many marked in yellow and highlighting specific dates. A magazine photograph of Peter Smith, with his business card, were tacked in one corner.

Aiden stepped close to the desk, his gaze perusing the board.

"This is your sister?" He pointed to the five-by-seven picture sitting in the center of the board.

"Zoe's college graduation photo."

"There's a resemblance around the mouth and chin."

"We had different fathers." She opened the top desk drawer and handed him a faded photograph. "This was our mother." A stunning blonde grinned back at the camera as if she'd just been told a naughty joke. She held a toothless, smiling baby wearing only a diaper. Standing next to them, a serious-faced little girl with her hands folded in front of her.

"I can see how you both favor your mom. What were you here, about ten? Eleven?"

"Ten. Zoe was eight months."

He gave the photo back to her and turned his attention to the board. "You've done a lot. I can tell you're a research junkie."

She sighed. "It's what I'm good at."

He slanted her a glance and a grin hot enough to make her stick-straight hair curl.

"Okay, let's get started. Do you have another chair for me to sit in?"

"Take that one, and I'll go get one from the kitchen."

Brontë lifted her head, and Lexi swore she had a

question in her eyes as they stared across the room at her.

"We need another chair," she told the dog. A second later she shook her head. "And I'm talking to a dog like she can understand me." Because her brain never shut down, the statistic she'd read stating three in one hundred people will experience a psychotic break or episode in their lifetimes flew through it, evidenced by fantastical and non-reality-based thoughts.

"Sounds dead-on," she muttered.

When she returned to the study, she stopped short in the doorway. Aiden had taken a seat and had already booted up her computer. Neither of those things surprised her. What did was the vision of him in glasses.

Without them, his face was a sculptor's masterpiece of classic planes and angles all fitting together in a gorgeous, masculine façade. With them…well, with them he was the sexiest thing she'd ever laid eyes on. Perfect in every way from his good looks to his broad shoulders and trim, athletic physique, she could honestly say there wasn't a thing wrong with him. But knowing he had one tiny flaw—his vision—made those little excited tingles in her belly bloom full force until she had a merengue band banging away inside her.

He glanced over his shoulder. "All set?"

Unable to stop herself, she blinked and said, "Forty percent of the U.S. population suffers from myopia. But only 5 to 10 percent are afflicted with farsightedness."

One corner of his mouth twitched upward before he said, "Good to know, but I'm neither."

"Then why the glasses?"

"I have, for lack of a perfect medical term, computer vision syndrome. My eyes hurt and blur if I focus on anything from three to five feet for prolonged periods. The glasses help prevent straining."

"That's got to be hard considering you must spend the majority of your work day staring at a computer screen." She slammed her lips together, felt the flush creep up her neck and jaw again, and the tingling in her stomach paralyze to a stop. "I'm sorry. That was rude and intrusive."

"It was neither, especially since it's the truth. Come on, sit down."

He rose and took the chair from her, placed it next to his, and then waited until she sat before taking his seat again.

The desk wasn't wide, so the sides of their legs slid against one another.

"The glasses help prevent eye issues," he said. "That includes"—he pointed to the wall—"your bulletin board. Take me through all this so I can get a feel for where you are, what you've done, and what you've been able to find out."

His smooth, calm manner went a long way in settling her nerves. She took a deep breath and then let the logical, analytical part of her brain speak. For the next hour, she related everything she'd been able to put together about her sister's life prior to her death. Aiden listened quietly, nodding at times, letting her get it all out in a logical progression.

"For someone who hadn't seen or spoken to her in a while, you've gotten a pretty good handle on her comings and goings," he said when she finally stopped. "I'm impressed."

Silently thrilled with the compliment, she shrugged. "Zoe was a creature of habit and a pack rat. It came from having such an unstable life before our mother died. We'd moved eight times before Zoe turned six. She tended to hold on to things. All things, no matter how inconsequential. Ephemera, you know?"

Aiden nodded.

"So it wasn't too difficult to put some of the pieces of her life together to form a timeline of the last few months. I'm her emergency contact on everything and was able to get all her mail forwarded here. I paid all her outstanding bills, like her rent, and I opened all her credit card statements when they arrived. Like I said, she was a pack rat, so she'd kept every one, plus bank statements and receipts for the past three years."

"The items you've lined with marker?" He pointed to the board. "What significance do they have?"

She glanced up them. "They're all from the month preceding her death. The dates on the parking stubs all correspond to receipts I found from a coffee shop matching credit card purchases for the place on the same dates."

"So your assumption is, what? She was meeting someone there? Or went to a meeting there? Or close by, maybe?"

She nodded. "It makes sense, doesn't it? You can see, every Tuesday she parks at a municipal lot at six in the evening. At seven thirty she makes a purchase in this place called Brewers, and then around eight thirty her credit card is charged for parking."

Aiden glanced back up at the board and nodded. "It's good work."

Why his praise infused her with such a sense of

pride and satisfaction was a mystery.

"Who is that?" He pointed to the photograph of Peter Smith.

Lexi swallowed, then tucked her hair behind her ear. "I found his picture and the business card among Zoe's things. I thought she knew him, but he told me he didn't."

"You questioned him?"

"I called his office after I found the card, explained who I was. He said he'd never heard of her. Had no idea why she would have his business card. But he did say he handed them out like candy on Halloween. He said maybe she came to one of his business presentations and he gave it to her. He meets so many people, he said, he can't possibly remember them all."

"The Kingman Group," Aiden read aloud the business listed on the card. "What is it?"

"A public relations firm. What I can't figure out is why she would need one. Zoe wasn't in the public eye."

"Maybe she was looking to up her professional profile? Get her name recognized as a journalist?"

"Maybe."

"You don't sound convinced. There's nothing else in her possessions to tell you why she had this?"

"Not that I've found yet. There are still a few boxes I haven't gone through."

Aiden looked back up at the picture, then turned his attention back to her. "Is he the lead you told me on the plane you went to Atlanta to pursue?"

This time she couldn't hide the flush galloping across her face.

"Lexi?"

His entire demeanor suggested he was calm and

relaxed, just having a conversation on a random morning. With his hands resting on his thighs and his shoulders dropped in a casual attitude, there wasn't an ounce of tension wafting from them. But when she looked into those piercing and probing eyes, she saw anything but calm. Focused, like a hunter with his quarry captured in the crosshairs, waiting for the perfect moment to strike. Lexi appreciated in this instance, she was the prey.

She swallowed again. "Yes," she said on a jagged exhale.

Aiden tipped his head to one side as he continued to hold her paralyzed in his stare. "And did you find out anything more?"

This time she nodded.

She gave him credit for the patience in his voice because she knew her one-word answers were annoying in their lack of information.

Instead of replying, she shooed him to move and when he shifted she typed a few strokes on the keyboard. The photo she'd taken of his credit card and driver's license popped across the screen.

"Why do you have these?" he asked. "And more importantly, how did you get them? I can't see anyone just handing over personal information like this to a stranger."

When his attention centered on her again, Lexi folded her hands together so he wouldn't see them shaking.

"In answer to the first question, because I was hoping to see if I could, somehow, get a digital copy of his credit card statements."

"To…what? See if there were any charges similar

to your sister's? Maybe he was the one she was meeting on those nights?"

"Yes, actually, that's the very reason."

"So you don't believe he never met your sister? Didn't know her?"

"In all honesty, when we spoke over the phone I got the impression he wasn't being honest with me. There was something in his voice, some kind of, I don't know"—she flipped a hand in the air—"hesitation, in his answers." She shrugged.

"You felt he was evading."

"Yes. I wanted to meet him, face to face, to see if he'd tell me anything. People tend to have an easier time dodging and lying on the phone than when they're standing in front of you."

"That's been my experience as well. And did he react the same way?"

"He wouldn't see me. His secretary kept stonewalling me. Finally, after I called four times, she told me he was leaving for Chicago on a business trip the next day and wouldn't be back for weeks. I knew I had to do something, so…"

When she went no further, he said, "I think it's time you told me how you got this"—he pointed to the screen—"information."

Chapter 4

If he touched her face, he'd bet his fingers would come back singed from the violence of heat suffusing her cheeks. She wouldn't meet his eyes, drifted her gaze off to their almost-touching knees, instead. He'd turned in the chair to fully face her and tried to keep his grin of the memory of her in a skintight dress and heels, contained.

She swallowed. Then did it again.

"Lexi?"

"It's a felony in all fifty states to steal a credit card."

He nodded. "It's even worse if you steal it and then use it."

"I didn't...steal...the actual card. Merely took a picture of the numbers."

"For the purpose of gaining access to his account statements. Yes, I get it. But you still haven't told me how you came to have it."

Just as he thought she wasn't going to confess something he already knew, she huffed out a breath and rubbed her eyes.

"I distracted him and took a picture with my camera phone. He never knew I did it."

"I thought you said he wouldn't meet with you?"

"He wouldn't."

"Then—"

"He didn't know who I was when we…met."

"I think you'd better explain."

It all came out in a rush. No arcane trivia added in with the telling, no embellishing.

"I felt he wasn't being truthful," she said, "about Zoe, but I also knew if I confronted him in person he'd probably keep denying it. So I approached him as he waited to board his plane."

"How did you know what airline? What plane? Even what time he was leaving? Certainly not from his secretary."

The blush crossing her cheeks intensified. "I looked up the human resources number on the website, called, and told them I was confirming some last-minute travel details for Smith. I must have sounded convincing because they gave me everything I needed to know. Didn't even question me or ask for any kind of identification. They just accepted who I told them I was."

What did it say about him he was more impressed with her by the moment?

He nodded. "I've found, in my line of work, the more certain and assured you sound when you're lying, the less pushback you get from people. They're willing to believe you at face value."

The way she winced at his words, told him she'd never considered what she'd done as lying until right then when confronted with the truth of her actions.

"You would know, I imagine. Anyway. I found him at the airport bar, having a preflight drink. I knew what he looked like from the picture I found in Zoe's possessions, so I…approached him. Started talking. Flirting a little." She swallowed again. As a tell, it was as prominent as the earlobe swipe.

Oh, babe, you did a lot more than a little flirting. "Go on."

"I convinced him to buy me a drink, and when he took out his wallet to pay, I snapped a photo with my cell camera."

"And he didn't realize you did it?"

She shook her head.

"How did you do it without him knowing?"

Instead of answering, she stood and left the room, to return a moment later, her phone in hand.

"Do you like magic tricks?"

"Who doesn't?" he said.

With the phone in her left hand and angled under the desk, she said, "Pick up one of those pens." She pointed to the right side of the desk, and Aiden did so. Once he had it in hand, Lexi lifted her phone and showed the photo she'd snapped of him holding it.

"The whole concept of a magic trick is misdirection," she said.

"While my focus is diverted, you strike."

She nodded. "He never saw my phone because he was focused on something else. And he never heard it click because I'd turned it to silent mode. It was busy and loud in the bar, so he probably wouldn't have heard it anyway."

She still hadn't confessed the disguise, but he figured he'd hold on to that little nugget of knowledge a while longer since he already knew what Smith's attention had been *focused* on.

"Extraordinary." He gave her the full benefit of his smile. "You'd make a great PI."

For the first time in a while, her features relaxed,

her shoulders following suit. A darling curl tugged on a corner of her lips, and Aiden felt as if he'd been dropped kicked in the gut.

"I'm taking that as high praise," she told him, a sparkle lighting her eyes.

Their gazes held for a few beats. Aiden's second favorite word drifted across his mind again.

When Brontë promenaded into the room and tried to shove between them, Aiden blinked out of imagining Lexi's legs wrapped around his waist and scratched his fingers behind the dog's ears.

"She needs to go out," he said when the dog laid her head down on his thigh. He glanced at his phone and noted the time. "You up for some lunch? We had breakfast a while ago. I need to take her for a walk. You could join us, grab something to eat along the way."

It amazed him in the short time they'd been together how astute he'd become at reading her. The tiny thought line springing up between her eyes told him she was considering his offer, and the hand that slid to her temple and then tucked a stray hair behind her ear, squeezed the lobe, proved she was nervous about it. He didn't think it had anything to do with what they working on. No. Her little anxious tics had more to do with…him.

Was she uneasy around men in general or him, specifically? He'd sacrifice his left nut to know.

There certainly hadn't been any apparent apprehension when she'd been conning Peter Smith at the bar. Dressed in her seduction-wear, she'd been the epitome of a confident, take-what-you-want, in-charge female, not afraid to put her sexuality on the forefront or to use it to an end.

He appreciated that in a woman.

Without the benefit of her disguise, though, she seemed less sure of her appealing, alluring side. Which struck him as ridiculous considering how physically attractive and sexy she was.

"Why don't you go walk her," she said as her free hand found its way to absently scratch the dog's neck, "and I'll throw something together for us. We can keep working while we eat."

Twenty minutes later and after stopping at his car to get the food for Brontë he always kept with them when they traveled, he lifted his chin once they were back in Lexi's apartment and asked, "What's that amazing smell?"

"Sub sandwiches. I made a batch of meatballs and sauce before I left for Atlanta, froze it all, and just put some in the microwave for a few minutes. I bought the sub rolls last night on the way home from the airport."

"Homemade meatballs and sauce? Woman, where have you been all my life?"

Making her blush was rapidly becoming a habit. So was seeing the pleased uptick of those fabulous lips.

"A recent study showed 98 percent of Americans prefer a homemade meal to eating out. Unfortunately, only about 10 percent of those surveyed admitted they actually liked cooking."

"I'm betting you fall in the minority."

She handed him a plate with the steaming and delicious-smelling sandwich.

"I love to cook. Even though I cook for just myself, I always feel better knowing I put what I'm eating together. It's all self-taught, though. Someday I'd like to take a professional cooking class when I find the time."

"I'll be your taste tester," he told her, taking a seat at the small kitchen table. Brontë ambled up to him and settled down at his feet. "I'm one of the 98 percent. My mom still cooks everything from scratch, and every Sunday she makes a family meal we're all invited to. I've missed out on those since I've been away."

Her wistful sigh tugged at his heart.

"My mother wasn't much for cooking so I learned early on how to make easy stuff like mac and cheese, minute rice. Cereal became a big dinner item a lot of the time. After she died, I strived to ensure both our diets were more nutritious. Zoe was still growing, and I wanted her to be healthy, so I took a bunch of books out of our local library and just"—she flipped a hand in the air—"found recipes I thought might be easy and affordable."

He'd been impressed when she'd told him she'd raised her sister. To assume that kind of adult responsibility when she'd been little more than a child herself he found commendable. Picturing himself at eighteen, he knew there was no way he could have handled raising a younger sibling on his own or been responsible for anyone other than himself.

In the span of two minutes, she'd humbled him with her simple acceptance of having to be an adult and assuming charge for someone else's life.

Aiden cleared the unexpected emotion from the back of his throat. "Is that when your devotion to library science developed?"

Her full-faced smile made him glad he was seated. If standing, he knew the force and power of her grin would have knocked him back a few paces.

"I always loved going to the library. Always. It was my safe haven after school because my mother couldn't afford a babysitter to care for me. The librarians were like my adopted grandmothers, and they instilled in me a love of reading and research."

"Which you made your life's work. That's pretty amazing." He took a bite of his sub and groaned. "So is this," he said after swiping at his mouth with the napkin she'd handed him with the plate.

She thanked him, her gaze drifting down to his dog. "She's so well behaved. Did you have to teach her not to beg?"

"Begging is a learned response. If you give an animal food from the table, and it likes it, it will, naturally, want more. I've never done that. She only gets the food she's meant to have."

It had been one of the sticking points he'd made before he'd allowed Dylan to care for her in his absence. Brontë could only have the specialized food he bought from her veterinarian. Aiden had no intention of coming back home and finding his well-behaved dog had suddenly adopted habits he didn't want her to have like eating people food, swilling beer, and being lazy.

That longing sigh blew from between Lexi's luscious lips again. Aiden held the sub, poised between the plate and his mouth, as he zeroed in on her mouth.

"I always wanted a dog, but my mother wouldn't allow it. Too much work when she already had two kids to care for, plus another mouth to feed when money was tight."

"You could get one now," he said. "There's nothing stopping you."

Her gaze drifted down to Brontë. The dog must

have known she was being scrutinized because she lifted her head, her soulful eyes locked onto Lexi's.

"If I could be guaranteed a dog as wonderful as yours, I might consider it. Oh, my God, she's smiling at me again."

The corners of the dog's open mouth lifted as she turned her head to him, then back to his dinner companion.

"She likes you," he said, dropping a hand down to rub her behind an ear. "Don't ya, girl?"

For an answer, the dog sat up on her haunches, shifted, and placed her head down in Lexi's lap.

What did it say about him that a tiny bullet of jealousy shot through him because he wished it was his own head nestled between Lexi's legs and not his dog's?

"You really are a beautiful girl," she said, dropping a kiss on the dog's snout.

That tiny bullet turned into a cumbersome cannonball. He imagined what her lips would taste like pressed against his and was hard as granite in the time it took to take a breath.

The image of her mouth, taking him in and running up and down his full, erect length burst clear and bright in his mind as if it were a memory and not merely a wish.

Blinking did nothing to chase it away or slow the blood pumping to his pelvis.

"Aiden?"

He shook his head left and right a few times. With a monumental effort he was sure would result in a headache, he called for internal calm.

"Is everything okay?"

"Yeah, why?" he managed to say, thankful the timbre of his voice remained steady and smooth.

"You looked a bit…lost there, for a moment."

"Just thinking about all the work we've got waiting for us in there." He ticked his head toward her study. "Let's finish up and get back to it."

With a nod, she diverted her attention back to her meal. Brontë let out a doggy sigh of her own, then slid back down to the floor, this time settled at Lexi's feet.

When they were finished, the dishes in the dishwasher, they took their seats again in front of her computer.

"So you got this guy Smith's info," Aiden said, putting his glasses back on. "Have you called up his statements yet?"

The tops of her cheeks went pink when she said, "I tried. But I need a password to access the account. I guess I didn't think this all the way through. Of course it's a password-protected account. Everything is nowadays."

With a nod, Aiden turned to the screen. "There are ways around it, but I'm reluctant to use your computer to do it. I can't vouch for its security, and any attempt we make to access a private account could set off a signal to the company. You wouldn't want that."

"Oh, good Lord, I never even considered that." She dropped her head into her hands. "This was the stupidest idea I've ever had."

"I don't think the word stupid can be applied in any context to you. Don't worry. I've got a way, just not through your computer. We need mine."

Her head whipped up so fast he felt a breeze shunt past him. "Wait. You…hack?" She lowered her voice when she said the word and looked equal parts of horrified and excited. He let out a full belly laugh.

God, he wanted to kiss her.

"Not quite," he said when he got control of his thoughts lest he give in to the impulse and press his mouth against hers. "It's a grey area for sure, but I won't be getting arrested or put on any watch list, so don't worry. Remember Lexi, this is what I do for a living. And I'm very good at it."

"I have no doubt about that at all," she said immediately. When her gaze did a quick dip down to his mouth and then shot back up to his eyes, her neck turning a lovely shade of rose, the tension low in his belly erupted again.

He pulled deep for calm as she sat back and squared her shoulders. He wasn't a bit surprised when her hand swiped around her ear and pressed the lobe.

"I'll access his info from my home desktop later on," he said. "For now, you mentioned there are some boxes you haven't gotten to yet?"

She nodded.

"Do you think there might be something in them to help us find some answers?"

"I honestly don't know. They're mostly books I packed up from her apartment. I didn't have time to look through them."

"No harm in doing it now."

She rose and Aiden followed suit.

Brontë was back to her resting spot underneath the window, but she lifted her head and tracked them when they walked into the room.

Lexi opened a hall door filled almost to the top with banker's boxes.

"These are all books?" he asked.

"The one thing Zoe and I shared was a love of reading. She was the type to stroll into a used bookstore and buy something just because the cover struck her fancy. Her apartment was filled with books, strewn everywhere, on top of furniture, under her bed. Like I said, I just gathered them all up and packed them. I figured I go through everything at one point, see if any called to me to read, and then donate the rest to the local library. I know how tight money is to purchase books these days."

"Kind of giving back."

Surprise jumped into her eyes. "Yes. Exactly."

"Okay. Since I'm here and I'm another set of hands, let's go through these, see if we can find anything useful."

He hauled out the top two boxes and, from the heft, imagined them filled with textbooks.

They worked in her living room with him sitting on the couch in front of her cocktail table, she on the floor opposite him and Brontë under the table between them. Once again the dog rested her head against Lexi.

"Oh, goodness."

"What?"

"This"—she held up a small paperback—"was Zoe's favorite book as a tween."

"*The Case Files of Jenny Pertwiddy*," he read. "Sounds like a kiddie mystery."

"It is. About an eleven-year-old girl who's an amateur sleuth." She sighed and placed the book down on the table. "Zoe loved it."

With a shake of her head, she grabbed another one.

He hit pay dirt when he opened the last of the two

remaining boxes.

"This isn't a book. It's a day planner." He held it up to her.

The hardbound book, covered in roses, and the title—*A Day in My Life*—gave the impression to the casual eye it was some sort of fictional tome. The inside, though, held a calendar and planner, the pages divided into weeks and months with each page an individual day. Most of the pages were covered in notes, appointments, even phone numbers.

"Let me see." She stood and reached for the book. "This is the current year." She flipped a few pages. "Goodness, she was a busy girl. I never realized how full her life was. Every weekend has two or three things listed." She flipped to the center of the book, a gasp flying from her.

Aiden's body went on alert, his dog's as well as Brontë lifted her head and gave her full attention to Lexi.

"The last entry is the day before she…died."

Her voice broke, the quiet pain in it screaming at him to give comfort. Rising from his perch on the couch, he moved next to her and threw an arm around her shoulders, cuddling her to his side, just as tears spilled down her cheeks and heartbreaking sobs erupted from within her. Brontë came out from under the table, sat, and leaned her weight against her thigh. Aiden knew the move well, since the dog made it every time he had a headache.

While Lexi cried, he held her, his lips skimming her forehead. She turned to face him and burrowed into his chest, the book wedged between them.

Growing up with a horde of brothers and a mother

who invented the phrase *backbone of steel*, he'd never been witness to emotional crying jags. Even when his health had gone to hell, his mother's terrified tears were something she'd never allowed anyone to see.

As he ran his hands up and down Lexi's slim back, he marveled at how small and fragile she appeared when he'd seen her as nothing less than steadfast and strong.

The other thought flittering through his mind as he held her was how wonderful she felt in his arms and how perfectly she fit within them.

And you're a first class asshole for thinking that as she's crying her eyes out.

"I apologize," she said after a few moments. She swiped at her cheeks with the tips of her fingers and pulled in a jagged breath. "I don't usually fall apart this way." Embarrassment tinged her face as she lifted her watery gaze to his. "Just seeing this"—she lifted the planner—"and realizing it was the last connection to Zoe just…hit me hard."

"Totally understandable. Please don't ever apologize for your emotions." He squeezed her arms. "You've lost your sister, someone you shared blood and history with. A good cry is deserved."

Shaking her head, she dropped her free hand down to pet the dog's head. Brontë flicked her tongue over it, her head tilting to one side as she regarded Lexi. "It's as if she can read people," she said. "Identify their emotions."

"I'm no expert and you can probably quote me a study to either prove or disprove it, but I think dogs are more intuitive than people. They're certainly kinder."

His heart thudded against his chest when one side

of her mouth quirked.

Good. Her smile, even a small, lopsided one, was easier to deal with than her tears. He'd wanted nothing more than to gather her up in his arms and sit them on the couch with her in his lap while he kissed and cooed away the sadness. He wanted to be a balm and ease the pain of her sister's death, quiet the torment he sensed she felt about it.

He knew next to nothing about her, bare bones in truth, yet he'd never felt such a strong desire to comfort and protect a woman before.

Nor had that need to comfort ever been so mixed with arousal.

The moment he touched her, every nerve in his body fired like an internal switch had been flicked on, serving to heighten his already skyrocketing awareness.

The subtle aroma of vanilla in her hair tickled his nose. The smooth, supple, and intoxicatingly warm skin he brushed over made his fingertips tingle. She barely came to his shoulder. When she tilted her head against his chest and pressed in, the knowledge she trusted him with her honest vulnerability barreled through him.

He wanted to be her protector, her source of comfort, and lose himself in her all at the same time.

Lexi shifted, and he let her go.

"Okay now?"

"Yes, thank you." She crouched down to eye level with his dog. "And thank you, too." She was rewarded with both a face lick and a doggie-smile.

Hauling in a deep breath, she held it for a moment, then let it out.

"We should go over this." She held up the planner.

"Let's go through the rest of the box first, and then

the last one, just to ensure there's nothing else. We don't want to miss anything pertinent."

Once they'd cleared the boxes, it was apparent the planner was all they were going to find of interest.

Seated at her kitchen table, they opened it to the beginning and began reading it page by page.

"The same notation is made for every Tuesday night at seven," he said. "*Group.* It corresponds with the credit card and parking receipts. Do you have any idea what it means?"

Instead of answering him, she said, "Look at this." She leaned in closer and shoved the book nearer to him. "Starting in April, she writes *Meet with Kim* underneath the group note." She flipped the pages forward. "Same thing, every week. There's no phone number or address listed for her, though." Her eyes were shining with excitement when she lifted them back to his. He was getting used to the swift, hard jab to his abdomen every time she focused her full attention on him.

"Think they're connected?"

She leaned back in the chair. "Remember when I told you Zoe had a bit of trouble as a teen?"

He nodded.

"She got herself out of it when her counselor referred her to an AA meeting."

"Alcoholics Anonymous? You didn't say she had an issue with booze."

"She didn't, not in the true alcoholic sense. But she did have impulse control issues and didn't possess the tools to rein in any compulsions and deal with them. One drink would lead to ten. One hit of a joint would lead to a night of them. Going to meetings to deal with her demons was more a way for her to be accountable and keep a lid on her destructive actions. And it worked."

"And she still attended them after all this time?"

"I'm convinced she did even though we hadn't spoken about it since she was in college."

"And…what? You think this Kim was part of those meetings? Another member, maybe?"

She nodded.

"Come on," he said, rising and moving back to her laptop.

"What are you thinking?" she asked.

"Of a way to see if you're hunch is correct."

He keyed in the name of the coffee shop from the credit card receipts, then the parking garage. When he added the addresses, he plotted them on a map search.

"They're within a block of one another," Lexi said, her eyes watching the screen.

Then, Aiden did a search for all the self-help and addiction group meetings in a five-block radius. Fifteen different groups popped up along with the addresses and times they were held.

"She never had trouble with her weight," Lexi said, "so you can eliminate the three eating disorder ones. Same thing with shopaholics and postpartum depression meetings."

"There are two AA groups and one Narcotics Anonymous gathering listed," he said, "all within one block of the coffee house listed on her credit card receipts. Only the NA group meets on Tuesday nights. Would she have attended that one and not the AA meeting?"

When she bit down on a corner of her lip, Aiden had to shift position in the chair lest she see the effect she had on the lower half of his body.

"In all honesty she could have gone to either," she said after a few moments. "Both promote living one day at a time and giving yourself up to a higher power, which is what helped Zoe initially."

Her gaze turned thoughtful as she turned to him. "Kim could have been a member of the group or even Zoe's sponsor. Accountability is key in ensuring backslides are kept to a minimum or eradicated completely."

He held his tongue on something his brother Dylan had told him once when they'd been discussing a celebrity client the firm was charged with protecting. The guy had already done three stints in a ridiculously expensive treatment facility for the infamous and addicted. Dylan had been hired to protect him from rabid fans and prying paparazzi while he finished shooting a movie.

"Once an addict, always an addict," Dylan had said, sagely. "They never stop feeling the urge; they simply learn how to control the impulse to feed it. Or they don't. Recovery is a lifelong struggle and process."

"Although," Lexi added, interrupting the memory, "the rate of relapse with addictive behaviors is estimated at between 40 and 60 percent. Which is probably the reason Zoe continued with group counseling."

Aiden could appreciate the inability to control urges because at that moment he wanted to kiss her more than he'd wanted to a few minutes ago.

Kiss? Hell, he wanted to get lost in her and hope never to be found.

"I wish we knew how to find this Kim person," she

said on a sigh. "But without a phone number or any other kind of identification, we can't."

"There is a way," he said, tugging his glasses off and twirling them between his fingers.

"How?"

"Well, it depends," he said, leaning forward and holding her gaze prisoner. "How do you feel about a road trip?"

Chapter 5

It was difficult to believe she was back on an airplane less than forty-eight hours after arriving home. Once again she had a window seat with Aiden to her right, his eyes closed, but the seats were immeasurably more comfortable now, since they were in first class.

Her shock at the seating assignments was just one more thing in the past twenty-four-hour period that had been filled with surprises.

After asking how she felt about a road trip, Aiden explained the reasoning behind his question.

"We have a pretty good working theory about Zoe's last days, based on her planner," he said, while petting the dog who'd nuzzled her way between them. "It's a place to start, to see if we can make some sense of what happened to either cause her to take her own life, which you don't believe, or to find out who killed her and why."

He planned to attend the Tuesday Narcotics Anonymous meeting to locate Kim, if she was in fact, connected to Zoe through the group.

Before agreeing, Lexi did a quick calculation of her upcoming expenses and bills in her head. If she walked to work for the foreseeable future and ate a sandwich every day at her desk instead of ordering a salad, she'd be able to swing it. Of course she didn't share this with Aiden. He didn't need to know how little available cash she had, especially when she was still trying to come up with a way to repay him for helping her.

Aiden

The first surprise of the morning had been when she was picked up at six a.m. by Aiden, his brother, and a smiling Brontë.

"Dyl's driving us to the airport and then getting us when we return. That way we don't have to deal with parking," Aiden told her once she'd shaken his older brother's hand and received a good morning lick from the dog. The second surprise had been Dylan, himself. If not for the subtle difference in their height, they could have been twins. The same jet black hair, although Dylan's was shorter, and the identical piercing blue eyes prompted her to say, "Blue eyes are a recessive trait, so if both of you have them your parents are blue-eyed, as well."

Dylan's grin—another twin to his younger brother—came fast and bright, Aiden's taking a slower stroll until it bloomed.

"Our older brother, Josh, has blue eyes, too," Dylan told her and then flicked his brother a quick glance. "Brain said you were smart."

Her face heated at what he meant as a compliment. For the thousandth time in her life, she wished it wasn't such a dominant feature of her personality.

"He failed to mention, though, how beautiful you are," he added with a grin.

"Dylan." There was a warning in Aiden's voice.

"Brain?" she asked.

"Ignore him," Aiden said. "It's a stupid nickname. You don't want me telling her what we call you, do you?" he asked his brother.

The grin disappeared in a heartbeat, and Lexi had to stifle a giggle at Dylan's abashed features.

Brontë placed her head on Lexi's lap as they flew

through the early morning traffic. Absently, she petted the dog's head and got another surprise at how calming the action was.

"I booked us a hotel for two nights," Aiden said, turning around to face her. "If we find something that needs further looking into, we can extend the stay."

Lexi flicked a glance in the rearview at his brother.

"I explained everything to Dylan," he said.

"Oh. Oh, okay then."

"I'm gonna do a dive into your friend Smith," Dylan said. "See what I can come up with. I'll text if I find anything."

Lexi nodded and once again grew nervous about how she was going to reimburse them for their time. Between the airline tickets, a hotel stay, and everything else she figured would come up regarding their investigation, she was beginning to question pursuing what might lead to nowhere.

They arrived at the airport a short time later.

"Take care of my best girl," Aiden told his brother while they gave each other a man-hug, complete with enthusiastic back thumps. "She's not used to me leaving so soon after coming home. Pay her some extra attention today."

"Don't worry. I've already got our route planned for our run." The grin he tossed him again was steeped in mischief as he wiggled his eyebrows.

"Do not use my dog to pick up women." Aiden jabbed his brother in the chest with his index finger, but she could see the humor shining in his eyes.

Lifting his hands in an aw-shucks gesture, Dylan replied, "I can't help it if she's a natural chick magnet."

"You're an asshole." Another hug and then he

grabbed both of their overnight bags from the back seat.

"It was nice meeting you," Lexi said. "Thank you for picking me up."

"Don't mention it. And in this family, we hug." He ignored her outstretched hand and tugged her into his tree-trunk muscled arms before she realized what he was doing. He embraced her the same way he had his brother, although he was much gentler with his back pats. Releasing her, he told them, "Safe travels."

"Talk later," Aiden said.

They managed to get through the security line without any issues. Only when their flight was called did Lexi realize where they were seated.

"It's more comfortable for me to fly first class," he explained while they walked down the jetway, "because of my height."

"But you were in coach the other day."

He dipped his chin and averted his eyes.

"Last-minute booking," he said as they entered the plane. "You take what they have available."

"Wasn't this a last-minute booking, too?"

His shrug looked awkward as they took their seats. "Better availability today, I guess."

They cabbed to the hotel after landing, and once again Lexi's nerves came full force. This wasn't the one-star, low-cost economy motel she'd booked the last time she'd been in town but an upscale, five-star hotel she'd never be able to afford even if she skipped lunch for year.

"What's wrong?" Aiden asked in the elevator. "You look upset."

She shook her head, then swallowed, keeping her gaze glued to the wall panel as they ascended to their floor, even knowing Aiden's attention stayed focused on her.

"This is a suite," she cried the moment she entered the room. Her bag fell from her hand, and she spun around to confront him. "Aiden, I can't afford this."

"I can." He shrugged off his duffle and tossed it on floor.

"But you're not paying for all this"—she flipped her hand around the room—"I am. You're working for me, remember?"

"I'm helping you, not working for you," he said, shaking his head. "I'm still off the clock for a few more days, so you're not responsible for the cost of any of this. And that includes the airfare in case you're nervous about that, too."

Dumbfounded, she gaped at him. "I can't let you do that."

"Why not? I can more than afford it, and besides, it's already done."

"Why are you helping me? You don't even know me, never met me before two days ago, and now you're flying across the country in first class, staying in a five-star hotel—in a suite, no less—and you're not even going to charge me for your investigative services? There has to be some reason you're doing this other than you're a nice guy."

"First of all, we didn't fly across the country. It took less than two hours to get here. And I like a suite when I travel because my hours are usually hectic which makes eating a problem if the hotel restaurants are closed for the night. Having a suite with a kitchen included is easier for me." He strode to her, his long legs eating up the carpet as his gaze paralyzed her in place. "And as far as the reason I'm helping you goes"—he slid his hands around her upper arms—"I *am* a nice guy, and you don't need to be worried about my intentions, if that's what you mean."

Heat ramped up her neck and scorched her cheeks.

"I understand how concerned you are about the circumstances surrounding your sister's death, Lexi. In your position, I'd feel the same way if one of my brothers died suddenly. I'd have questions, too, I'd want answered. I happen to be in the unique position to help you get some of those answers."

"It's really that simple for you?"

"Yeah, it is."

When he dropped his hands and turned from her, she had the ridiculous notion to grab them back and make him hold her again.

"Things are usually more simple than people make them out to be. Now, I'm gonna put my stuff in my room and set up shop out here. Give me a few minutes and we can plan the day, okay?"

Sighing, she nodded.

"Why are we going to see Zoe's editor?" she asked him twenty minutes later when they got into the cab the doorman had called for them. "I already spoke to him."

"We've got some time to kill before tonight's meeting, and I've got a few questions rolling around in my head about her work situation. You said her editor wasn't forthcoming when you spoke to him originally, right?"

She shook her head. "So?"

Aiden settled back in the seat. "So now we've got an idea something was going on in her life which may be connected to her group meetings. Since she was a journalist, I'm willing to bet whatever it was, she'd do some research on it or maybe talk to someone at the magazine about it. About the potential of a story. To her editor, maybe. All stories have to be approved by an editor, so…" He left the rest unsaid.

"That's a fairly large leap in logic, don't you think?"

The grin he tossed her had her pulse jumping.

"Sometimes the answer is right in front of you. You just need to know the correct questions to ask in order to see it."

He certainly made sense. She hadn't asked Zoe's editor anything other than if she'd been working on something dangerous. She could see now how she should have pressed him harder.

"Do you think he'll be honest with us? He never gave me any indication she was writing anything other than the stuff she was assigned. If she was, he might just…lie to us."

Aiden nodded. "He may. He may think it's in the magazine's best interest to keep quiet. If Zoe was working on something that got her killed, he wouldn't want the publication to assume any liability or responsibility for that."

"How will we know, then, if he's being truthful?"

His lips lifted slowly, starting in one corner and then gliding to the other. She couldn't look away from his mouth while it moved into a captivating and cocky smirk.

"Do you trust I know what I'm doing?" he asked.

She didn't need to think before replying, "Yes."

Aiden nodded. "Don't worry. He'll be truthful."

From the look of steely reserve in his eyes, she had

no doubt of it.

They were silent, each lost in their own thoughts, as the cab meandered crosstown.

At one point, Aiden said, "Since you've met the editor already, I'll let you take the lead when we get there."

"The last time he was brusque and treated me like he couldn't be bothered speaking to me. As if I was taking him away from something important. It was rude, that's for sure, and it's why I didn't think he knew anything. Wouldn't he act cagey, or try to figure out what I knew if he were hiding something?"

"Maybe. Maybe he simply assumed you didn't have a clue what your sister did at the magazine."

"Well, is there anything, specifically, I should say or ask him this time?"

He cocked his head and considered her for a few seconds. From the way his piercing eyes narrowed in on her face, she got the strangest sensation he could see inside her, deep, deep inside, read her mind, know all her secrets and…desires.

Her hand rose and her fingers brushed the hair at her temple behind her ear while she licked suddenly parched lips. A shudder ran up her spine, and it took her a moment to realize her nerves had nothing to do with fear and everything to do with excitement.

His lower jaw twisted as he bit down in the inside of his cheek. "Then depends," he said.

Lexi swallowed. "On what?"

He snuck a glance at the driver, then bent his head so she could hear his lowered voice. It took all the will she could muster not to melt into him.

"How good an actress would you say you are?"

****

Her eyes widened and filled with fear at the same time her cheeks went pale. Aiden was playing with fire by asking the question. He'd never told her he knew about her seduction act in the bar and from the concern wafting across her brow he wondered if she suspected he did.

"I need to know because I've got an idea and I'm wondering how comfortable you're gonna be going along with it."

"What—what did you have in mind?"

When he told her, her eyes widened, and then he swore he could hear the gears grinding in her head about how to pull it off. Excitement jumped from her expression when she said, "You're sure about this?"

He tried to make his shrug casual. "I think it'll work. You think you're up to it?"

She told him she was "all-in," and for the life of him he couldn't help the pleased sensation sluicing through him.

"We're here to see Cameron Monroe," Lexi told the receptionist stationed outside the glass partition leading to the magazine's offices.

"Do you have an appointment?"

"Yes," Aiden said before Lexi could tell the girl they didn't. He gave his name, and they stepped back while the receptionist called the office.

"When did you make an appointment?" Lexi whispered.

Clamping down on the urge to run his nose along the slender column of her throat and inhale even more of the sweet vanilla flavor drifting toward him, Aiden lowered his own voice. "Yesterday afternoon after I left your apartment. I knew we'd have easier access if we had one. It's better than showing up unannounced."

"What did you say you wanted to see him about?"

She turned her head a fraction and lifted her gaze to his. Standing this close he could make out every shard of green, jade, and amber surrounding her pupils—pupils that dilated when he snuck a glance down to her lips.

"A personal matter," he said, happy the desire running wild in him wasn't apparent in his voice.

"He'll see you now," the receptionist told them.

It took him a good two seconds to break his gaze from Lexi's. A complete sense of joy shot through him when she gave her head a little shake and took a breath while they followed the receptionist.

Going with the scenario he'd outlined for her, he reached down and slipped his hand into hers, gave it a gentle squeeze, and felt her return it.

Cameron Monroe looked, Aiden imagined, like what a middle-aged magazine editor in chief should look like: stocky, hung over, and as if the weight of the world were carried on his substantial shoulders. The scattered red tracks in his eyes bespoke a late night drinker, the paunch nestled above his belt buckle that of a man used to sitting. Dark skin, dark eyes, and just going grey, close-cropped hair completed the look.

The downtown Atlanta skyline backdropped him from where he stood behind his desk. Tired eyes scanned Aiden up and down, then slid to Lexi. He squinted. "Ms.…Buckley, isn't it? What are you doing here?"

Aiden jumped in before she could answer. "Thanks for seeing us. Aiden Keane." He held out his hand and waited until the editor took it.

"Your name is in my appointment book," the man said, then turned to Lexi. "Yours isn't."

"I'm Dr. Buckley's…friend." He stretched a hand over and tugged one of Lexi's into his. "We're only in town for a day, and I didn't want to spend any time away from her, so I asked to tag along today," Aiden said, grinning and knowing he looked affable and harmless doing so.

Monroe's eyebrows crawled up to his hairline. "I thought the appointment was with you," he said, addressing Aiden.

Aiden shrugged, said, "I guess there's been a mix-up."

Monroe stared at him a beat, then indicated the chairs in front of his massive desk.

"Why, exactly, are you here again, Ms. Buckley?" he asked while they sat. "I was under the impression our business concerning your sister was completed."

As he'd instructed her to in the cab, Lexi took over. Gone was the pleasant, soft-spoken woman he was coming to know, replaced by a peeved pixie with an ax to grind. With her free hand fisted in her lap and murder in her eyes, she leaned forward and glared at the man. "That's where you're wrong," she said in a voice cut from glass. "The last time you wouldn't give me any information on my sister and basically gave me the bum's rush out the door, like you couldn't be bothered with me."

"I answered your questions." He looked down his nose as if she were a bug he wanted to squash, and Aiden clamped down on the desire to smash his fist into the man's face.

"No, you didn't. I want to know what she was working on for you, and don't insult my intelligence again by telling me it was wedding announcements and birth notices."

"That's exactly what she did for us. I don't know why you don't believe that."

"I know that's what she *did,"* Lexi snapped. "What I want to know is what else she was working on."

"Nothing."

"I don't believe you."

"I really don't care whether you do or not, but it's true. Your sister was contracted to this magazine for a specific reason and nothing more."

"Oh, there's more," Lexi, said her voice harsh and deathly rigid.

On cue, Aiden squeezed her hand. "Babe?" Lexi turned her glare on him. What did it say about him he was so turned on felt he might have to cross his legs to keep the effect she had on him concealed? "Take a breath. Getting your blood pressure up isn't gonna help you find out what happened."

She did, and Aiden sent her a tiny wink.

When she—apparently—had herself under control again, she turned back to Monroe. "I would greatly appreciate it if you could tell me what you know about my sister's death."

"I told you the last time you were here I don't know anything about her suicide—"

"She didn't kill herself."

"The police think she did."

"And how do you know what the police think?" Lexi asked, eyes narrowing as she leaned forward again.

Good girl. Aiden mentally high-fived her quickness.

Monroe snapped his mouth shut. Then, after a moment said, "The detective in charge of her case. I don't remember his name. He came here, asked questions. He told me they considered it a suicide."

"They're wrong. Zoe didn't kill herself. Someone murdered her."

It was subtle, and if he hadn't been staring intently at the man, Aiden knew he would have missed it. But the faint spark of worry that flashed in Monroe's eyes proved the man knew more than he was admitting.

Sitting back in his chair, the editor took a deep breath, his attention focused on Lexi. "Murdered? That's a helluva an allegation to make. Why do you think that?"

"I don't think it, I know it."

His eyes narrowed. "How?"

"Zoe was a journalist."

The condescending jeer in the man's single laugh heated Aiden's blood.

"She was," Lexi said. "And a good one. I think a story she was working on got her killed."

"You *think*? So you don't really *know* anything. Where's your proof, Ms. Buckley? Do you have any? Anything tangible?"

She flicked her gaze to Aiden, then back to him. "If you tell me what she was working on, I'll have the proof I need."

"So that's a no." He shook his head and crossed his arms over his chest. "I thought as much. Now, I am under no legal obligation to tell you what—if anything—she was working on while employed here at the magazine, but I have done so. Twice now. So I suggest you give up these ridiculous, potentially slanderous statements and accept the fact your sister killed herself. She was an unhappy, morose woman."

"You didn't know her at all if you think that," Lexi said.

"I knew her well enough to know what a mediocre writer she was."

Lexi's spine turned to hardened cement.

"I'm sorry she'd dead, but I've answered your questions and, as I've said, I am under no obligation to discuss anything else about her work while employed here." He stood again and lifted a hand. "Now, you're both here under false pretenses, so before you waste any more of my time, I suggest you leave, or I'll need to have Security remove you."

Aiden sat back in the comfortable visitor chair, one leg resting on the other, his shoulders relaxed and said, "You may think you're not legally liable, but if you're in possession of any research notes, flash drives, or personal emails, anything at all, that could prove to be of vital information in the investigation into her death, you could be held accountable if you don't turn it over or make it known."

"There is no investigation into her death. I told you, the detective informed me they've ruled it a suicide. End of story."

"And we're in possession of information refuting that."

"What are you, a cop? Lawyer?"

Aiden laughed, outright. "Nope to both. I'm merely Dr. Buckley's friend."

"Then I'm done listening to you." He pointed to

the door. "Now I want you both out of my office. You've wasted enough of my time already—"

"It wouldn't be a bad idea for you to call a lawyer, though. A good one, too. Maybe even more than one."

"What are you talking about?"

"Well, for starters..." Aiden leaned forward and rested his elbows on his knees, his gaze staying locked on the editor's face. "There are the gambling debts to a local...businessman, and I use the term loosely, who I believe knows you quite well. Those debts were recently paid in full with funds garnered from the magazine. Over ten thousand dollars' worth. Magazine expenses which were, well, we'll say *shuffled*, to another account. A private one. In your name. You'll need a good criminal lawyer once it's made known to the owner of the magazine his editor in chief is embezzling."

Monroe's cocoa-colored skin turned the color of ash. "What—"

"Then, there's the little pied-à-terre you have here in the city I'm pretty sure your wife doesn't know about." Aiden grinned again. "But your girlfriend does, because she lives in it. Rent free, too. I'm thinking you'll need a good divorce lawyer when the wife finds out about her."

Sweat drenched Monroe's face and shirt.

"And of course you'll need another lawyer once the feds come after you when they hear about all those videos you've got stored on your office computer. You know the ones I mean. As I understand the law, filming women in the bathroom is an unlawful invasion of privacy and, I believe, subject to over a dozen different prosecution statutes. Come to think of it, you'll probably want to engage an entire firm so all those specialties can be covered."

"How…?"

Fear had many looks, Aiden thought as the man in front of him physically shrank behind his desk and plopped back down in to his chair.

He felt Lexi's eyes on him, knew she was astounded by what he'd just divulged, but he kept his own attention focused on the man they'd come to see.

"Now, I think it's time you answered Dr. Buckley's question and tell her exactly what her sister was working on for this magazine. Or what she was researching. If you continue stonewalling us, you won't have enough time to contact a law firm before hell rains down on you from all quarters."

Monroe swallowed several times as his color turned from fire-red to muted gray.

Several seconds passed. The moisture on the man's forehead and above his lips, increased. After swiping a hand over his brows, he addressed Lexi. "She came to me a few weeks before she…died." He licked his lips and swiped a hand across his sweating brow again. "Asked me a bunch of questions about one of the magazine's advertisers."

"Advertisers?" Lexi said.

"Which one?" Aiden asked.

The struggle to tell them warred all over his face with the fear Aiden would make everything he'd accused Monroe of public.

The fear won.

"The Kingman Group," he said on a loud exhale. "They're a public relations firm, and they've been one of our clients since the magazine first went into production. They advertise with us monthly, have a huge budget and a rotating ad campaign."

"Why did Zoe want to know about them?"

He swallowed. "She said she was interested in doing a story on the public relations industry."

Lexi nodded. "Okay, then, what did she ask about?"

He sat back in his chair, all the energy appearing to drain from his body. "Who was in charge of the company? What was the group's tie to the magazine? Many of our clients have personal relationships with William Bard, the owner. Zoe wanted to know who handled the Kingman account."

"And what did you tell her?"

"Nothing. I don't handle the day-to-day working of the magazine's advertising. We have individual departments and managers for the minutiae. I referred her to the advertising editor, Dewitt Carde. He's been in charge of the ad division since the magazine's beginnings."

"Do you know if she contacted him?"

"No, and that's all I did and all I know. Zoe never approached me with any kind of story idea, that's the God's truth. She merely wanted info on the Kingman Group. I swear it." He pulled a Post-It from a holder on his desk, scribbled something in a shaky hand, then handed it to Lexi. "This is Carde's number. He works, mainly, from his home office."

Lexi took the note, glanced down at it, then to Aiden, who nodded. "Thank you," he said to Monroe, then stood.

"Wait. That's it? Are you…? You're—you're not going to…"

Aiden smiled and placed a hand at Lexi's back when she stood next to him. "We'll be in touch if we have anything else."

Without another word, they exited the office.

"How—"

"Not here," Aiden said, his voice hushed as he slid a hand around her upper arm. "Wait until we're outside.

Chapter 6

Her entire body shook like margarita mix in a whirling blender. The crowded elevator forced her to keep her questions contained. Aiden kept his hand wound around her arm during the ride, so he had to feel her body quaking. Lexi glanced up at him while the floors ticked off one by one, his attention fixed on the numbers above the doors as they toggled downward, his chin lifted, his mouth composed and relaxed.

How the hell could he be this calm when her insides were jumping like popcorn exploding in a microwave?

Well, that's a stupid question, Alexis. This is what he does for a living. It makes sense he isn't acting like a nervous Nelly.

Lexi had a hundred questions banging around in her brain and felt she was going to explode if she didn't give them a voice soon.

Once they were outside the building, she let loose. "How did you know all those things about Monroe? And why didn't you tell me, beforehand?"

Aiden typed on his phone for a moment, the *whoosh* of a message sending audible in the noisy midday bustle around them.

"I just ordered us a ride. And to answer your question—Dylan. He spent most of last night deep diving through Monroe's life so we'd have something to use if he refused to tell you anything."

"A head's-up would have been nice. Was all that stuff you told him about lawyers, true?"

He shrugged. "It sounded good. I wasn't sure there would be a need to use any of the intel." He dipped his head toward her, a half grin tugging on a corner of his mouth. "You were handling him perfectly. Strong, persistent, and pissed. I figured he was gonna tell you what you wanted to know without me ever saying a word."

She folded her arms over her chest.

Glancing up, he thrust out his chin and said, "Here's our ride."

The back seat of the car he'd ordered was smaller than the previous taxi, so small the outsides of their legs slid against one another as the car pulled into traffic. An involuntary shudder slipped up her spine.

"I'm really impressed at the amount of anger you could call up when you spoke to him. Like a seasoned actress. I thought you were going to hit him at one point."

"I certainly thought about it," she mumbled and shook her head.

"So did I." He grinned across at her, reached out a hand, and tugged hers into it. "Did you perform in school plays as a kid?"

Stunned by how perfect his skin felt against hers, she fumbled for a moment before she could speak. "N-no. Not school. But…" She stared down at their joined hands.

When he squeezed hers, she took a breath and did something so out of character that she sent herself a mental note to think later why her willingness to divulge her past to him wasn't causing her nerves to spark.

"My mother had…issues. Money. Shopping. Men." She hoped her shrug came off less embarrassed than she felt. "More times than I can remember, I needed to help her out of a jam she'd gotten herself, and us, into. Missed rent payments, bringing home a man from a bar who decided he didn't want to leave the next morning." She tossed him a side eye to gauge his reaction and was met with an expression so understanding she almost wept. "A few times I pretended to go ballistic and all bat-shit crazy just to get a man out of our apartment. I figured no guy wanted a woman when she's got out-of-control kids hanging around, right?"

He squeezed her hand again.

"Sometimes I'll have to deal with a recalcitrant, demanding student, or even a professor or two who act high and mighty and rude. A few firm words said in a tone brooking no argument and that hints at retaliation usually defuses the situation and makes the person more cooperative. It's a sad commentary on gender bias that when a woman raises her voice, people tend to think she's gone off the deep end and most will make an attempt to quell her craziness by changing behavior."

His deep, soft chuckle ignited a fire in her belly that had her squirming in the seat.

"Remind me never to do, or say, anything to get on your bad side. Although"—his eyes turned to slits—"the…punishment…may be worthwhile."

All the moisture in Lexi's mouth evaporated, and her insides vibrated like an oscillating fan turned on high. This time she was certain he was flirting with her, and in truth, she didn't know how to respond. Give him a sexy retort to show she understood his meaning? Or ignore it and change the subject before he could detect the effect his words had on her?

"Did you know," she began after licking some moisture back into her lips, her gaze staying locked on his, "in medieval times, women were punished by having a device called a scold's bridle placed over their heads if they spoke out of turn, sassed, or spoke in anger toward men? It was meant to silence them until they agreed to apologize for their"—she lifted her free hand and made quote marks in the air—"'out of control and disrespectful behavior.'"

Lexi's pulse tripled when Aiden's eyes went to half-mast and one corner of his luscious lips inched upward.

Oh...my.

The man caused every nerve in her body to stand at attention and scream with longing, the likes of which she'd never experienced before. Lexi swallowed—again—and tried to quell the quivering overtaking her insides.

Aiden lifted the hand he held and dragged it against his chin, her knuckles grazing his skin, before he placed a sweet, gentle kiss along them. "Personally," he said, his voice a whispering smolder, his tone packed with gravel, "it's a good thing I live in the here and now because I love nothing better than verbally sparring, especially with my woman."

Oh, sweet baby Jesus.

Her toes curled inside her shoes, and when she pressed her shaking thighs together, liquid heat gushed through her.

"Here ya go," the driver said, breaking through the

sexual heat engulfing the back of the cab.

Aiden held her gaze for a beat, then pressed her hand, once, and let it go.

Lexi took the few moments to try and temper the raging emotions and sensations tripping through her.

"This place has an extensive menu, and it's quiet," Aiden told her after he once again took her arm and led her into the small establishment. "We can talk here without shouting to be heard."

When they were seated in a far-off booth, their orders taken, he rested back against the faux-leather seat, and Lexi took the moment to ask, "What are you going to do about the info you have on Monroe? Give it to the police?"

"What do you think we should do?"

She pondered that. "I'm not sure we can go to the cops and let them know because he could accuse us of blackmailing him into telling him about my sister if we did."

"I'm not sure blackmail's the right term, but I get what you mean. There are other ways, though, to let the people who need to know about his…deeds, without us reporting him."

"Do I want to know these ways?"

"Better off if you don't. You wouldn't want to tarnish your upstanding citizen and librarian crown now, would you?"

The wildfire heating her cheeks and neck at his words was unpreventable. Thinking of how she'd baited and fooled Peter Smith, Lexi knew her so-called crown was far from pristine and untarnished and wondered what Aiden would think if she'd told him exactly what she'd done to obtain the info she had on the man.

Thinking of him had her asking, "Where are we going next? To see Peter Smith?"

"No. He's for tomorrow. I want to know a little more about the group before we ambush him." He pulled his cell out again, along with the Post-It Monroe had given them. "I want to call Dewitt Carde and see if he'll meet us."

He was forced to leave a message and did so.

"Think he'll call back?" she asked.

"It's anyone's guess. Hopefully, he will. After this we should head back to the hotel. I've got a few things to do before we head over to the NA meeting."

"That's still not for four more hours."

He nodded. "Enjoy the free time. Go shopping. Read. Take a nap. I'm sure you can quote me some statistic about adults needing to nap as much a kids do."

Automatically, Lexi said, "Experts in the field of sleep study have found adults who nap during daylight hours can decrease their stress, boost the creative center of the mind, and enhance motor skills and accuracy. It also helps with weight loss and even lowers the risk of heart attacks."

She blinked twice and then dropped her gaze to her plate of food.

"See?" he said. Daring a peek at him, she found his smile bright, his eyes lit with humor. "Alexis Buckley, you're a walking encyclopedia."

Most of the time she was able to shake a comment like his off, admit it as fact, and then move on, secure in her memory skills. Why having Aiden say something she'd heard dozens, if not hundreds of times, bothered her, wasn't a mystery. She wanted him to see her as a desirable woman, not a walking flash drive of facts and minutia.

"Hey." He reached across the table and rubbed his fingers along the back of her hand. "Why do you look upset at me saying that? It's a compliment, not a dig. I've told you before how I feel about smart women."

She lifted her gaze to his. Her thoughts must have been telegraphed on her face because he threaded his fingers into hers. For the thousandth time since they'd met, she thought how good he was at his job. Without saying a word or asking a question, he got her to say things she ordinarily kept hidden.

"Have you ever wanted to be seen as something other than what you are? Something..." She shrugged. "Different? *More?*"

He stretched his free hand across the table and held both of hers.

"I have what's called eidetic memory," she said. "I can recall memories, dates, full books of information after reading or seeing them one time. I can tell you what day of the week a certain date fell in any year, and I know where I've been every single day of my life."

"I have to think that's a blessing because of your occupation, but I'm sensing you feel it's also, what? A curse? A burden?"

"An inconvenience more than anything." She shook her head and dropped her gaze to their joined hands. "Being the smart girl in class was fun in middle school. My home life wasn't exactly normal, and there were so many times I was made fun of because my clothes came from secondhand stores, or my shoes were a little too big when I walked. Being smart made me"—she shrugged again—"special. Not so much in high school and college. Guys don't routinely like a girl who's smarter than they are. Their egos can't take it."

"Not true," he said immediately. "At least, not in my case or in any of my brothers. My sister-in-law and her own sisters are all wickedly smart, much smarter than my brothers about certain things."

"But I'm sure they're all gorgeous, as well."

"I can't deny that because they are. But so are you, Lexi."

"No. I'm not. I'm…average, at best. Add in the computer-chip brain and it's a real turnoff for men."

"You've been around the wrong men if you think, a., your brain is a turnoff, and b., you're not gorgeous. You are. Beautiful, in fact. Your facial features are perfectly symmetrical, something most professional models can't even boast of. Your eyes are the most amazing mix of colors I've ever seen, and I swear I could stare at them all day long. You may not be tall, but what you lack in height, you make up for with flawless proportions. In fact"—he tugged on her hands, yanking her toward him a bit, and lowered his voice—"when I placed my hand on the small of your back in Monroe's office, all I could think about was how nice you fit against me."

For the first time in her memory, Lexi's brain went silent.

No facts, no lines of seemingly useless information, no words formed.

A slow, seductive smile spread across his mouth as she sat there, mute and motionless.

"I get the impression no man has ever said that to you before."

With a few quick blinks first, she shook her head.

"Like I said…" He let go of her hands and sat back

while their food was served. With a quick head bob at the waitress, he then focused his attention back on her. "You've been hanging around the wrong men."

That said, he lifted his burger to his mouth, the mouth she wanted to kiss more than she wanted to take her next breath.

"Eat up." He ticked his head in the direction of her sandwich. "We've got a long afternoon and evening ahead of us."

Chapter 7

The basement of the old church stank of bitter coffee, cheap donuts, and cigarettes. It always struck him as odd in a room filled with substance abusers, smoking was an acceptable, alternative addiction.

Dylan referred to it as the exchange of an illegal habit for a legal, socially acceptable one.

Either way, Aiden mused, the person was still dependent on something.

He'd arrived at the Narcotics Anonymous meeting a few minutes before the stated time, shook hands with the group leader, and gave the cover story he'd fashioned for himself—visiting for the week with a cousin, didn't want to miss any meetings while away—and then took a few moments to scope out the room. Three women in their twenties or thirties, any of whom could be Kim. Or not. When the meeting was called, he sat on one side of the circle, able to see all three clearly.

The introductions clued him in to his target.

Late twenties, dishwater hair pulled into a high ponytail, gaunt face with jutting cheekbones, and flat blue eyes. Her body needed a good twenty pounds to even be considered thin. Seated across from her in the circle, he got a good bead on her while the rest of the intros were made.

At his turn, he recited the spiel he'd written and then accepted the room's welcomes.

An hour later, the meeting ended with a prayer. Kim didn't wait around and talk to the others, but quit the room after tossing her Styrofoam coffee cup in the garbage can. Aiden followed her. Out on the street, she stopped to light up a cigarette. He called her name, said his own quick prayer, and then while her eyes narrowed and suspicion colored her features, he made his way to her.

Moment of truth.

Ten minutes later, he walked into the coffee shop listed on Zoe's credit statement, with Kim in tow. He spotted Lexi seated in a corner table in the back, facing the door where he'd left her earlier. When she lit on him, relief shining on her lovely face, a warm sensation seeped through his system. It had been a long, long time since a woman had depended on him, had looked at him with real expectation in her eyes. In the span of a few days, he'd come to know more about Lexi, and care more, than he had for any other woman he'd dated in recent years.

He pointed her out to Kim, and then the two made their way to her table.

Quickly, he made the introductions, then held a chair for their visitor.

"I'm so glad you came," Lexi told the woman.

"Like I told your boyfriend, here"—she cocked her thumb at him—"I don't know how much I can tell you. I haven't seen Zoe for a while."

Lexi's gaze shot to him, a question bounding in her eyes. Aiden gave her a quick head shake. "I didn't tell her."

"Tell me what?" Kim asked. "Is this some kind of con or game? If so"—she started to stand—"I'm out."

"Please." Lexi stood as well and laid a hand on the woman's arm. "Please stay. We have some questions about Zoe we hope you can help with."

The young woman's wary glance tripped from Aiden to Lexi.

"Would you like something to drink?" he asked. "The coffee at the meeting wasn't fit for human consumption."

"You ain't lying." She gave him her order, adding a chocolate muffin along with it.

"Be right back."

While he went to the service counter, he heard Kim ask Lexi, "Where's Zoe? And who, exactly, are you to her?"

He'd decided to let Lexi take the lead since Kim appeared more comfortable with her than she had with him when he'd approached her. One mention of Zoe Tremont's name, though, and the girl's mistrustful scowl had softened, then filled with curiosity. She'd agreed to follow him to the coffee shop after first telling him she had *protection* in her bag should he try anything.

For all his assurance he was on the up and up, she hadn't really relaxed until introduced to Lexi.

When he returned with two coffees, Kim's muffin and a handful of creamers and sugar, he heard Lexi saying, "Zoe probably never mentioned me—"

"Alexis," Kim said, nodding. "The *Lexi* threw me off. Zoe talked about you in group."

Surprise engulfed her face. "She did?"

Kim doctored her coffee with enough sugar to make him wince before saying, "How you're way older and you raised her after your mom died. Told how you were the reason she wanted to stay clean."

"I was?"

Kim sniggered, but Aiden saw kindness shine in her world-wary eyes. "She didn't want to disappoint you, seeing as you were more like her mom than her sister."

"Well, that part is true." Lexi glanced at Aiden again.

"So where's Zoe been?"

Carefully, and with a great deal of gentle kindness, Lexi told Kim about her sister's death. The young woman's surprise felt genuine to him. He'd been around too many liars and fakes in his career not to recognize false shock, and according to his brothers, he possessed an excellent, inbuilt bullshit detector.

"I should have known something happened when she stopped coming to meetings and our sessions without getting in touch. When I called her, all I ever got was her voice mail."

"Sessions?" he asked.

"Zoe's my sponsor. We used to come here after each meeting and she'd check in with me, find out how my week had been. Kept me focused and on track, you know?"

"I didn't realize Zoe acted as a sponsor," Lexi said.

Kim nodded again and took a sip of her coffee. "She was a good one. Knew when to call me on my crap. Knew when I was hurting." She closed her eyes and hung her head for a moment. "I can't believe she killed herself. She seemed like she had it all together. Great job. Staying clean. Being an example to others." She shook her head again. "She helped me get my life back on track, even helped me get into a GED prep course so I could get my high school diploma."

"Zoe was a big believer in education," Lexi said.

"Said she got it from you," Kim told her. "You've got a bunch of initials after your name, Zoe said. She was proud of that. Of you."

Aiden spotted the sheen sprout in Lexi's eyes at the praise, and he grew sad no one else in her life had ever told her how wonderful she was.

"Did Zoe talk to you about her personal life?" he asked, drawing the younger woman's attention to him. "You mentioned she had a great job. Did she ever talk about it?"

"She mostly let me talk. Your sister had a great gift for listening," she said, settling back on Lexi. "She made me feel comfortable when I told my story in group. No judgment, you know? Not like a lot of people who, once they hear about how you got hooked and what you did to pay for your addiction, they don't want to hear anything else, figuring you're a loser and not worth the time. Zoe wasn't like that."

"Would you mind sharing some of what you told her with us?" Lexi asked.

Kim peered at her, then Aiden.

"I can leave if I make you uncomfortable," he said.

Her eyebrows lifted. "Babe, I don't think you make any woman with a pulse uncomfortable."

His quick smile finally pulled one from her. It was amazing how her entire face changed with the simple uptick of her lips. She looked ten years younger.

Kim sighed and tore the wrapper off the chocolate chip muffin. Lifting it, she said, "A trick to help fight the cravings. Sugar. It works, too."

"Dopamine, a chemical neurotransmitter released

in your brain when you take certain drugs, is also released when you eat sugary substances. It causes feelings of pleasure and euphoria when it floods your system, which is why it's often referred to as a sugar high."

Lexi blinked a few times, the tips of her ears going pink, as Kim stared at her, open-mouthed, for a few moments.

After clearing her throat, Lexi added, "Zoe loved chocolate chip muffins, too."

"Yeah. She's the one who turned me on to them. Anyway." She stretched her neck to the right, then left, as if working out any kinks. "My story's the typical one you hear a lot. An abusive home life, a drunken stepdad who liked to hit us when we were little, then do other things when me and my sisters got older. I hit the road at fourteen after he started coming into my room at night. My mother was passed out drunk most of the time, so she was no help."

"I'm sorry." Lexi reached out and laid a hand over Kim's outstretched one.

Kim tossed her a casual shrug Aiden knew was anything but. "There's not much you can do as a teenager and a runaway to make money. Panhandling and begging get you spotted by the cops and tossed into juvie, so I started hooking when another girl told me you could make quick, fast cash. I was young, and guys like 'em young. But it's a hard life, and pretty soon I started using and getting high to…escape, I guess is the best word. I started sharing an apartment with another girl, older than me. She'd been in the life for a while and was an escort. Better money in that. She cleaned me up, offered to let me stay with her."

"She took care of you," Lexi said.

"Kinda. I mean, she was older and knew the tricks and the ropes. She kept me…safe, you know? She got me into NA, which is where I met your sister. When she died, I decided it was time to turn my life around for good."

"She died? How?" he asked.

"Cops called it a junkie suicide—O.D.'d. They found her body downtown in a flophouse where street addicts go to score. But I never thought that was right."

"What do you mean? What part?"

"All of it. She was getting outta the life. Found herself a man, a real hotshot. Loaded. Said he was gonna set her up. Marry her. She was floating on a natural high and had been clean for months. She wouldn'ta slipped back."

"So what do you think happened?" Lexi asked.

"For real? I always the thought the hotshot had been stringing her along. Shel—that's my friend, Shel Bushman—she wasn't the type of girl guys take home to Mom, if you know what I mean. No picket fences and happily ever after. This ain't the movies."

"Do you think he had something to do with her death?" Aiden asked.

"Honestly? It wouldn't surprise me. Zoe thought so, too."

"She did? When did she tell you that?"

"Couple weeks before I saw her last."

Aiden could feel an excited wave drifting off Lexi.

"She knew Shel from group. They were friends before I came in. I called her when she went missing, then when they found her. I told her I didn't believe she offed herself. Zoe asked me a bunch of questions about the guy." She shrugged. "Their relationship. Stuff like that."

"Did she tell you why she was asking?" Aiden wanted to know.

Another shrug. "I figured she was just being supportive, you know? Letting me talk out my thoughts like she always did. Like I said, Zoe's a great listener."

"When did Shel die?" Lexi asked.

"About two months ago, maybe a little more. She wasn't found for a while after she went missing. I reported her gone to the cops, but they flipped me off. They knew what she was, what she did for a living. Told me she was probably holed up somewhere with a john and getting high. Stupid fucks. The guy at the coroner's office told me, when I went down to ID her, he figured she'd been dead about a week, maybe two. I didn't recognize her, but they told me it was her. They found her ID on the…body."

Aiden digested that, knowing it would be easy for him to access the medical examiner's records if he needed to. The fact it would be an illegal access he wouldn't share with Lexi.

"Did she happen to ask you the name of the man Shel was seeing?"

"Yeah. I told her I didn't know. Shel never told me. Obviously didn't tell Zoe, either. Wanted to keep it a secret. I don't know why, but he was probably married and she didn't want me to know. When she died, the police gave me her personal stuff. Shel didn't have any family. Zoe asked me to let her see it all, and I was gonna give it to her when I saw her again. Only, I didn't see her again. And now I know why."

"Did she indicate why she wanted to see Shel's

belongings?"

"No, but I figured she was gonna see if she could find out who Shel's guy was." She shrugged, then squinted across the small table at them. "Why all the questions?"

"I know this may seem like a weird request," Lexi said instead of answering her, "but do you think we can see Shel's belongings? Maybe go through them? If you still have them, that is."

"I do, and I guess you can. I mean, I was gonna give them to Zoe, anyways." Kim pulled her phone from her pocket and glanced down at it. "I've gotta be at work in an hour, though. I don't have a lot of time to get back to my place, then back here. I've got late shift tonight, and my boss is a real asshole if I'm late. Not that I ever am, but still. The trains only come one every half hour after seven thirty."

Aiden turned to Lexi, then back to Kim. "We'll send you to work in a car," he said. "I promise you'll be on time, if not early."

Fifteen minutes later, the three of them alighted from a cab and walked up the three flights to Kim's small, but clean and tidy apartment. She tugged a shoebox, taped shut, from a minuscule closet by the front door and handed it to Aiden.

"This is everything she had on her when she was found. I had to move because I couldn't afford the rent by myself, so I sold most of the furniture, but I kept some of her clothes 'cuz they were nice. I didn't think she'd mind."

"I'm sure she wouldn't," Lexi said. "Thank you, Kim, for this. And…thank you for being Zoe's friend."

"She was one of the good ones. I hope you find out

why she killed herself."

Before leaving, Aiden called up a car to bring Kim to work and then shook her hand.

"Thank you," he said, "for your time, and for speaking to us."

When they were in their own car on the way back to the hotel, Lexi turned to him and asked, "What did you slip into her hand when we said our goodbyes?"

He stared at her across the darkened back of the car.

"What makes you think I slipped her anything?"

The glare she tossed him had all his blood shunting to his lower body. The image of her playing hot librarian, complete with cat's-eye glasses and bouncing a ruler between her palms to his bad-boy, overdue book borrower, jumped to the front of his mind and all the nerves below his waist went haywire.

"Anyone ever call you eagle eyes?" he asked, his lips twisting in the corners.

She quirked her left eyebrow at him, so with a grin and a shrug, he told her, "I gave her a couple hundred bucks and my business card. I figure it takes her a while to make that in tips, plus I wanted to pay her for her time. She could have sent me packing and refused to speak to us when I all but ambushed her after the meeting."

"I don't think many people refuse to speak to you when you ask."

"You'd be surprised. Gazes automatically turn cold, distrust coats the eyes, and some even take a complete step away out of fear. Stranger danger isn't a thing only babies and kids go through."

"Your idea to join the meeting, then, was a good

one. She most likely didn't see you as a threat since you'd attended."

"Maybe. She was suspicious, though, until I mentioned Zoe's name. Then she was suspicious, but curious. I gave her the money because she's trying to make a new life for herself and it doesn't seem like she's gotten too many breaks. The fact she's able to hold a job, keep an apartment, and stay clean are pluses in her favor. It wasn't much, but it may make it a little easier on her to pay the rent next month."

He felt the heat and weight of her stare across the seat. "What?"

Her eyes softened as they regarded him. "You're one of the good guys, Aiden Keane."

The praise warmed him in ways he couldn't begin to understand. "Don't let my brothers hear you say that. I have a reputation as a hard-ass to live up to."

"Why do I think that's just a bold-faced lie?" she asked. Her quick and bright grin lit up the back of the cab like lights on a Christmas tree.

Aiden cleared his throat. "No idea." Then, wanting to divert the conversation away from himself, he said, "When we get back to the hotel, we can eat something and go through this." He thrust his chin at the box in his lap. "It's not heavy, so I imagine there isn't much in it."

"I'm hoping there's at least a phone with some contact info."

"Kim might have sold a phone," he said. "It's one of the things you can pawn and get fast cash for."

"Let's hope not."

Once they were back in the suite, Aiden said, "I had the hotel deliver some supplies while we were out. The fridge should be filled with enough for dinner and breakfast tomorrow. I'm gonna go get my laptop and then we can get to work. Okay?"

"I'll see what we've got and put something together. We had a late lunch, so how hungry are you?"

He grinned at her over his shoulder. "I can always eat. Especially if a beautiful woman is doing the prep work."

When he walked into his room, he was sure she was thinking about some research concerning gender roles.

Chapter 8

"Okay, the good news is there's a phone," Aiden said right after he slit the tape on the box with a knife. "But the bad news is the battery's dead," he added after removing it and trying to turn it on.

"Here's a charger." Lexi pulled it from the box. "See if it fits."

When they discovered it did, he plugged it into the hotel room desk outlet.

"This'll need a few hours." He rummaged through the box again. "Here's her purse. Pens, a few lipsticks," he said after opening it. "Condoms. A lot of condoms."

The way her face heated at the word was annoying. She was a grown woman, not a child. She shouldn't be embarrassed at what they represented. "She's got business cards in here." She held up a small rectangular piece of plastic to divert them away from the subject of sex.

"Hers?"

"And a few others. Car service. Chinese restaurant. Walk-in clinic," she said, ticking them off as she removed them. "Bail bondsman. The rest are hers. Name and a phone number. Nothing else on the card."

"Did you think it was going to advertise what she did for a living?" he asked.

Why the adorable smirk on his face made her want to slap it off and kiss him at the same time, was troublesome.

"There's something in the inside pocket. Feels like a book." Aiden unzipped the hidden compartment inside the bag and pulled out a small spiral notepad, the cover torn.

Lexi moved closer as he flipped through the pages. When he shifted so she could read along with him, his arm brushed against hers. The simple, innocent contact sent the heat on her face dancing down her neck.

"It's a makeshift date planner," he said, obviously unaware of what his touch did to her. "Names, phone numbers. Names of hotels. There are cash notations next to each entry, too." He glanced up at her, excitement shimmering in his eyes. "I think this was her date book."

"Date book?"

Aiden shrugged. "You know what I mean. This"—he lifted the note book—"is how she conducted business." He flipped through a few pages.

"You'd think she'd be more apt to conduct it online. The latest studies show 85 to 90 percent of sex work is done over the internet." As soon as she said it she wanted to take the words back. She could imagine he'd wonder why she knew a statistic like that off the top of her head.

To her immense relief, he simply shrugged. "Guess she preferred to go old school. There are a lot of names in here."

"Any labeled 'hotshot'?"

His grin made her knees lock in place.

"That would be nice, wouldn't it? But too easy."

He turned to the end of the notepad. "There's only one name for the last few pages. And believe it or not, this name I recognize."

"Richard Deveroux?" she said when he pointed it out to her. "Who is he?"

"I'm surprised you don't know. He's been on every talk show there is for the past three months since his book came out."

"He's a writer? Then it is weird I haven't heard of him."

"Not a writer, not like you're thinking. Until a few years ago he was a stockbroker. When the market went haywire, he was able to keep his clients' money and their investments intact using methods nobody had used before. A book editor, who happened to be one of those clients, contacted him and encouraged him to write about how he did it."

"What's the title?"

"*The Money Whisperer*. It's a how-to and how-I-did-it book about not losing your shirt when you invest."

"And his name is the last one in Shel's book for several entries. How…interesting."

"Bet you five bucks she wasn't seeking his advice on investment strategies."

Shaking her head, she returned his grin. "I'm not taking any part of that bet because I have a hunch you're right. Think this is Mr. Hotshot?"

"The guy is loaded, his name is the only one in what looks like her date book for the last"—he flipped to through the pages—"two months, according to these dates. And after the first two times, she doesn't list any cash payments next to his name. Makes me think he went from being a client to…" He shrugged.

"Something more." She thought for a moment then

asked, "Can I use your laptop?"

Without questioning why she wanted to, he nodded, opened it, and typed in his password. While she sat in the desk chair and entered her own password for the search engine she used for work, Aiden went into the adjoining room, returning with another chair.

He'd slipped his glasses on and just like it had while they'd worked side by side in her apartment, Lexi's entire body came to attention after one glance at him.

"He's married," she said after calling up his media profile. "Three kids, all teens. Homes in New York, San Francisco, and on Sanibel Island. Worked for Harcourt Able, the investment firm, for fifteen years before his book came out. Hmm, that's interesting."

"What is?"

She turned to find his eyes magnified behind the glasses and peering at her. The riot of differing blue hues was mesmerizing. Every statistic and known fact she could call up about eye color, genetics, even the rate of lash growth got stuck in the back of her throat as his gaze honed in on her face. The urge to lean across and press her lips to his was so profound she licked her mouth in anticipation of doing so.

Why did this man make her feel things no man in her memory ever had?

Yes, he was good-looking. A sight-impaired person could see it. But looks weren't everything.

Yes, he was kind. The way he treated and loved his dog proved it. He was gentle and patient, two qualities she hadn't found in many men.

Intelligent? Without a doubt. Quick-witted? Yes, in spades.

Aiden

She could add sexy as hell to the mix. All great qualities in a man, but none to explain why she went from having trivia-Tourette's one minute to dull-witted and speechless the next from one quick look at him.

"Lexi?"

She blinked, while heat rose up her cheeks when she realized she'd been staring, speechless, at him. "Um…yes?"

One corner of his mouth quirked upward, revealing a darling dimple in his cheek. Like a hummingbird to nectar, she was drawn to it. "You said something's interesting."

"I did?"

When the other corner lifted and a twin dimple appeared, and his eyes crinkled under the glasses, it dawned on her why Aiden had such an unusual effect on her psyche. No man had ever looked at her the way he did: completely and with an all-consuming gleam in his eyes. As if he could read her mind. As if he saw her. Really saw…*her*.

The notion he did boggled her mind and was so wickedly arousing she felt her nipples pull and tighten against the satin of her bra cups.

"Oh. I did. Yes." She shook her head and blinked a few times. "He's quoted as saying he received his master's degree in economics from Corolean College."

"And that's interesting, why?"

"Because he couldn't have. Corolean didn't have a masters of economics until five years after he states he received his."

"I'm not gonna even ask how you know that, but I'll take it as fact simply because you said it. So he lied."

"If he supplied the bio, then yes, he did."

"It's a stupid lie when it can be easily fact-checked. Makes you wonder what else he's lied about. And publicly, at that."

Lexi agreed. "So what does this mean for us? For the investigation into Zoe's death?"

Aiden sat back and slid his glasses up onto his head. Cradling the back of his neck with his hands, he stared off past her and bit down on the inside of his cheek.

That desire to kiss him bounded through her again.

"Honestly, I don't know. Kim mentioned she didn't think Shel took her own life. She said Zoe agreed, and she was going to give all this"—he swiped his hand at the box on the table—"to her, but never got the chance."

"She also said Zoe didn't know who Shel's 'hotshot' was. She wouldn't know who to look into or where to look for any info."

"Not necessarily."

When she asked him what he meant, he said, "First, let's eat something. I've got an idea I want to let run around in my head a bit."

She wanted to press him, but her stomach rumbled.

"Looks like I'm not the only one hungry," he said with another grin.

The hotel had stocked the suite's refrigerator with a room service selection. Aiden brought utensils and drinks to the table while Lexi plated both their selections.

"I never knew you could do this in a hotel," she said after taking a bite of her mouthwatering salmon salad.

Swallowing, Aiden nodded. "My brother Josh used to travel a lot when he first opened the business, and his hours were erratic. One of his clients was a hotelier who clued him in to having the hotel stock the fridge. It's easier for them because they don't have to make room service meals on the fly, the markup is good for the hotel's bank account, and you can have something any time you want instead of gorging on minibar snacks."

Lexi's mind immediately got stuck on one part of his sentence. "The cost is more than room service would be?"

He shrugged. "Usually."

"So this"—she circled her fork in the air around her full plate—"is one more thing I can't afford to reimburse you for."

"I've told you before, Lexi, this is on me. I'm the one who likes this convenience, and I don't think it's fair to ask you pay for it. And don't worry about the cost." When he tossed her a cocky grin, her toes curled under the table and her knees slammed together. "I'm having the bill sent to my brother."

"That doesn't seem fair to your brother."

His grin broadened. "Fair has nothing to do with it. Josh owes me for the last job I did. The one that got me stuck here for eight weeks when I was promised it was only gonna take two at the most. He won't raise an eyebrow at this cost, trust me."

"You said he used to travel a lot more. Is he more home based now?"

"Since he got married, yeah. Josh is a homebody at heart. His wife just had their second kid a few months ago. Sophie Grace."

"What a beautiful name. Sophia was the fourth most-popular baby name last year for girls."

"Why am I not at all surprised you know that." Laughter filled his face, while kindness graced his eyes. "Kandy named her after her grandmother Sophie, the one who helped launch her into the cooking stratosphere."

"Wait. Kandy? As in Kandy Laine, the television star?"

He nodded.

"She's your sister-in-law?"

"Married my oldest brother four years ago. She's definitely out of his league," he added, good-naturedly.

"I used to watch her show any time I had a chance. I learned so much about cooking from her. She made everything look easy and doable."

"She makes everything she does look easy. When I got home the other night, my fridge was packed with food she'd made so I wouldn't need to shop or cook for a while. She's really thoughtful that way."

"And gorgeous," she blurted and immediately felt her face redden.

He nodded again. "All her sisters are. She's got six. One of them is getting married to my adopted brother, Rick, next month. Abby. She's a lawyer. Specializes in women's and family rights. She's pretty passionate about it."

"I'm still in awe Kandy Laine is your sister-in-law." She shook her head as she stood with her now empty plate and brought it to the sink.

Aiden was right on her heels, his own plate and utensils in hand.

"Stick them in the dishwasher," he said when he

saw she was getting ready to wash them. "That's what it's there for."

All set to argue she didn't mind washing dishes, she stopped at the sound of his phone ringing. He grabbed it out of his back pocket and walked back toward his room.

"Hey, Dyl. S'up?"

Lexi stacked the dishes while the brothers spoke. Sadness filtered through her when the thought she'd never speak to Zoe again sprouted. While they hadn't had the closest relationship in recent years, Lexi loved her little sister with all her heart, and her absence caused a void in her life that would never be filled.

For all intents and purposes, she was now an orphan. No family at all to spend holidays with, travel with, share all the fun things family shared with one another. A tiny thread of envy wove its way through her at the easy and loving rapport Aiden had with his family. While she'd only met one of his brothers, the way he spoke about the rest of them indicated what a close-knit connection and bond they shared. She and Zoe had never been *that* close, the age difference barring any kind of a close-as-twins association, but they had shared a great deal, and once Zoe got her life together, their relationship had benefitted from it.

But her death had killed any future they could have had.

"Dylan says hey," Aiden said as he came back into the room. "Brontë, too."

She called up a smile and bit back a sigh. No use pining over things she couldn't have. Better to concentrate on the here and now.

"So." She leaned back against the kitchen counter

and crossed her arms over her chest. "What are you thinking about Deveroux, Shel, and any connection to my sister?"

****

He joined her and settled back against the opposite countertop, mimicking her cross-armed stance. Something was different about her. During the time he'd gone into his room to talk to his brother to right now, her eyes had turned sad, her posture had stiffened.

He could chalk it up to exhaustion, but he sensed that wasn't the cause of her sudden emotional deflation. He wanted to ask about it, but from the determined glare in her eyes and the flat line she'd pulled her mouth into, he'd probably meet resistance.

"What if Zoe started to dig into Shel's death and came across Deveroux's name?"

"How? She didn't have any of the info, any of the things we do. Kim was going to give them to her, but now we know Zoe died before she could."

"Right, but she didn't have to be in possession of the phone or the notebook. Shel's death record is on the books. All your sister had to do was conduct an online search to find out the details of how she died."

She shrugged. "Granted, but I don't see how it could have led her to Deveroux."

"Maybe not directly. But it could have led her to Peter Smith." When her eyes widened, he knew she hadn't considered the thought. "Zoe was asking questions about Smith from Monroe."

"How do you make the leap from Zoe asking about Smith to Richard Deveroux?"

"This is why it pays to have brothers. I texted Dylan after we met with Monroe today because I knew he was doing a deep dive on Smith. More than you and I have already done. I wanted to know more about the business and his role in it. A few minutes ago, Dylan went over a few things he found, one of which is the Kingman group represents—"

"Deveroux."

He loved how lightning-quick her mind was. "Exactly."

"So Zoe was asking questions about Smith, who has a professional link to the former broker, who, we think, has a link to a dead prostitute who we know is linked to Zoe through an NA meeting. It's not exactly linear."

"It's all supposition is what it is, and it gives us even more questions. But when we meet with Smith tomorrow, we'll have more info to confront him with than you did when you originally spoke with him."

Two cherry-red dots popped up on her cheeks, and Aiden had to physically stop himself from reaching out and stroking the back of his finger across them. He knew the cause behind the blush and for a quick second thought to confess he knew what she'd done in the airport. If he could be certain she wouldn't grow even more embarrassed—or worse, angry with him for keeping his knowledge hidden—he'd tell her in a heartbeat.

Lexi had to be the one to come clean to him; he felt it down to his marrow. She was nervous about their meeting with Smith, but even so, she kept silent on what she'd done. Springing his knowledge on her now wasn't the way to handle the situation.

"So you're...what? Going to ask him about Deveroux?" she said. "About Zoe? He's already told me he didn't know her. If it's a lie, he's bound to continue telling it."

"Maybe. When you spoke to him before, you didn't know she'd been asking questions about him. They may not have actually met, but the fact she was researching him is telling."

"But how is he connected to Zoe's death? That's what I want to know."

"Ultimately, it may not have anything to do with her death. But it's still information you didn't have before and that's leading us to, hopefully, find out what really happened to her. If she took her own life, or…"

"Or someone took it from her." The cavernous sigh she expelled bounded around the room, and once again he had an overwhelming desire to grab her up in his arms, hold her close, and erase all the sadness from her eyes.

Why he wanted to was obvious, as was the reason why he shouldn't act on his impulses.

Lexi was a client. True, he'd volunteered to help her and no money had changed hands, no contract signed to be followed to the letter of the law which could subject him to legal action. But his own internal code of ethics forced him to think of her as such. Otherwise, if he didn't keep the boundaries between them contained behind professional lines, he knew without a doubt he'd pursue her in a personal way. If she remained a client in his mind, he could keep himself in check.

"Either way, we'll see where we stand after meeting with Smith tomorrow morning, okay?"

She nodded.

He closed his eyes, lifted his arms above his head,

and stretched. Fatigue was starting to gnaw at him, and he knew he needed to sleep and recharge for tomorrow's confrontation. If Brontë had been with them, she would have already been nudging his legs, coaxing him to get to bed. When he opened his eyes again, Lexi's quick glance askance told him she'd been checking him out. A warm and arousing sense of comfort shot through him, boosting his ego a bit. Good to know she wasn't immune to him, just like he wasn't to her.

Maybe, when they'd taken this case as far as they could…

He'd think more about that later. For now, he pushed forward from the counter and said, "I think I'm gonna head to bed. We've got the meeting with Smith bright and early, and then we have to get to the airport and head back."

Lexi nodded, her top teeth biting down on a corner of her bottom lip as she stared over at him. It didn't take an expert in reading body language to know the tiny crease bifurcating the skin between her brows was from worry. His brothers teased him time and again for how in tune he was to the unsaid emotions of others, but even they'd come to know how valuable a trait it was, especially when it came to their business.

"Hey." Aiden moved to her and slid the back of his hand down her cheek. "What's wrong?"

Her eyes widened at his touch, and the chaos of green in them was almost obliterated when her pupils grew. He was insanely aware of the sweet fragrance of vanilla drifting up from her hair and tickling his nose.

"Lexi? Tell me what's wrong." He lowered his voice, using the tone he used when thunder spooked

Brontë. Lexi had the same frightened look to her his dog did when she was scared.

The breath she dragged in pulled all the air surrounding him toward her. He wasn't even sure she realized she made a quick head bob right, then left, before lifting her shoulders and releasing the breath she'd taken. It was fascinating watching her take control of herself. Fascinating, and wildly appealing. Desire thrummed low in his belly, and he had to clamp down on the urge to lift her chin and put his mouth on hers.

"Nothing's wrong," she said.

"I'm pretty good at reading people, and your words aren't lining up with your body language right now."

In a heartbeat, she schooled her facial features.

He couldn't help but grin at her. "Too late, sweetheart. I saw the worry fly across your face. Now tell me what's got you so nervous."

"You really are good at reading people, because nervous is what I am."

"About meeting Smith?"

She nodded. "Everything, actually. From that, to the discussions with Kim and Monroe. I'm terrified Zoe was involved in something she shouldn't have been, or discovered something that got her killed."

"Don't get ahead of yourself. All this may turn out to be circumstantial."

"You don't really think that, do you?"

He didn't but felt saying it would add to the worry bouncing through her.

"Your silence speaks volumes," she said. After a few moments, she dropped her gaze to her feet and said, "I feel so…guilty."

"About what?"

"I really wasn't a very good big sister when all is said and done. I didn't know anything about Zoe's current life other than superficial, meaningless stuff. Where she lived. Where she worked. Surface things. I don't know if she had a boyfriend, or any girlfriends for that matter. I didn't even know she'd become a sobriety sponsor. And I wish I had." She lifted her gaze to him, tears shimmering in her eyes. "She'd gotten her life together, and because she didn't need me anymore to bail her out when she got into trouble, I simply"—another shrug—"stopped paying attention. And now she's dead."

When he drew her into his arms, he told himself he'd comfort any emotional client in exactly the same way. The moment she melted against him, he recognized it for the lie it was.

No other client had ever felt as perfect as Alexis Buckley did when she cuddled against him, her tiny body engulfed in his arms, her head resting against his chest. Every nerve ending in his body charged when he felt the warmth of her arms circling around his waist.

"I regret, so much, not being more present in her life these past few years. I can tell myself why, using any number of reasons, from my job to the fact we lived in different cities, but every one of them is a feeble excuse. I failed Zoe. Horribly."

A sob broke from deep within her, and he tightened his arms, prepared for a deluge of tears.

None came.

Shocked at her well of control, and awed by it too, he stroked one hand up and down her back. Tiny frissons of excitement shot through him as his hand moved against her.

"First of all," he managed to say, thrilled his voice didn't betray the bounding lust jumping through his system, "I happen to think you were a wonderful big sister. I don't know anyone—and I know a lot of people—who, as a teenager, would have been able to keep a younger child under their care safe, fed, and loved. That's remarkable in my book. In anyone's actually. Second"—he continued keeping her bound to him when she moved to shift away—"you've faced what every parent faces when their kids are grown. There's a fine line between continuing to treat them like children, and respecting the fact they're adults and letting them go off to forge their own lives and make their own mistakes."

She stopped trying to pull away from him, and when she actually burrowed in closer, Aiden couldn't prevent his body from responding to the feel of a warm and luscious woman in his arms. Especially this one.

He swallowed. "Third," he said, his voice now sounding a bit choked to his own ears, "I don't know anything about being a big sister, but as a little brother, I can tell you point-blank that even when my brothers aren't around, I always hear them in my head, encouraging me, or berating me, and telling me how much they care about me. I'll bet it was the same for Zoe. You two might not have talked on the phone every night, but I'm sure your influence and the sacrifices you made for her when you were both kids weren't unnoticed or forgotten."

It was a testament to his ability to remain calm in most situations that he didn't lose the tether he had on his control when her shoulders shifted and her body completely relaxed against his, nestling even closer. He desperately wanted to haul her up and carry her to his side of the suite and do every dirty little thing he'd been imagining doing to her for the past two days, despite the fatigue escalating by the moment through him.

Instead, he took a breath—mental and physical—patted her back and gently pushed her away from him. The tiny sound of protest escaping through her lips almost had him pulling her back.

"I think you're being too hard on yourself," he said once she stood across from him again. He shoved his hands into the front pockets of his trousers and leaned back again against the counter. "It's understandable, I know," he added when she started to say something. "You felt responsible for your sister, and now she's gone. But you're being proactive and you're trying to find out what happened, so in my book, you didn't fail at anything."

Lexi shot both hands through her temples, clutching on to small tufts of hair, then pressed one earlobe between her fingers, her emotional tell on full blast.

"I know you're right," she said after a few beats. "Here." She touched her head. "But down here"—she pointed a finger at her heart—"I'm having difficulty accepting that."

Aiden nodded. "Perfectly understandable." He couldn't stifle his yawn. "Look," he said. "Let's sleep on all this. It's been a big day and we learned a lot, most of which we don't understand yet. Let's look at everything with fresh eyes in the morning."

Her gaze darted across his face, that tiny crease popping up in between her brows again. "Are you feeling okay?"

"Yeah. Why?"

"In the past few minutes, your color has paled considerably."

Aiden nodded and then pushed off the counter. "My body runs hot for a long time, but when it needs rest, I crash quick. So, on that note, I'll say good night."

As he walked by, he pressed his hand to her shoulder, gave it a reassuring squeeze, and then went to his room.

The memory of the confused and bemused expression on her face did a whole lot to boost his ego as he shut the light and crawled into bed minutes later.

While exhaustion took over his body, his mind drifted to just how good she'd felt snuggled into his arms.

Chapter 9

"Oh. I didn't know you were awake. You're so quiet."

Aiden turned from the coffee machine, a cup in one hand. His gaze took a slow stroll from the top of her head, all the way down to her toes and back before setting on her face.

She knew what she looked like, standing there with her freshly showered hair twined in a makeshift towel turban and covered from neck to calves in the oversized hotel-issued plush robe and slippers. The only thing on her face was moisturizer, and the only thing under the robe was a pair of panties.

"Growing up in my house it paid to be stealthy and early," he said, handing her the mug he'd filled. He reached into the cabinet for another for himself. Lexi's gaze followed the arch of his muscular back, the extension of his shoulders and arms as he stretched up. Aiden Keane's shirtless torso and the low-riding sweats covering his narrow hips sent her brain into lust-ridden convulsions. She had to concentrate—hard—on not losing the grip she had on the mug.

"If you were the first up in my house, you were guaranteed an extra helping of whatever Mom cooked for breakfast. My brothers could eat like men starved for a decade. They still can, so I had to learn to wake up early and be quiet doing it. Since I shared a room with

Dylan, who woke if an owl hooted three blocks away, stealth was a goal of mine."

Lexi said the second thought to pop into her head because she couldn't give a voice to the first and keep any scintilla of dignity around this man. "Stealth is a characteristic of historic warriors of the ninja clan. They had to be able to move silently and tread soundlessly in order to carry out their deadly assignments without detection."

When his grin popped across his mouth, she almost let loose with her first thought.

"If I ever need to switch careers, I guess I can apply to be a ninja."

"No doubt you'd make the cut."

His deep, sensual laugh sent a tidal wave of carnal thoughts through her brain. She gulped the coffee, lest she say them aloud. Surprise had her blinking.

"How did you know how I like my coffee?"

He leaned a hip against the counter. "I'm a trained observer, remember? Filing away little things about a person is second nature to me." He took a sip of his own hot brew. "I've seen you drink enough cups over the past few days it was easy to remember how you take it. Lots of cream, no sugar."

"But you were making this for yourself when I came in."

He nodded. "Turns out I like mine the same way."

Why that thrilled her was a conundrum.

"You sleep okay?" he asked, studying her.

"Like a rock." She shook her head and tossed him a twisted grin of her own. "It's surprising how well I did, considering my mind was going in a million directions last night. But from the moment my head hit the pillow,

I don't remember anything else before waking up."

"You've been running around for several days, taken two flights back-to-back, plus yesterday we got a lot accomplished. It's no wonder your body wanted to crash. You needed to recharge."

"Most adults require seven to nine hours of sleep per night in order for the brain and body to restore, repair, and reenergize. Only 25 percent of the population gets the required number of hours, though, which leads to problems with focus, memory, and even changes in the immune system. Shift work and working during night hours contribute to chronic fatigue from lack of sleep."

Lexi slammed to a halt when she caught the amused, *tolerant* gleam in Aiden's eyes.

Great way to bore the guy to tears, Alexis.

"Sorry." She lifted her mug again and took a gulp. "Sleep deprivation is a pet project of mine."

"Pet project?" He cocked his head while he regarded her.

"Since I work at a college, most of the students and even a large number of the faculty are chronically sleep-deprived. The psych department has been conducting an ongoing study about the effects, causes of, and treatments of sleep loss and deprivation. I'm on the committee for their funding, so I get a firsthand read of all their research."

The amused expression on his face turned thoughtful.

"What?"

He shook his head, then tossed her an eyes-half-closed perusal that made her stomach muscles contract. "Nothing."

Before she could challenge the statement, he added, "Shel's phone should be fully charged about now. Let's take a look."

She followed him into the living area and watched while he unplugged the phone and then swiped the screen.

"Charged and, thank you, Lord, not password protected." He plopped down on the sofa, Lexi following suit and sitting next to him so she could view the phone, too. Acutely aware she was, for the most part, naked under the robe, she tucked the collar up under her chin and pinned the slit together with her hands so her legs would stay hidden, before settling.

"Lucky for us. Can you access her call log, in and out?"

"Yup. Well, lookie here. Recognize him?"

He turned the device toward her. Peter Smith's name ran across the screen.

He scrolled through the rest of her phone. "There are multiple calls to one number." He turned to her. "Where's Shel's date book?"

Lexi rose and crossed to the desk. "I put it in her purse last night and stuck her purse back in the box Kim gave us." She handed it to him.

Aiden flipped the book to the final pages and then put the phone next to it.

"I knew it looked familiar. It's Deveroux's number."

Lexi took the phone from him and glanced over the numerous calls in the log. "There aren't any texts between them, only calls. Most are less than a minute, except for the last one. That's"—she leaned closer to see the screen—"almost ten minutes."

"Most of them are probably 'dates.' " He put the word in air quotes. "Again, it would be too easy, wouldn't it, if there were stored texts alluding to an affair. But this is a definite link to the two of them. The last call is dated a little over two months ago."

"And Shel, we think, died soon thereafter."

"We need to get the police reports of her death."

"Can you do that? Aren't there privacy laws attached to them?"

"In many states, they're part of the public record." He tugged his phone from the pocket of his sweats and typed in a series of keystrokes. "It's a documented closed case, but here's the record number and the links."

She had to lean in to see the screen clearly. The scent of his skin, still warm from his bed, had her fingertips tingling. The desire to lean closer and run her nose along the column of his throat, kiss the pulse beating there, then drag her lips over his morning stubble was so intense, she had to physically will her body to stay still.

"Here's the date she was found."

"That's almost three weeks after her last call to Deveroux. What do you think it means?"

"Again, it's all speculation and circumstance, but the last time she speaks to someone, it's Deveroux, she goes missing, then winds up dead. It has to mean…something."

Lexi ran all the statistics about sex workers, physical abuse, and even murder through her head. She kept a clamp on sharing them, though.

Aiden glanced at the phone, then turned to her, the stark blues in his eye sparkling. "I'm gonna go grab a shower and clear out the sleep fuzz. Our appointment with Smith is at nine thirty. Plenty of time to get dressed, have breakfast. The fridge is loaded, so we can look through this more while we eat. Sound good?"

She nodded, then watched as he sauntered back to his room, appreciating the subtle, utterly masculine sway of those slim hips and waist. If she wasn't mistaken, the muscles in his ass were as tight and toned as the rest of him. What she'd give for a feel to determine if they were.

Stop thinking about his body parts, Alexis. They're of no concern to you, and you won't be seeing or feeling them in this lifetime or any other.

But oh, how she wanted to.

****

From across a crowded airport bar, Peter Smith had looked like a middle-aged businessman who'd had too much to drink and anticipated getting laid. Up close, seated not three feet away from him now, Aiden thought he looked more like a middle-aged, *tired* businessman with a grandiose sense of himself.

After being escorted into his corner office by a secretary who looked straight out of central casting for the role of office bimbo, Smith rose and shook hands with them both. When he took Lexi's, he squinted and stared at her face for a few beats.

Thinks he recognizes her, but can't tell from where.

"Thank you for seeing us," Aiden said, drawing the man's attention back to him.

The confusion lifted to be replaced with a questioning glare. The practiced smile he plastered on his face didn't lift to his eyes.

"I must say, I don't have many private

investigators make appointments. What can I do for you? My secretary was a little muddled about why you wanted to see me."

Aiden bit back the retort the woman probably appeared muddled about most things and said, "We're conducting an investigation into a death, and your name came up during our research."

"My name? I'm sure you're mistaken. I don't know anyone who's died in the past"—he shrugged—"two or three years. What was the person's name?"

"Zoe Tremont."

After opening his mouth to give them what Aiden was sure had been an immediate denial, Smith cocked his head and scrunched his brows together while clamping his lips closed again.

"That name sounds familiar in some vague way," he said after a moment. "I don't know why. When did she die?"

"A little over a month ago.

Smith sat back in his chair and crossed his arms over his chest. All at once, his brow smoothed and his vision cleared. He nodded. "Someone called me. Recently. I don't remember who, though, inquiring about this Tremont woman. That's why I recognize the name. I told the caller I didn't know her."

"I was the one you spoke with," Lexi said for the first time since entering the office. "Zoe Tremont was my sister."

Smith turned his full attention to her, and once again, his brow quirked into quizzical groove. "Yes. You called, and we spoke over the phone," he said. His gaze ran around her face as his head cocked a bit to one side. "Did we…meet, in person, too?"

They'd gone over what she should say in the event Smith, somehow, recognized her. Aiden was confident, after seeing how she'd dealt with Monroe, she'd stick to the script he'd outlined.

"I didn't come to your office because I was only in town for a few days," Lexi said, neither statement an outright lie. "I informed you I'd found your business card in her personal effects and you said—"

"I hand those things out like candy at Halloween." He nodded again. "It's true. But I didn't know your sister. I believe I also said she may have gotten my card after attending one of my conferences. We've already discussed this." He turned back to Aiden. "I don't know what else I can tell you."

"Bear with us for a few minutes, please. Ms. Tremont was a journalist here, in Atlanta," Aiden said, watching Smith for any sign he had knowledge of the fact. The man's face remained impassive.

"So perhaps she was doing a story on the public relations industry?" he offered, his head weaving left and right. "Maybe that's why she had my card. Did she work freelance or for a publication?"

Lexi told him the name of the magazine.

"I don't recognize it. But again, maybe she came to one of my conferences to gather info. I give informational workshops about our firm once a quarter. They're open to the public."

"Do you take attendance?" Lexi asked.

"No. But we ask attendees to sign up beforehand so we know the head count."

"And I'm sure you keep a list of those attendees because you'd want to do a follow-up email afterward to garner new clients," Aiden said.

"Of course. The first rule of business is to grow a satisfied client base."

"We'd appreciate it if you could check to see if Zoe's name shows up on any of your attendance lists," Aiden said.

Smith's mouth pinched in annoyance. With a deep inhale signaling what a waste of his time it was, he tugged his keyboard from across his desk and typed in a few strokes. After a few moments, he said, "I don't see her name listed for this year or last as an attendee."

"So she didn't get your card at one of your conferences," Lexi declared.

"Even so, I can't tell you why she had it or how she got it. As I've said, I hand those things out wherever I go." He stood and buttoned his suit jacket. "Now, I don't know how much more help I can be, but if that's all, I have other meetings today I need to prepare for."

"Richard Deveroux is a client of your firm, is he not?" Aiden asked, keeping his seat.

Either the abrupt change in topic or the mention of the name, surprised Smith. His eyes widened, and his back snapped to attention while he stopped fastening his jacket.

"I'm sure you can appreciate I'm not at liberty to discuss whether someone is a client or not."

"A denial like that just confirms he is," Aiden said with a grin. Before Smith could negate it, Aiden added, "His name also came up in our investigation into Ms. Tremont's death."

A visible shudder slid down Smith's back.

Bingo.

"So you can see," Aiden continued, "why we came here today. Both you and your client have a link to a dead woman, and we're trying to ascertain what the connection is. "

They had no tangible proof Zoe had ever interacted with either man, but Aiden had confronted people with less evidence only to discover later his instincts were dead on. And right now those instincts told him there was a connection between all three.

"I don't see any link," Smith said. "I know thousands of people, as I'm sure Deveroux does. What's that old saying about six degrees of separation between everyone on earth? Whatever link you think there is, is probably a coincidence. I'm sure of it."

Aiden slid a side-glance at Lexi. Perched on the edge of her chair, her eyes focused on Smith, she had a look of extreme thought on her face.

"I don't believe in coincidences," she told him.

"Well, whether you do or not, that's all this is. A coincidence."

"Zoe never approached you and asked about him?"

Smith let out a long breath. "No."

"Never asked to meet him? Have you introduce her to him?" Aiden asked.

"No."

"And you have no idea how she came to have your information? Your card?"

His head bounced back toward Lexi.

"How many times, and in how many ways, can I say no? The answer will be the same every way you ask the question." He shot his cuffs, then tugged at the hem of his jacket. "Look, Mr."—Smith glanced down at Aiden's business card—"Keane. I've told you, both of you," he added, thrusting his chin at Lexi, "I've never met Ms. Fremont—"

"Tremont," Aiden said.

"—and I have no knowledge if Richard Deveroux has either. So, again, if there's nothing else, please." He lifted a hand toward the door. "I have other appointments and will not keep my clients waiting."

Aiden stood. "We won't take up any more of your time, then. You have my card." He took Lexi's hand and guided her from the room. Before exiting, he stopped, turned and said, "Oh, one more thing."

Smith sighed, dramatically, then gave him a perfunctory nod.

"Cameron Monroe says hello."

All the color in Smith's face drained.

"Thanks for your time." With Lexi's hand in his, he propelled them from the room. Once again they were silent as the elevator descended. Aiden took the time to check his phone.

The moment they alighted on the street, she pounced. "Why did you say that to him?"

Aiden shoved his phone back in his jacket pocket. "He said he'd never heard of the magazine. The way he reacted to Monroe's name proves he knows him, or at least who is, so it stands to reason he knows the man runs the magazine. That seals it in my mind he lied to us at least once. And if told us one lie—"

"The probability he told us more, grows."

Nodding, Aiden's gaze tracked the car pulling up to the curb. "Yeah, it does. Come on, here's our car."

Once they were settled, he turned in the seat to face her and asked, "How imperative is it you head back home today?"

"Why?"

"While we were in with Smith, Dylan texted me

something interesting that we might want to jump on." To the question crossing her lovely eyes, he said, "Deveroux's got a book event this afternoon at four, downtown."

He got lost in the intensity of the colors in her eyes as she considered the information.

"You want to go speak to him," she said after a moment.

It wasn't a question, but he nodded anyway. "I don't usually believe in coincidences either, but I'm gonna consider it serendipitous he's in town the same time we are. We'd be foolish not to take advantage of an opportunity like this."

"What do you propose we do? Introduce ourselves, then ask, oh by the way, did you date a hooker who went missing, then wound up dead after texting you?"

His laugh came quick and full. Tugging her hand into his, he gave it a squeeze. "I'd like to think I'm a little more professional and subtle than that."

She blushed scarlet and bit down on her bottom lip. "Sorry. That was rude. You *are* more professional than that. I've seen it for myself numerous times over the past few days."

Her words had a warming effect on the space around his heart. The urge to tug her on to his lap and kiss away the embarrassment on her face was palpable, despite the fact they were in a cab and not someplace private. Each moment he spent with her helped chip away at his resolve, so much so he knew he was in serious danger of forgetting his promise to consider her a client.

He wanted Lexi. There was no denying it or brushing it aside. And it wasn't just because he hadn't gotten laid in a while.

A long while.

She intrigued him. Challenged him. Made him feel what he was doing was worthwhile. Too many times over the years since he'd first started working with his brothers, he'd felt his skills were wasted on the cases he was assigned. He knew his expertise at digital finances helped grow the company's reputation, but he hadn't wanted to be stuck behind a computer all day long, deep diving into client concerns. The issues that had plagued him earlier in his life fostered in him a need to be around people, interact one-on-one, talk. Help them, personally.

Aiding Lexi, even though she wasn't technically a client, had brought a continual smile to his lips and a sense of contentment in just a few days he hadn't experienced in the past few years.

So, yeah, he wanted her in his bed, no denying it, or the attraction simmering between them. But he'd come to realize he wanted her *out* of it, too.

Just as he was about to discuss what he planned to accomplish with Deveroux, his cell pinged.

"It's the magazine's advertising guy, Dewitt Carde," Aiden told her, after glancing at his screen. "This is Aiden Keane," he announced into the phone.

By the time he disconnected, they were stuck in traffic.

"That sounded interesting from my perspective as an eavesdropper. What did he tell you?"

"Basically, Zoe came to him a little over a month ago, maybe six weeks? He wasn't sure on the dates. And asked him a slew of questions about the Kingman Group, Peter Smith, especially."

"Did she indicate why she was asking?"

Aiden nodded. "Said Zoe told him she was doing a freelance article on the public relations industry."

Lexi cocked her head and peered at him across the table. "Smith and Monroe said the same thing. *Exactly* the same thing."

"They did.

Jesus. He could get lost in her eyes all day. Through them he could practically see the gears grinding in her amazing brain. His grin took its time blooming, but when it did he was delighted as her pupils dilated and her mouth dropped open a tiny bit when she zeroed in on his lips.

"Makes you wonder about some sort of coordinated effort to get their stories straight, doesn't it?" he asked.

She stared down at her lap and shook her head. The frustrated sigh that blew through her lips had his grin fleeing.

"Hey." He reached across the tiny distance between them and pulled her hands into his. "What's wrong?"

"What does all this mean?" Her smooth brow wrinkled. "Why are they lying to us?"

"Obviously, because they feel they need to. Something's connecting all three of them, maybe Deveroux as well."

"Shel Bushman? Or Zoe?"

He shrugged. "Maybe. Maybe not. We don't have enough intel to make a solid argument, but if I had to guess, I'd say when Zoe started asking questions about the Kingman Group, it triggered something. It's the only thing making sense right now. What it is, we don't know. It could be anything, not necessarily something to do with Shel's death."

"Do you think approaching Deveroux when he's at an event is the right way to proceed?" she asked after a bit. They were still stuck in traffic, the annoying blare of horns around them muffled inside the car.

"I do. Blindsiding people is a great way to get them to reveal something they wouldn't if they had foreknowledge they'd be questioned." His good-natured smirk returned. "It's one of my most effective investigative tools. "

"I'm starting to realize how many effective investigative tools you possess. And that you're good at all of them."

Accompanying a cute eye roll, a tiny grin of her own bloomed on her lips, and when it spread full force across her face, Aiden swore a bell chimed.

"Okay." She tugged her hands from his, then dug her cell phone from her purse. "I agree we should go see Deveroux. But I need to call my provost first, to let him know I won't be coming back tomorrow as planned."

While she did, Aiden took the time to figure out the best way to approach the former stock trader.

Lexi blew out a breath moments later and re-stored her phone.

"Problem?"

She shook her head. "He wasn't what I'd call happy I was taking another day, but I assured him I'd be back the day after tomorrow to attend a mandatory university budget meeting." She pierced him with a determined glare. "I need to be at that meeting. No matter what we discover."

He pulled one of her hands back into his when his own grew lonely. "You will be. Promise. Now, here's what I've been thinking."

Chapter 10

She'd never hated someone at first sight before until she'd spent two minutes watching Richard Deveroux meet and greet his so-called fans.

An entire dictionary of descriptions from pompous to entitled, arrogant to obnoxious, with a generous helping of condescending and rude mixed in, defined the one-time Wall Street strategist. The man possessed an immense ego he didn't even try to shield. Lexi had, unfortunately, met many visiting professors in her job who fell into the same category. None of them, though, had made her flesh crawl like Deveroux had when she watched him accept a fan's gushing praise, a predatory glint in his glare as he eye-raked the woman.

"Guy's a tool," Aiden said close to her ear from his position behind her.

She nodded as the sensitive skin on the nape of her neck warmed from his breath.

"He doesn't even hide the fact he's undressing her with his eyes. If he looked at my woman like that, he'd be missing a few teeth about now."

"The woman standing to his right?" she said, attempting to control the speed of her breathing, because having Aiden this close always sped it up. Plus, imagining herself as *his woman* added a few beats to her heart.

"Red dress, auburn hair?"

"That's his wife, Margo. She's a financial wunderkind. Started trading at her daddy's knee when she was barely out of diapers. MBA from Wharton by the time she turned twenty-one. I read an article on my phone last night after you went to bed, referring to her as 'Mankiller Margo.' "

His quiet chuckle, soft and bold against her neck, had her stomach muscles contracting. "Not very flattering. Why the nickname?"

Lexi swallowed, took a cleansing breath, then alternately flexed and relaxed her hands to keep them occupied, lest they grab on to him. "Apparently, she obliterated several seasoned male traders when she appeared on the stock exchange floor. Mowed them over and left them in her dust as she skyrocketed through the ranks. Stole clients. Pulled in new ones. She became a top trader, even pushing some of the old guard out of her way. Took no prisoners. She met Deveroux at a cocktail party, and from then on they were inseparable. Married quick, and they've been together ever since."

"She's a stunning woman, and I imagine she knows, and uses it, to her advantage."

She turned around and a hot stab of foreign jealousy cut through her system at the way his eyes narrowed, subtle lines fanning toward his temples, those blue colors bright and focused intently on Margo Deveroux.

Give it up, Lex. You've got no right to be jealous. The man is a free agent in every sense of the word. He can lust after anyone he wants to, and it's no concern of yours.

"Even from this distance," he said, still staring at

the woman, "it's easy to see she's got a controlled and calculating coldness in her."

"It is?"

His shrug was easy. "She hides it well, but if you look closely, you can tell who's controlling the flow of people to the desk and the amount of time each person spends with her husband, despite the store manager standing right there. Look at the way she smiles at each fan. It doesn't make it to her eyes. And her eyes are watchful in a possessive way. Like she's protecting her asset, and God help anyone who tries to take it away from her. She's paying lip and teeth service to be seen as accommodating and supportive of her husband. It's an act. A good one, but an act, nonetheless."

When he stopped, Lexi was incapable of calling up one trivia factoid or piece of information from her encyclopedic knowledge base. He turned his attention to her, a quizzical line blooming between his brows, as his eyes swept across her face.

"What?"

She shook her head, dropped her gaze to her shoes to give herself time to form a coherent response that wouldn't make her seem like a love-crazed teenager fawning over a rock star.

"Lexi?"

"You are, without a doubt, the most attuned and insightful man I have ever met."

He cocked his head, a ghost of that sexy grin lifting one corner of his mouth. "I think that's a compliment."

"It is. Believe me, it is." She clasped her hands in front of her, her own smile finally making an entrance. "You just put into words what I've been thinking but felt if I said it out loud I'd come off like a total bitch."

He took a step closer, bringing them almost into contact. Lexi willed herself to stay put and not dissolve against him like she so ardently wanted to.

"I don't think that word can ever apply to you." He lowered his voice and dipped his head a bit, giving her the impression his words were only meant for her to hear. Fixated now on her and not the man—and woman—up ahead of them, his pupils grew in size, shoving the riot of blues to the edges, as he gazed at her face. The opposite corner of his mouth lifted, mimicking its twin, to create the most charming and seductive of grins. "In fact"—he was so close his body heat warmed her from head to toes like a blanket fresh from a hot dryer—"I don't think you've ever had a bitchy thought or moment in your life."

"You'd be surprised," she mumbled. Of its own free will, her gaze dipped down to his mouth. She licked her lips at the thought of how they would feel against her own, and the rush of air he sucked in pulled her along with it.

Without warning, Aiden lifted a hand, caressed her cheek with the back of it, as he sighed her name.

The notion he was going to kiss her barreled through her, and she couldn't think of one reason why she shouldn't kiss him right back.

He swiped his tongue across his bottom lip, his lids dropping half closed as he continued to concentrate solely on her. It didn't matter a whit they were standing in the aisle of a crowded bookstore surrounded by books and people and waiting to speak to a man who may be able to answer some questions about her sister's death. All that did matter was the attraction crackling in the air between them—an attraction growing hourly since he'd sat himself down next to her on that first flight.

Just as he bent a bit more toward her, and she responded by lifting up on the balls of her feet, the moment shattered.

"Excuse me, but can you move up?" An irritated voice from behind yanked them out of the sexual fugue they'd both drifted into. Aiden's eyes opened wide again, his lashes beating a rapid tattoo against the top of his cheeks. He shook his head like a dog shucking water from its back, turned to the woman with the annoyed voice and said, "Please. Go ahead of us."

Without waiting for a response, he wrapped a hand around Lexi's arm and gently tugged her off the line. Silently, he propelled her to the back of the store, down a secluded hallway near the restrooms. With a furtive glance to the right, then the left, assuring they were alone, he spun her so she faced him.

Brows pinched together and looking at her through inquiring eyes, Aiden took a breath, let it out slowly, then said, "I have to ask. I'm pretty sure of the answer, but I have to hear it from you first, Lexi."

She stopped him before he could give a voice to his question by rising up on her toes and fusing her lips to his.

For the second time in the span of a few minutes, her never-resting mind went completely still. No data spewed forth about how humans were the only species who kiss, or the crazy laws about kissing still on the books and punishable by fines or imprisonment in some states, or even that, on average, each person spends about 330 hours of their life engaged in the art of kissing.

No, just as she'd thought she would if ever put in this situation, Lexi kissed him without any thought why she shouldn't.

It took him less than a millisecond to realize he didn't need to ask permission at all. His hands dropped from her arms and with subtle speed, wove around her waist, his palms flattening above the dip in her spine, while her hands bolted up his chest to link behind his neck. Torso to torso, hipbone against hipbone, there wasn't enough room for a sigh to slip between them.

She wasn't surprised he was a superb kisser. Not that she had a wealth of practical data behind her to compare to, but by virtue of the way her bones liquefied and her heart galloped like a Kentucky Derby frontrunner charging the last quarter-mile stretch, it was enough to convince her he knew what he doing.

Boy, did he ever.

She'd pondered the notion no other man had ever looked at her the way Aiden had. Now she knew no other man had ever kissed her the way Aiden was kissing her, with an all-consuming passion and devotion that brought her to her knees.

Heady stuff.

His tongue slid along the seam of her lips, parted them, and then...*plundered*. There really wasn't another word she could call up from her cephalic dictionary to describe it. Although, admittedly, she was a more than willing participant. Warmth engulfed her, and she didn't need a mirror to know her face—and the rest of her body—was flushed scarlet.

Aiden lifted one hand to cradle her jaw, tilted it back, and then deepened the kiss even more.

Good golly was the only coherent phrase tripping

through her mind. Being flattened up against his solid tank of a body was more intoxicating than she'd imagined it would be. The earlier view of the sculpted definition of his naked chest and arms, his trim and tight hips and waist, and the carved washboard corrugations in his abdomen had been food for her eyes. Aiden took care of his body, and thank goodness for that. But to be pressed up against all his strength and hard-bodied sinew and held there with the most gentle and tender of caresses made every fantasy she'd ever had pale to this reality.

If he pulled her into one of the nearby restrooms, flipped the lock on the door, and then took her against it, fully clothed, she wouldn't have protested one whit.

Straight-laced librarian? Yeah, that description was fleeing fast from her professional résumé.

The whoosh of a door swinging open and the sound of giggling teenagers drifted over them. Embarrassment at being caught in such a public display should have overwhelmed her, made her pull out of Aiden's arms and run to the nearest exit.

But she didn't, because for the first time in her adult life, Alexis Elizabeth Buckley didn't care what others thought of her, how they saw her, or what they believed about her.

Lexi didn't care if they stood in the hallway all afternoon—*hell, all night*—if it meant Aiden would continue kissing her as if both their lives depended on it.

It seemed he didn't share her thoughts on the matter because when the chortling teens moved past them he ended the kiss.

Terror kept her eyes closed. The idea he would

look repulsed—or worse—exploded through her like a cannonball roaring out of a cannon.

"Open your eyes."

His soft command had her clamping them shut tighter.

"Sweetheart, open your eyes and look at me."

Knowing it for a cowardly move, Lexi winked one open, keeping the other closed.

Okay. He didn't look repulsed—or worse. He looked…confused? Worried, maybe?

Aiden took a deep breath, all his attention focused on her as he smoothed his hands down her arms and gathered her hands in his. "Are you okay?"

All she could do was nod since her voice had decided to take a vacation.

"We're gonna need to talk about what just happened." He squeezed her hands. "But it has to wait. Right now we need to concentrate on why we came here."

Lexi swallowed. "Deveroux," she managed to say in a voice that barely registered.

Aiden flicked his gaze from her face to the end of the corridor. "The line is almost at the end. We should get back on it, be the last ones so we can spend some time with him without his wife hustling us along. Okay with you?"

She must look like a bobblehead with the amount of nodding she found herself doing. To hide how truly discombobulated she felt from that mind-blowing kiss, she swallowed, stamped down on the surge of emotions drilling through her, then lifted her chin. Praying her voice had returned to some semblance of normal, she gave him one final, brisk nod, let out the breath she'd been holding and said, "Let's go."

****

Focus, man. You've got a job to do. You can't let yourself get preoccupied right now.

Easy to say, not so easy to do.

Holy shit, that kiss.

As a man who appreciated every nuance about a woman, Aiden considered himself well versed in the art of kissing. The heady rush of blood that coursed through him at the notion he was going to press his lips against a pair of soft and willing ones, the powerful wave of expectation the moment before he did so, even the way he held his breath for a fraction of a second as his lips took their first taste of another, then released in a slow and seductive exhale, all added to his enjoyment of the simple act.

Aiden liked kissing, knew he was good at it, and since it often led to his favorite four-letter word, he took his time to ensure the moment proved memorable.

It took him exactly one second to appreciate that kissing Lexi for the very first time was like no other kiss he'd ever experienced before. If he lived to be a hundred years old, he'd never forget the instant her lips fused with his. She tasted like no other woman ever had. A mix of innocence, determination, and desire all wrapped into one.

If they hadn't been standing in a public hallway, the kiss would certainly have led to getting horizontal as soon as possible. It had taken every ounce of will he could muster to put an end to it. Her disappointed expression did wonders for his ego, but he had to put it aside, do the job they'd come to do.

But he promised himself, they were going to talk

about that kiss and what it meant. And hopefully, they were on the same page for where it took them in the future.

With one hand circling her upper arm, Aiden guided her back to the end of the line.

"You feel comfortable taking the lead?" he asked, quietly, keeping his eyes on Richard Deveroux. "Cuz if his creep vibe is too uncomfortable, I can do it."

"I'm good," she said, after first clearing her throat. "If there's one thing I've learned by being a female department chair at a major university, it's how to deal with predatory and vile men. Professors and students alike."

The steel in her voice proved it. He had no doubt she could defend herself against the unwanted advances of lecherous academics and troublesome students. Even knowing it, the hot need to punch the shit out of every man who'd ever done or said anything off-color or who'd made a lewd pass at her, shot through him, setting his blood on boil mode.

He squeezed her arm in solidarity.

At last their turn came. Lexi moved to stand in front of the table while Aiden stood off to the side between two book stacks, giving the appearance she was solo, a tactic they'd discussed before arriving. Aiden thought if she presented as a woman alone, Deveroux might be more inclined to drop his guard than if they approached him together.

The oily smile plastered on the man's upturned lips as his eyes slowly dragged down from Lexi's face to settle in the area of her breasts had Aiden biting back the snarl wanting desperately to unleash itself. The man didn't even mask his eye-rake. That took some kind of balls, especially with his wife standing next to him, watching every move he made.

"Well now," he said, turning his attention back to Lexi's face, "your lovely hands are empty. Have they sold out of my book already?"

The deep, huskiness in his voice, like the rest of him, screamed phony.

"Actually, Mr. Deveroux, I'm not here for an autograph."

"Oh?" His eyes went from lascivious to alert. His wife took a step closer, her attention on Lexi, while the store manager remained on the other side of the table. All three stared at her.

"I read online you would be signing here today, and I thought I'd take a chance and come down to talk to you. My name is Alexis Buckley, and I'm investigating the death of my sister. I believe you knew her. Zoe Tremont?"

His eyes gave him away immediately. For someone with the reputation of a financial shark, it was a telling sign. He knew Zoe, or at least her name. The swift flick of his lids proved it.

"The name is familiar." He squinted over Lexi's shoulder as if trying to place it. "I believe she called a while back, asking to do an interview for some publication, or something. I can't remember." He turned to his wife. "That's the name she gave, wasn't it, Margo?"

Water cascading over a cliff face didn't move as fluidly as Margo Deveroux did when she maneuvered closer to her husband. She placed a hand with talon-like red nails on his shoulder as she leaned against his seated body, one bony hip sliding alongside him. She gave his shoulder a solid, visible squeeze. Aiden wondered if it was a sign of reassurance or one of warning.

Interesting.

"What does this have to do with my husband?"

Again, interesting. And telling. Doesn't answer the question, but puts forth one of her own.

"Your name," Lexi said, continuing to address Deveroux and ignoring his wife, something that warmed Aiden's heart, "along with several others, came up during my investigation."

"Investigation? Are you a cop?" he asked.

"Merely a concerned sister. I'd appreciate anything you can tell me about your interaction with Zoe."

"I didn't have any interaction with her other than one very brief phone call. How she got my private number I never discovered. She called one night and requested an interview. I don't handle media requests, so I referred her to my publicist."

"Peter Smith of the Kingman Group?"

If he was surprised she knew who represented him, Deveroux didn't show it. "Yes. The firm handles all my media appearances. I get so many requests every day I couldn't possibly do it myself."

"Did you meet with her?"

"No. Smith thought, because she was an unknown name, an interview with her wouldn't do anything to elevate my public profile." He shrugged inside his four-thousand-dollar tailor-made suit.

"I always thought any publicity was good publicity."

That condescending smirk returned. "Only when it serves a purpose. Smith didn't believe being featured in such a small publication would do me any good with increasing sales."

"I thought you didn't know what kind of venue she was doing a story for?"

Aiden's heart turned over with pride. *Good girl.*

"My husband has already told you he referred her to Smith. It was he who told us your—sister, was it?—worked for some inconsequential publication." Margo flipped a hand in the air, a practiced and elegant move to convey boredom. "Now, if you'll excuse us, we need to be at a business dinner since we're finished here."

Lexi wouldn't be deterred, something a woman like Margo wasn't used to. Her perfect, plump lips pressed into a flat line as Lexi ignored her.

"So you never met Zoe?" she pressed Deveroux.

"No."

"And you only spoke with her once on the phone?"

A dramatic sigh barreled up from him before he said, "Yes."

"Did she actually state she wanted to interview you about your book?"

The question seemed to surprise him. He blinked a few times and sat up straighter. "I don't remember her saying those words precisely, but my book is a national bestseller. It stands to reason she was looking to get some eyes on her work and wanted to use the book's notoriety, and me, as a way to do so."

Arrogant, superbilious, and condescending. Aiden shook his head. The creep hit all three personality traits on his version of the biggest asshole list.

Lexi nodded. "Okay. I can see where you would think that."

Deveroux shrugged.

"So you never actually met my sister."

It wasn't a question, but he took it as one. "No. As I've said. Repeatedly."

"Okay, well, what can you tell me about Shel Bushman?"

Oh, the man really had to work on blanking his expressions. Aiden smirked.

"Excuse me?" He recovered quickly, his brows tugging toward one another, his chin dropping a hair. But everyone in close vicinity of the table had witnessed the surprised gasp he let out upon hearing the name.

Lexi repeated her question.

"Nothing," he said with a spastic shake of his head. "I don't know the name."

"Really?" Lexi cocked her head to one side. "I find that strange since your private number shows up repeatedly in her phone. Calls placed to you over a period of months and occurring at all hours of the day. And night."

Once again, his wife pressed her fingers into his shoulder. This time Aiden knew it for the warning it was.

Deveroux looked up at her. Some unspoken communication drifted between them in their intense gazes, and after a moment he gave her a quick nod. Margo dropped her hand. Deveroux rose from the chair and made a production of buttoning his suit jacket while he stared down his nose at Lexi, annoyance drifting across his face.

"I don't know where you've gotten your information, but obviously, you're mistaken since I've never heard of this person. Now, as my wife"—he turned to her and took her hand—"has said, we need to be somewhere. I can't be of any help to you. Margo?"

"Miss Bushman is dead, too. Just like my sister."

Deveroux stopped in his tracks and turned back around to her. Aiden would bet ten bucks the surprise in his widened eyes and grooved brows at hearing the news was a true reaction. Regaining his composure, Deveroux said, "I'm sorry for your loss and for this other...woman's, but none of it concerns me."

"Two dead women with your name linked to them, and it doesn't concern you?" Lexi's voice rose as the couple moved away, the store manager trailing behind them, shooting Lexi nasty looks over her shoulder.

He stopped short again, said something to his wife, turned, and strode back toward Lexi. Aiden wasn't mistaken when he caught the look of rage in the man's eyes. He was all set to move from his vantage point and place himself in front of Lexi, but one glance at the determined glare in her eyes and the rod of forged metal shooting up her spine, and he knew she could handle herself. Still, he edged closer to the aisle as a precaution.

Deveroux's height gave him an intimidating advantage as he towered over the pixie librarian. She never wavered though, staring straight into his eyes, her hands relaxed at her sides. Her entire demeanor, in fact, reflected a cool collectiveness and not a whit of fear.

"Now you listen and you listen good." A thunderous cloud of menace had wormed its way into his tone. "I've answered your questions and repeatedly told you I don't know anything about your sister. Your insinuations otherwise could get you arrested for slander, and don't think I won't pursue prosecution if you make me."

"It's not slander if it's the truth." Her voice, in contrast to his, remained calm.

Like his wife, Deveroux was obviously not used to being challenged. His face turned the most vibrant hue of apple red, his ears following suit. Audible and rapid breaths blew from him as he balled his hands into fists at his sides.

"Darling? We need to go."

Margo's voice broke through the man's ire. Leaning down so his face was mere inches from Lexi's, he growled, "Stay away from me or you'll be sorry."

"I don't respond to threats, Mr. Deveroux."

He took a step closer, and Aiden was all set to spring. If it were possible for someone so short to look down their nose at someone so much taller, Lexi managed to. From the bored look in her eyes to the pursed pout on her lips, her expression told Deveroux just how ridiculous she thought him.

Aiden's heart turned over and that bell chimed again.

Sputtering with rage, he turned on his heels and strode back to his wife. Taking her arm, he ushered her down the aisle toward the back of the store, the manager still imprinted on to them.

Once they were out of sight, Lexi's shoulders dropped down and the breath she sucked in drained the air surrounding her.

"You okay?" Aiden cocked his head and traced a hand down her arm.

When she turned those gorgeous green eyes his way, her pupils were constricted with anger.

She dragged in another deep breath, closed her

eyes a moment, and when she opened them again, zeroed right in on his face. Her lips set into a firm flat line and, *Jesus*, he wanted to kiss them plump again. If they were somewhere private he would, because he wanted to do so much more to her than simply kiss her sweet mouth.

"I can tolerate almost anything but being lied to," she told him, her voice filled with more emotion than her eyes.

Aiden nodded. "He was definitely lying. And he's not good at it, which is surprising."

Her brows tugged together. "Why is it surprising?"

"Come on." He wrapped his hand around her arm because he needed to touch her. "Let's get out of here and I'll tell you why."

****

"Do you think his wife knows about his relationship with Shel?" she asked.

They were seated on the floor in the suite's living area, Aiden's back against the couch, his legs stretched out under the coffee table and crossed at the ankles, while she sat back against the opposing wing-back chair, a glass of wine in her hand. The room service meal they'd reheated of braised pork, fingerling potatoes, and a veggie mix was now a memory, their empty plates spread across the table in front of them.

"Fifty-fifty chance she does. You noticed how she dug her nails into him when you asked about Shel?"

"Yes, I did, which made me think she did. But you don't look convinced."

"I can go either way." He shrugged, then stretched his arms over his head. Lexi tried valiantly not to swallow her tongue when his shirt slipped up from the waistband of his trousers, giving her a brief glimpse of his defined abs. "She was either showing support or making sure he didn't say anything to incriminate himself. I tend to think she's the power behind the throne, and he's just the front man."

Lexi blinked a few times and concentrated on lowering her heart rate back to normal. They hadn't discussed *the kiss* yet, and Aiden had promised her they would. "Woodrow Wilson's wife, Edith, took over many of his duties in the White House after he suffered a stroke while in office. She kept the truth about the severity of his illness from the press and many in Wilson's own cabinet. There are more examples throughout history of the powerful partner being the one in the background, taking a more Machiavellian role."

The grin he tossed her looked more tired than tolerant.

"It's interesting he didn't deny any knowledge of your sister. Owned up to speaking to her without showing any signs of deception."

"Do you think he didn't know Shel was dead until I told him?"

"I tend to think in this instance he was telling the truth. We've already established he's a shitty liar. What he said about Zoe and his limited interaction rings true."

She sighed, then took another sip of her wine. "Where does this get us? I mean, we stayed here, hoping he'd be able to tell us something about Zoe. I feel like I'm no further along now than when I started looking into her death. I keep hitting walls."

Aiden's eyes softened as one corner of his fabulous

mouth lifted. "First of all, *we* know a lot more than when *we* first started."

Her cheeks heated.

If he noticed her blushing, he ignored it. "If we believe Deveroux, then Smith flat out lied. Deveroux referred Zoe to him, so that means he knew the name before you contacted him. We know Deveroux's lying about something, as are Monroe, Smith, and maybe Carde. What it is we don't know for sure, but I'm betting it has something to do with Shel Bushman, her death, or both. Zoe was looking into it for Kim, and she probably asked the wrong person the wrong question. All that makes sense if, as you believe, your sister didn't commit suicide, despite the evidence to the contrary."

"I know she didn't. I just…know it. Here." She fisted her hand over her heart.

Aiden nodded, then stifled a yawn. "And I trust your instincts. If we go on the thought someone killed Zoe, then whoever did it had something to hide, the skills to carry out an involved plan, and the ability to include others as accessories."

"That sounds like it's someone with means, money, and something to lose."

He nodded. "Deveroux fits the description."

"So do Monroe and Smith."

He shot his finger at her, and this time yawned fully. "Sorry. The lack of sleep and not being in my own bed for so long is starting to catch up."

"Don't apologize. It's my fault you aren't home in your own bed right now."

As soon as she said the words the image of him in *her* bed, naked, aroused, and doing wild and wicked things to her body shot to the front of her mind so fast she knew the current flush on her cheeks wasn't from embarrassment, but lust.

Aiden's phone chirped and when he answered it and said, "Hey, Dyl," Lexi took it as her cue to remove herself and give him some privacy. With their empty plates in her hands, she went into the kitchen. As she loaded the dishwasher, she overheard Aiden say, "Mild headache this morning, but I'm fine. Stop worrying. You're worse than Mom."

Headache? He never said anything about having a headache.

Guilt shot through her. If he weren't helping her, he'd be home right now and nestled in his own bed, probably with some tall, lithe model or gorgeous actress lying beside him.

On that depressing note, she went to her room and readied herself for bed. Minutes later, she realized she'd neglected to ask what time she should be ready to fly home the next morning. Donning a robe, she went back out into the living area to find Aiden, sprawled out on the length of the couch on his back, his feet draped over one of the arm rests, his head settled against the other, with one arm bent beneath him, supporting it like a pillow.

He was sound asleep.

Taking a moment to stare at him without needing to hide her mounting desire from his inquisitive stare, Lexi thought he looked younger than his thirty-two years. His face was completely relaxed and expressionless, his eyelashes fanning across the top of his cheeks and his lips slightly parted. The previous pallor had abated.

Not wanting to wake him, she did want him to be comfortable, though, so she went into his room and grabbed the bedspread and one of his pillows from the bed. From the corner of her eye, she spotted a trio of medicine bottles on his bedside.

Curiosity got the better of her and, with a quick side-glance at the door, she picked one up, read the label, and frowned. She did the same with the other two, memorizing the unfamiliar names.

After she draped the comforter over him and managed to replace his arm with the pillow without waking him, Lexi went back to her room and typed the drug names into her phone, then stored them in a file. She could do a search on them now, but her own fatigue was setting in fast.

Her last thought before she succumbed to sleep was to wonder if Aiden could be sick in some way.

Chapter 11

"I feel like I should be paying your gas bills," Lexi told Dylan as he helped her down from his jeep the next morning.

He grinned at her and tipped an imaginary cap. "It's my pleasure to be your chauffeur, Doc. Any time you need a ride, you call me."

Alighting from the car, Aiden's eyes narrowed, then he shot a quick punch into Dylan's gut. His brother barely flinched.

"Stop flirting," he ordered.

Dylan's grin grew wider. "You hit like a girl."

"Hey," Lexi exclaimed.

Dylan touched his invisible hat again. "Present company excluded."

With a warning glare aimed at his brother, Aiden took Lexi's bag from her hand. "I'll see you up."

He could tell she was all set to tell him he didn't need to, so he lifted his brows and stared hard at her.

The dull headache he'd woken with had him cursing the fact he'd neglected to take his meds before falling asleep on the couch. He woke covered with the comforter from his bed, so he knew Lexi'd made sure he was okay before retiring herself. That ache had grown in the shower, and the moment the plane lifted off, with the shifting cabin pressure, it now resembled a bongo drum line. He'd been taciturn and uncommunicative on the flight, something, if Lexi noticed, she'd thankfully ignored. All he wanted to do was make sure she got back to her apartment safe and sound, and then he planned on crashing in his own bed with his dog at his feet for the next several hours until the pain subsided. Watching his brother flirt with Lexi had done nothing to ease his grumpy attitude.

She must have recognized he was in no mood to argue because she gave him a quick head bob, said, "Thank you," to his brother, and added a side hug, before she preceded him into the building.

In the elevator, Aiden told her, "I'll call you later, and we can figure out where to go with the investigation. There are still a few avenues open to finding out what was going on in Zoe's life."

With her keys in her hand, she stared up at him, a frown line between her brows.

"Don't worry, Lex," he said. "We're not done yet. I promise, we'll figure out what happened to your sister."

Once they exited the elevator, Lexi slid her key into the lock. Before opening the door, she turned to him. With a corner of her bottom lip tucked between her top teeth, she started to say something, then stopped. If the pain in his head wasn't escalating by the moment, he'd have pressed her. But he really needed to get to bed, a.s.a.p.

He dropped the suitcase down next to her, squeezed her upper arm and said, "I'll talk to you later."

With a sigh, she nodded, pushed the door open, and shrieked.

****

The baby-faced cop couldn't have been greener if he'd admitted, "I'm a rookie and this is my first day," when he arrived at the apartment.

Kneading his right temple with his first two fingers, Aiden wanted to scream. Not from the pain, although that was bad enough. But when the cop asked the same question for the fourth time, and Lexi gave him the same exact answer, Aiden knew he was in serious danger of letting loose on the guy. Trust Dylan to have his back and prevent him from being arrested for threatening a law enforcement officer.

"Dr. Buckley has already told you she'd been gone for two days, Officer McCormick," his brother said, "and she doesn't know everything that's been stolen because she hasn't gone through all her belongings yet. The first thing we did when we saw the apartment had been trashed was call the precinct to report the break-in. We knew we shouldn't touch anything before you got here."

McCormick nodded. "You got any idea how the perp got in?" He ticked his head toward the door. "No sign that's been jimmied. Any windows you left open while you were in"—he glanced down at his notepad—"Atlanta?"

"All the windows in the apartment are painted shut," she told him.

When she'd screeched after opening the door, Aiden's first instinct was to get her out of the way of any danger. Going on pure instinct and adrenaline, he grabbed her arm, tugged her back into the hallway, and shoved her behind him.

"Go get Dylan," he commanded before pushing the door open wide. Someone had done a number of the front room. The couch and chairs had been turned upside down, the fabric sliced and shredded down to the wooden underbelly. The coffee and end tables were upended and the lamps shattered, the pieces covering the carpet like confetti. Every cabinet in the kitchen was thrown open wide, the contents scattered and splattered across the countertops. All the books they'd gone through before leaving for Atlanta were strewn about the room. Cautiously, he crept into the apartment. The destruction followed into the room where she'd held her research into her sister's death. The pictures and papers she'd placed on the wall above the desk had been sliced, the desk drawers pulled open and lying empty on the carpet. Her laptop was gone.

He turned at a sound, braced to defend himself against the intruder, and instead found Lexi, a knife he recognized from her butcher block in her hand and poised to strike.

"I told you to go get Dylan," he barked.

Her back snapped straight and her shoulders squared as she glared at him. "Don't take that tone with me. I was covering your back. You had no idea if someone was in here."

If his head wasn't splitting and all the scenarios of what could have happened to her if he'd left her to come back up to the apartment alone weren't running through his head, he would have laughed at the notion of this hundred-pound pixie coming to his assistance. But the fact that she'd put herself in potential danger sent terror shooting down his spine. With equal measure, he wanted to kiss her until her bones liquefied and alternately shake some sense into her. After telling her he'd cleared the apartment, he took a deep breath and called Dylan.

The officer glanced around the wreckage that was

once Lexi's neat and tidy living room. "So no idea what, besides the laptop, has been taken?"

The pain in his head combined with the greenhorn officer's repetition tic finally got to Aiden.

"Listen." He slid his hands into his pants pockets for fear he'd sucker punch the guy. "Why don't you give Dr. Buckley your card and she can call you when she's got a full list of what's been taken? So far, it's only her laptop. For now, just write this up as a routine break-in and you can fill in the rest of the details later, okay?"

The young man turned to Lexi. "That okay with you?"

She told him it was and took the card he offered.

Once the three of them were alone in the apartment, Dylan asked his brother, "Connected?"

"I'm sure of it."

"What are you talking about?" Lexi asked, hands on her hips and her gaze ping-ponging between them. When she settled on his face, her brows tugged together. "Are you okay?" she asked, taking a step toward him, her hand outstretched.

Hating to show any kind of weakness, he brushed her hand aside and said, "I'm fine. And I don't think this is a random break-in, despite what I told McCormick."

"You think it's connected to our investigation." She nodded. "I thought that, too. It makes sense, especially since my laptop's gone. But why did they trash everything?"

"They were looking for something other than your computer," Dylan said.

"What?"

He shrugged. "Anything belonging to your sister that might be incriminating for whoever did this. Who knows what it was?" He flipped his hand to the strewn book pile. "Something in a book, like a letter, or even a note. A flash drive."

"We didn't find any of those things when we unpacked her boxes," Aiden said.

Lexi snapped her fingers. "Her day planner." She crossed to where she'd tossed her purse on the floor. "I bet that's what they wanted. I didn't leave it here when we went to Atlanta. I brought it with me." She pulled it from the bowels of the bag

"Why?" Dylan asked.

"I have no idea. I just stuck it in my purse before we left for the airport."

Dylan nodded slowly, then looked over at him, his gaze tracking over his face. "You need to get home."

"I'm fine—"

"*Brain.*"

The warning in the hated nickname filtered through.

"Okay. But first"—he turned back to Lexi—"you can't stay here. If this is connected to Zoe—and I'd bet my last dollar it is—whoever did it knows you, knows you're looking into her death, knows you live here, and may come back if they didn't find what they were searching for."

A flicker of fear flew through her eyes, then fled again, leaving the determined, penetrating stare he was coming to really like seeing there in its place. Nodding, she pulled her phone from her bag. "I can book a hotel close to the college—"

"You're staying with me."

Her eyes went wide. "Aiden, that's not necess—"

"No arguments."

He could tell she didn't like his tone, but he wasn't in the mood for niceties or a battle of wills.

"It makes sense," Dylan refereed, glancing from one of them to the other. "You can't stay here, Doc. It's not safe. This way"—he thrust his chin at his brother—"you two can keep digging, and Aiden can keep you safe by keeping you close. Besides…" He pulled out all the charm Aiden couldn't muster at the moment, by grinning and adding, "You'll have Brontë there, too. Believe me, nobody's gonna get to you with her around. Dog's the most protective animal there is."

She wasn't happy about it, but in the end she saw it as the best option. "I need to pack a few things since I have to work tomorrow."

When Aiden told her to bring enough for at least a week, her color dropped, but she went into her bedroom to get some things together.

Dylan was on him like white on rice a millisecond later, his affable air flown, his face a mask of intense concern.

"You look ready to drop," he said. "How's the pain?"

"It'll be better once I can crash for a few hours. I forgot to take my pills last night, woke up with a headache, and the flight made it worse. And now this." He swept a hand across the debris-cluttered room. "*Jesus.*"

"It's obvious Lexi's instincts were correct, and her sister didn't kill herself. She knew something about somebody."

"And might have had proof," Aiden added.

"Any thoughts on who?"

Quickly, he told his brother about the interaction with Deveroux. "He's definitely hiding something and he outright lied to us about knowing Shel Bushman.

"Yeah, but that could have been him wanting to keep his relationship with the hooker from his wife. She was standing next to him, right?"

"I thought of that. But I'm not sure that was the reason he lied. We need to keep digging. What I *am* sure of is Zoe's death and Shel's are connected. I can't see the why of it, yet, though." He sighed and rubbed at his temple again.

"Stop thinking," Dylan said. "Get some rest and look at everything once the headache's gone and you can function again."

He blew out a breath. "That's the plan."

****

Forty minutes later both brothers carried Lexi's bags into Aiden's guest room, a watchful Brontë following them.

"The bed is comfortable and the closet's a good size, so you should be okay here for a few days," Aiden said.

"This room is as big as half my apartment," she said, glancing around at the space. "I'm seriously jealous."

Brontë whined as she nuzzled against Aiden's thigh. Sweeping his hand across the dog's head, he said, "I hear ya, girl. Look..." He addressed her again. Fatigue swamped his face, and his eyes were glassy. He wore the headache she was sure he had for all to see. "I'm gonna go crash for a while. The fridge is stocked, so help yourself to anything you'd like. There's coffee, all sorts of stuff in the cabinets. Feel free to watch tv, or if you want to work you can use the desktop in the living room. Okay?"

Dylan shook his head in mild disgust and fisted his hands on his hips. "You definitely rate in his book. He doesn't even let me watch his precious flatscreen, so take him up on the offer."

"I feel like I'm imposing—"

"Stop."

Her lips slammed together.

Aiden dragged a hand through the side of his head. "Sorry. I don't mean to be so short."

"He can't help the fact he didn't get any of the charm in the family," Dylan said. Aiden shot him a speaking glance.

She folded her hands in front of her and nodded. "Thank you. For everything. I'll be fine while you go…rest."

"No thanks necessary." He nodded to Dylan and said, "Talk later."

Dylan grabbed him in for a hug and whispered something she couldn't hear in his ear.

Once they were alone, Lexi turned to Dylan. "I don't mean to pry, but is he okay?"

"Yeah. He's fine. Really. Every now and then he gets a killer headache, and it makes him crabby."

"Migraines?"

The answer flickered in his eyes. In the next second he'd banked them again.

"Like I said, I don't mean to be nosy." She wrung her hands. "I'm just concerned about him."

Dylan nodded. "You don't need to be, but it's nice you are. Aiden's good. Trust me."

Aiden

With that, he dropped a kiss on her cheek. Before leaving, he cocked his head and regarded her for a second.

"What?"

"It's not my story to tell, and Aiden's a ridiculously private guy. Clams talk more than my baby bro does. But if you've got any questions, just ask him."

He winked at her, then shut the door behind him.

Could he be any more cryptic? What, exactly, was it not his story to tell? She knew it must have something to do with the medicines she spotted. Should she do a little research now since she had a few hours free?

Brontë ambled into the kitchen and pressed her nose against Lexi's thigh. Petting her, she asked, "Aiden sleeping?"

She swore the dog nodded.

"Okay. Did you really just answer me or did I imagine you did? And why am I asking you like you're gonna talk to me?"

Shaking her head, she opened a few cabinets, mumbling, "I must be hypoglycemic. Lack of sugar in the bloodstream can cause hallucinations."

Brontë made a sound remarkably like a chuckle, then ambled off again in the direction of Aiden's room.

Armed with a strong cup of coffee and one of the scones she found in the filled refrigerator next to a tub of butter, Lexi sat down behind Aiden's desktop, powered it up, then keyed into a search engine.

A few hours later when he sauntered into the room with Brontë in tow, she was in the same spot, lost down the rabbit hole of research she'd tumbled into.

"Hey," he said, grabbing a mug from the cabinet

and then lifting the pot of coffee she'd made.

She glanced up at him and watched as he poured himself a cup. The pallor was gone, and even from this distance she could detect his eyes were once again clear. He stood in bare feet, wearing a T-shirt and jeans, and his shoulders had dropped back to their normal, relaxed position from where they'd been pinned to his ears earlier.

Everything she'd read for the past few hours simmered inside her head like a word jumble soup. She couldn't have stopped herself from blurting out "Craniopharyngioma" if she'd intentionally bitten down on her tongue to keep quiet.

Aiden stopped, mid-pour. With slow, measured movements he put the mug and pot down, then laid his fisted hands on the counter. Chugging in a deep breath, he looked across the counter at her.

Warning signs blasted from his pinched brows to the downturn of his full mouth, but Lexi was powerless to ignore them.

"A benign tumor located near the pituitary gland," she spat by rote. "Most commonly discovered between the ages of five and fourteen. They account for 6 percent of all brain tumors diagnosed in children. Most are curable if caught early. Treatment includes craniotomy to remove the tumor and/or radiation to reduce and eradicate it. Survival rates from early treatment are high."

She slammed to a stop, took a breath, and realized she was shaking, so she clasped her hands together and laid them in her lap.

Aiden tilted his head and after taking another breath, asked, "Dylan?"

It took her a moment before she realized what he was asking. "No. Goodness, no. Your brother didn't say a word. I just, well…"

He didn't push, which made her feel all the more guilty about her nosiness.

"I-I saw the medications on your bedside table last night at the hotel, and I, well, I did a search on what they're used for."

"And you came up with the diagnosis of a benign brain tumor?"

Her cheeks flushed hot. "It was a circuitous road to that, but yes. Headaches and migraines aren't uncommon after treatment and neither are changes associated with eyestrain. I remembered you said you have computer vision syndrome."

Aiden stood, silent, studying her for a few moments. Worried she'd overstepped and wishing she could control this endless tic of exclaiming facts the moment they turned into a thought, her hands grew slick with sweat. When Aiden shook his head, the ghost of a grin materializing across his lips, she thought maybe, just maybe, he wasn't upset with her after all.

"You really are a brilliant researcher," he declared as he started filling his mug again. "It's almost a shame you work for the college because I know we could use someone with your skills at the firm."

"You're not mad at me?"

He tilted his head and squinted. "For?"

She lifted a shoulder, then swiped her wet hands over the fabric of her pants. "Prying."

With his mug filled, he joined her at the desk, leaning a hip against it. "I'm not mad. Maybe a little self-conscious that you know. It's not like I talk about it. But I'm not mad."

There were so many questions she wanted to ask, but for the moment she surprised herself by keeping silent.

After drinking some coffee, Aiden said, "When I turned nine, my mother realized I wasn't growing at the rate my brothers had. By that age, they were all four or five inches taller and much heavier. I didn't even know my vision was so blurry because the deficit had come on so gradually I simply accommodated for the changes. The pediatrician did a bunch of tests, felt like she took vats of blood. My hormone levels were off, so she suspected it was something to do with my thyroid or my pituitary. The actual diagnosis came when I turned ten, after an MRI my mother pushed for. Seems she's a pretty good researcher, too. Especially when it comes to her boys." His lips lifted. "One successful surgery later and a bunch of meds to correct the imbalances, and I grew almost six inches in a year and gained thirty pounds. The migraines and vision issues started in college. They're correctable as long as I pay attention to the warning signs."

He stopped, shot her a glance, then added, "Last night I was so tired I forgot to take my meds. I woke up with a headache that got worse with the flight."

"Atmospheric pressure changes."

He nodded. "Finding your apartment trashed didn't help the situation either."

"Is that why Dylan refers to you as *Brain*? Because of what happened to you?"

The slight hesitation before he answered sent her nosy senses on hyperalert. "One of the reasons," he said.

Brontë nudged against him and licked the hand he gave her. "It's okay, girl. I'm okay now."

Another lick and then she settled at his feet, her eyes watchful.

"She's more than a companion, isn't she?" Lexi asked, giving a voice to something that had occurred to her while she'd been reading.

"Again..." He shook his head. "Your deductive skills are the best I think I've ever seen."

This time when her face heated it was from pleasure.

"Brontë's trained as a medical support dog. She has the uncanny ability to predict the auras that come with migraines and seizures." As if she knew they were speaking about her, the dog barked, once, then rested her head on Aiden's foot. "She considers it her job to warn me when I'm not paying attention to any signs of fatigue which can spark a migraine. In essence, she protects me from myself."

"That's amazing. How did you discover she could do that?"

Aiden took another giant sip of his coffee, then said, "That's a conversation best for another time. I need to take her out and then get us something to eat. Are you hungry?"

She shook her head. "I had the most delicious scone while I was trolling medical sites."

"Kandy's." He nodded. "They're the best. Okay. Let me take care of Brontë, then we can get started."

"Started?"

"On figuring out who trashed your apartment and why."

He went back into his bedroom and came back a

moment later, shod and with a sweatshirt over his tee.

"We'll be back in about ten minutes," he told her as he hooked on Brontë's leash.

While he was gone, she exited the search engine, then began preparing something for him to eat.

"I sure wish Kandy Laine was my sister-in-law," she mumbled when she pulled container after container from the refrigerator. There were almost too many delicious choices, and she wasn't sure how hungry Aiden was. He hadn't eaten before leaving the hotel and had refused the breakfast snack offered on the flight. Now she knew why. Who could eat with migraine pain pounding through their head?

But he did look better after resting, so she wanted to make sure he ate something hearty.

When he and Brontë walked in minutes later, she had beef stew heating on the stove and had sliced a loaf of artisan bread she'd found wrapped in foil.

"It smells great in here," he said as he came into the kitchen, the dog at his side.

"Thank your sister-in-law." She pulled two bowls down from a cabinet and said, "I don't know where you keep Brontë's food."

"I'll take care of it."

She'd thought the kitchen spacious as she moved around in it alone. The ceramic countertops in a cerulean blue were wide and long, the room fashioned into an opened L design leading into the living area. With the addition of man and dog, it was still roomy, but when she turned, intent on lifting the stew from the stove, she rammed, face first, into Aiden as he reached up into a cabinet. For the briefest of moments she actually thought to stay put, with her nose planted squarely in his chest, the top of her head grazing his chin and her body pressed against his. It would take nothing to slip her arms around his waist, hook them behind, and hang on for dear life.

Or until he kissed her again. Whichever came first.

When his hands instantly shot to her upper arms and folded around them, the notion to stay still took root. Her never-resting mind went dormant when he kept her against his wide, cement-hard torso instead of pushing her away. In the slightest of moves, she tilted her face so her cheek pressed into his chest.

The thrum of his heartbeat, steady, strong, and oh-so soothing, had her eyes closing as she nestled against him and sighed.

A flutter of air broke above her, and when Aiden removed his hands and slid them around her back, caging her to him, her entire body relaxed.

Well, almost her entire body.

"You okay?" The deep, raspy timbre in his voice vibrated against her ear and shot straight to her core. The intense pressure of need that formed at the apex of her thighs caused the muscles in the area to contract.

"Shouldn't I be asking you that?" she managed to get out. "You're the one with the headache."

His chuckle sent another wave of desire through her. Sliding his hands up, then down, her back, a few times, his touch ignited her insides like a wildfire raging across drought-ridden farmland. Every inch of her skin vibrated.

"My head's fine now. But you were the one whose apartment was trashed and whose life's been upended. How are you feeling about that?"

While doing her research, she'd been able to forget

the catastrophe of her apartment. Cleaning it up and replacing the destroyed things, the furniture especially, was going to take a great deal of time—and money—both of which she had little of at the moment.

She mumbled a "not great," then rubbed her nose across his shirt.

He smelled delicious.

"I think that's Kandy's stew," he said, his quiet laugh telling her she'd said it aloud.

Mortified, she inhaled deeply. Pushing back from him, she pressed her lips together and kept her eyes closed, her head bent. She imagined strawberries, ripe and ready to be picked, weren't as red as her face probably was at the moment.

The touch of Aiden's knuckles trailing softly across her jaw prompted her to open her eyes.

No man had ever looked at her with such kindness, humor, and desire all rolled into one gorgeous expression before.

She needed to say something but for the life of her couldn't think of anything other than "Do me. Right here, right now."

Yeah, I can imagine what he'd say if I said that out loud.

Besides, the man was recovering from an incapacitating migraine that had flattened him. Even if he wanted to, he might not be able to…perform.

Okay, well, that's the stupidest thing you've ever thought, Alexis Elizabeth. The man oozes sex from every pore, even with a headache screaming through him.

Aiden turned his hand and cupped her chin, then lifted it. When his thick thumb scraped across her bottom lip, a moan pushed out from her she was powerless to contain.

"I'm sure if I asked," he said, humor dancing in his quiet voice, "you could quote me all the physiological reasons your cheeks are flushed, your skin's warm to the touch, and your eyes are sparkling with moisture."

She pressed her thighs together again.

"But I don't need to know the how of it, Lexi, because I know the why. I know why your pulse is tripping, your breathing's doubled, and your body's trembling."

She swallowed, her gaze mesmerized to his. "You do?"

One side of his mouth lifted. "Yeah. Because I'm feeling the same way."

"*What?*"

He nodded, leaned down, and pressed his forehead against hers, the tips of their noses touching in the sweetest of caresses. A cavernous sigh broke from him, and he closed his eyes for a moment. When he opened them again, he said, "I've been feeling all those things since the first moment I saw you in the airport bar. I've been trying to keep a professional distance between us, but it's getting harder every moment we're together."

Even through the erotic fantasies she was having of the two of them naked and busy on top of the kitchen counter, she was aware enough to be confused by his words.

"Wait. The bar? Don't you mean when you saw me on the plane?"

He pulled back and settled his butt against the counter, taking her hands with his as he did and tugging her to lie flat against him, then circling his hands around her back again. Her palms flattened over his chest. "No. I meant the bar. I saw you there before I ever sat next to you on the flight."

"You couldn't ha—"

"With Smith."

Her mouth slammed shut, and the sheet of ice sliding down her spine dowsed all the heat emanating within her. "What—what do you mean?"

"I was grabbing something to eat before we had to board, killing time, people watching. I spotted a gorgeous redhead having drinks with a guy across from me."

Lexi had trouble believing flames weren't shooting from her face right now from the level of embarrassment engulfing her.

"I watched the redhead saunter out of the bar, trailing a cute little blue suitcase behind her." A grin she could only describe as wolfish grew on his lips. "You have a very distinctive sway to your hips when you walk. Most people have an idiosyncratic gait. Yours was a pleasure to watch from behind."

Okay, forget flames. It was a nine-day wonder she didn't immolate on the spot.

His grin grew with her discomfort. "Twenty minutes later I spotted the same cute little blue suitcase in front of me, the same sensual walk with it, but the redhead had been replaced by a blonde pixie in different clothes. So, being the inquisitive guy I am, I followed. Serendipity had us booked on the same flight."

"And seated in the same row?" She considered it a miracle she got the words out in a coherent sentence. Her mouth and throat had gone as dry as tree bark while he spoke.

The wolf grin was replaced by a lopsided one reminiscent of a naughty boy caught with a hand where it shouldn't be. "Well, serendipity had nothing to do with that, to be truthful. I switched out my first class seat for the one next to you."

"Why?"

"The main reason? Natural nosiness. I wanted to find out why you were in disguise and what it had to do with the guy in the bar. I figured you were either some kind of con artist, grifter, or thief."

"Why thief?"

"I saw you slip your hand under the bar when Smith pulled out his credit card. I thought you'd stolen something from him."

She shook her head. "I can't tell you how many times I practiced that move so no one would know what I was doing, and you saw right through it."

"Yeah, but I'm a trained observer, remember that. Besides, I was having fun staring at you."

She shook her head again. Then a thought filtered through. "How did you know where I was seated on the plane? I know for a fact the ticket agents aren't allowed to divulge any info."

After he told her, she pursed her lips and lifted her left eyebrow as she looked up into his face. "Remind me the next time I fly to keep my boarding pass in my purse until the last possible second."

His hands tightened around her. The laughter in his eyes ebbed, replaced, again, by the raw need that made her knees weak.

"You were gorgeous as an undercover redheaded siren," he said, making her roll her eyes. "You had

Smith and every other guy in the bar drooling, me included."

"Simple playacting. I mean, obviously." With a shrug she added, "I'm no man-magnet."

"No, Lex. You're wrong. So wrong. You're as sexy as fuck, and the fact you don't even know it makes you more so. That, combined with your amazing brain and skills, are what I'm drawn to like I haven't been to another woman in a long, long time. When I sat next to the real you on the plane and we started talking, after two minutes all I could think about was hoisting you over onto my lap and kissing the hell out of you. It's been hard—no pun—to concentrate whenever we're close together like this. I've been trying to be a professional about it and keep my distance. But I've got to tell you, it's a struggle to keep my hands, and every other part, off you."

Dumbfounded didn't do justice to the emotions flowing through her mind from his declaration.

"Right before you kissed me in the hallway of the bookstore, I'd been wracking my brain to try and figure out a way I could tell you how I felt without scaring you off or violating every ethical code I've got. But then I didn't need to ask because you kissed me first." He chuckled. "What's that saying? Great minds and thinking alike?"

She wanted to believe him, she really did. He hadn't resisted when she'd thrown herself at him.

Resisted? Ha. He was a more-than-willing participant.

But a healthy dose of reality prevented her from completely accepting his words.

"Forced proximity, plus being involved in highly

emotional situations which can lead to personal danger, oftentimes causes an adrenaline surge, the physiological effects of which can mimic signs of desire or lust," she stated, staring straight into his eyes. "We've been together practically every moment for almost three days, most of it in close quarters. We've shared meals and living space, and we share a common goal in finding out what we can about my sister. And my apartment being broken into constitutes as an adrenaline-releasing event. So."

Without missing a beat he grinned, broadly. "Adrenaline-releasing event, huh? You keep telling yourself that. Now..." He ticked his head toward his dog. "She needs to eat, and so do I. I'm always starving after a headache. Why don't we sit down and discuss what we're gonna do about your apartment and where we go next with the investigation, okay? We can table this discussion for later."

It was the *later* that worried her. For all intents and purposes she was living with him now, living under his protection until her apartment became safe to go back to. Protection she needed because of her pursuit of the truth of Zoe's death. She had to keep that reason uppermost in her mind. The truth was what mattered, not the desire swirling in the air about them.

Chapter 12

"They've got your computer, so they've got access to all the research you've been doing," Aiden said, after spooning in a whopping helping of Kandy's delicious stew. Brontë had once again seated herself at his feet after eating her own meal.

"Plus a million other things I've been working on for the college. Luckily, none of it is classified, and I backed it all up so I can still access it."

"Good girl. You'd be surprised how many people 'lose stuff' "—he put the words in air quotes—"because they fail to back up. In college, I worked at a computer store specializing in retrieving data when clients thought they'd lost it."

"Is that what you majored in college? Computer programing?"

"No. Actually, premed."

He wasn't taken aback by the shock that leapt across her beautiful face, but he had surprised himself by giving his one-time goal a voice. He never spoke of it or the real reason he'd changed his mind once he'd graduated.

"Because of what happened to you?" she asked, then immediately blushed. "Sorry." She shook her head and dipped her spoon back in her bowl. "Intrusive."

"It's not. You already know about the tumor. It's not a big stretch to think I wanted to go into medicine because of it." He sat back and crossed his arms over his chest. "I think, like most kids who've gone through a medical crisis, I had some lofty goals about treating cancer patients. Of finding a cure."

"Lofty goals, indeed."

"I figured since I'd experienced, first hand, how horrible it was, I could offer some…I don't know." He shrugged. "Solace maybe, that things were going to be okay. Like, look at me, I survived and you can, too."

"That's really a lovely sentiment, you know. The desire to help others who are going through something terrifying by giving them hope all will be well."

His lips lifted. "It sounds better the way you say it." He was rewarded with another blush.

"In the end, though, you didn't go into medicine."

"No. I graduated with a bachelor of science, but I switched to computer science for my master's."

"You have a master's degree?"

He laughed. "Why do you sound shocked?" He took a sip of his water. "All my brothers have advanced degrees, including Rick. My parents were big believers in higher education. Hence, the desire to go to med school."

"Again, I didn't mean to sound rude, but you've never mentioned it and most people in my experience who have advanced degrees of any sort, do. Many of them, often. They look for ways to let someone know about the letters after their name."

He shrugged again. "You don't. *Doctor.*"

Her lips twisted, and she rolled her eyes. "A doctor of library science is a very different career path from that of a medical doctor. What made you change your mind?"

"I realized I couldn't stand the sight of other people's blood."

It wasn't quite the whole truth, but for now, that's all he felt comfortable revealing. When she burst out laughing, he joined her.

"I know? Pathetic, right? I had no problem with seeing my own, but someone else's?" He pretended to shudder. "The stuff of nightmares. Computers don't bleed."

She pressed her lips together and cocked her head in a manner that told him she was thinking seriously about something. "No, but they do get viruses," she said, deadpan.

"Look at you, all witty and quick. You're pretty proud of yourself for that one, aren't you?"

Yeah, making her face flush with heat was rapidly becoming one of his now *three* favorite things to do.

She shoveled in a spoonful of the stew and said around it, "It kind of just materialized in my head."

He kept his smile aimed at her while his hand dropped to pet Brontë's head. "Getting back to the start of this conversation," he said. "Whoever stole your computer will be able to access your saved data if he or she's a good hacker."

With a shake of her head, she sighed. "It's not necessary to be a hacker. My files aren't locked. The minute anyone opens to the home screen, they'll be able to see everything. And before you give me a lecture on cyber security"—he slammed his mouth closed, because that's exactly what he'd been about to do—"save it. I know I should be more careful, and my only excuse is a stupid one. My laptop never leaves my apartment. I have another one at the college that houses all my work files, and I share the data between the two."

"Okay, I'll save the lecture for later, but that may make it easier to find out who's got your computer. Or who's accessing the data, anyway."

"How?"

"We'll need to hook up your work computer to mine. Then I can backdoor into your cloud account and run a program to allow me to shadow your files."

She looked cute, lost in thought for a few moments, her color returning to normal. "So if you shadow them?"

"Yes?"

"You'll be able to tell which ones are opened and then…"

"Then I can run a trace on the IP address of the computer accessing them."

"And it'll tell you who's reading them?"

"Theoretically. What it will actually do is tell me from where the files are being viewed. Once we know that we can try and locate the computer and, hopefully, the one running it."

"And all this is…legal?"

He stretched a hand across the table and twined his fingers into hers. Squeezing them, he said, "You need to trust I'm really good at my job."

"That's not an answer."

He tugged the hand to his lips and kissed her knuckles, rewarded when her eyes turned soft and a tiny sigh broke from between her lips. "Yeah, it is."

"Aiden—"

"Do you trust me?"

"Yes."

Okay, no hesitation at all. That's an ego booster if ever there was.

"Then don't worry. Now, I figure there are three people who would want to know what you've got on your computer. Monroe, Smith, and Deveroux."

"What about Carde? Or Margo?"

"Carde has no apparent skin in the game. He's just one of the people Zoe talked to. And I'm lumping husband and wife together for Deveroux."

"And you think Shel Bushman is what connects them?"

"Honestly, it makes the most sense, and if it's true, I'd say Richard is the main suspect. He seems to have the most to lose."

"What do you mean?"

"First, he was involved with a prostitute, and keeping his wife in the dark seems like a good motive to hurt Shel. Remember, she told Kim 'Hotshot' was gonna marry her. My guess? He was stringing her along."

"But would he kill her to keep that quiet? It seems over the top to me."

He shrugged. "People have done more based on less. The man's book recently became a national bestseller, and his reputation will sell more books. If it got out he was involved with a hooker…" He shook his head.

"What about Smith and Monroe? Where does Shel fit in with them, if she is, in fact, connected?"

"That's the money question and one we need to figure out. But Monroe connects to Zoe, who was asking questions about Smith. Smith is connected to Deveroux, whom Zoe wanted to interview. Shel is connected to Deveroux and Zoe, who's connected to all four, so it makes sense whatever bound them all together is what got Shel and your sister killed."

"If she truly was killed and didn't commit suicide like I've been led to believe."

"Correct."

"Laid out like that, in a linear fashion, it does make sense."

He nodded and finally let go of her hand. Grabbing both their empty bowls, he brought them to the sink. "Do you want to head over to the college now? Or wait until you're scheduled to be there in the morning? I vote for now. The quicker we can find out who's accessing your stuff the better. But it's up to you."

She followed him to the sink and placed their glasses into it alongside the dishes. "I guess now is better than tomorrow. I won't have a moment free from the second I get there until the end of the day. Probably beyond that. My desk, I can only imagine, is piled high." Her sigh echoed around the space. "I'll wash these."

Before she could reach for the soap pad, he laid a hand over hers. "That's what dishwashers are for."

Her gaze dipped to their joined hands. She bit down on a corner of her mouth, worked the area with her teeth. The tiny move, an emotional tell much like when she grabbed her earlobe, bounded through him.

With a quick flick of his wrist, he had her against his chest again, his hands twining around her slim waist to settle at the dip of her spine. In his arms, she felt as delicate and fragile as a piece of spun glass. He'd seen, firsthand, she was anything but.

"What's wrong?"

Another exhale, then she laid her head against him and burrowed. The move, so trusting and innocent, had him starving again. This time, Kandy's stew wasn't even a thought to quell the hunger deep inside him.

"I keep asking myself if I'm doing the right thing in trying to find out what really happened to Zoe."

"Why are you questioning yourself?"

Her shoulders lifted a bit. The top of her head came just to his shoulder line, and he couldn't resist the urge to gently rest his chin on it.

"Mainly because I don't see it ending well. My apartment has been trashed. My laptop and God knows what else has been stolen. I've missed enough work for no valid reason in the college's eyes, which might get me an official censure."

"The provost tell you that?"

"He hinted at it. Broadly. Plus…"

"Tell me."

"Well, now I've dragged you, and by extension your brother, into it. I can't possibly pay you for all the time and effort, hotel rooms, and airfares you've laid out. Not if I want to pay my rent on time and eat for the next decade."

"I've told you, numerous times, I'm not on the work clock right now, Lexi, so nothing is billable."

"But if you weren't helping me, you'd be doing something fun, something relaxing. You've just come off a two-month job without a break. You told me that yourself. You shouldn't be stuck with me and in all my drama—most of which is of my own making since I decided to push about Zoe's death. None of it seems fair to you."

"Fairness has nothing to do with why I'm helping

you, Lexi." His hold on her tightened. "Yes, I could be at the beach right now, snoozing the day away, catching some rays. Yes, I could be making my way through the dozens of books I've been meaning to read and haven't found the time for, or hanging out with my brothers. And yes, I could even be doing nothing, just sitting around with Brontë, waiting to go back to work and vegging in front of the tv. But I'm not, and it's *thanks* to you, not because of you."

She pulled back. Deep lines furrowed her usually smooth forehead.

"I'll admit, freely, when I first spotted you and knew you'd been the girl in the bar, I was intrigued and because I like a mystery, I decided to find out what you'd been up to."

Her color shot to ruby-red again.

"Once we started talking and you told me about your sister, I decided I wanted to help you. *I decided.*" He stressed the phrase and pushed against her with his hands. "I wanted you to get answers to your questions, and I'm in the position to help do that. Besides…" His lids went to half-mast, and he dipped his head closer to her. "It's more fun to hang out with you than my brothers. You're prettier."

She pursed her lips at him and rolled her eyes.

"And way sexier," he added while he ran a hand up to the middle of her back, then down again. When she shuddered, a rush of pure male satisfaction bolted through him.

With a shake of her head, she pushed against his chest and leaned backward. Aiden let her go.

She cleared her throat, then said, "In answer to your question, I think you're right and we should go to the college now."

Nodding, he said, "I'll get my keys."

****

"Dylan wasn't kidding when he said Brontë was a chick magnet," Lexi told him as she unlocked her office door. "Not one of those female students has ever said hello to me when they've seen me on campus or in the library. But the moment they spot me with a cute guy and a gorgeous dog, they treat me like a long-lost friend." She shook her head and tossed her purse on her desk.

"Did you just call me cute?"

The smug look on his face when she turned back around to him had her own lips lifting. She glanced down at her desk. As predicted, piles of mail, letters, envelopes, and interdepartmental mailers covered it. She blew out a breath and fisted her hands on her hips. "This is going to take hours to go through."

Aiden gave Brontë a hand signal that had her sitting. "You can work on diminishing it while I clone your computer. Okay?"

Seated behind her desk, Aiden removed a cable from his pocket, hooked it up to the laptop he'd brought with them, then plugged it into one of her desktop computer's ports. While he got busy, Lexi dragged the clutter of mail to her coffee table and plopped down on the couch to go through it. Brontë slid under the table, facing Aiden and keeping a watchful eye on him, while she laid her head on Lexi's feet. She stretched her hand down and fluffed the fur around the dog's neck.

A half hour later she had everything separated into three stacks: recycling, items she knew could wait a few days to deal with, and ones she needed to open as soon as possible. The last batch, unfortunately, proved the largest.

She glanced over at Aiden, and her heart rate shot up a good thirty beats. He'd donned his glasses and through the lenses his eyes were focused on the screen, his body taut, every movement of his fingers flying across the keyboard methodical, precise, swift.

What would it feel like to have all that fervid energy focused solely on...her? The two times he'd held her in his kitchen, she'd let herself melt against him, just relinquished over any and all of the control she judiciously clung to on a daily basis.

How wonderful it had felt.

She didn't have one memory of ever being able to cede control of her life to someone else. She'd been more than a mother to not only her baby sister, but most of the time to their own mom as well. Never once had Lexi shirked her duty in caring for either of them. It was, she'd mused more than once, why she depended solely on herself and no one else.

But with Aiden, she'd felt none of that protective instinct to take charge of a situation, to be the calmest one in the room when making decisions, to take care of everyone else to the detriment of herself.

And, yes, it had felt wonderful.

"I can feel you both staring at me," Aiden said never lifting his head, but flicking a glance over the tops of his glasses in her direction.

"Did you find who's got my computer yet?"

"Working on it. Whoever took it isn't logged on, so there's no activity I can trace."

"What have you been doing, then?"

"Setting up roadblocks and some research into

Richard Deveroux's finances. I'm looking for any payouts to Shel, or any hinky payments to third-party corporations."

"It amazes me how much information can be accessed digitally without anyone being the wiser."

"Which is another reason you still need a lecture on your own cyber security."

The image of Aiden, standing over her giving that lecture, naked except for his glasses had her squirming in her seat.

"I'll be right back," she said. "I need to use the restroom."

Aiden made to rise from the chair, but she stopped him with a shake of her head. "It's literally ten feet from this office. I don't need an escort."

He sat back down.

One look in the bathroom mirror while she washed her hands had her wishing she'd brought her purse in with her. Her hair, never her best feature, was a shock and riot of spikes. With her hands still wet, she finger-combed it into some semblance of order, when the door to the communal bathroom opened.

Lexi paid no attention to the person entering, since school was in session. Before she could wave her hands under the touchless drier, a hand clamped over her mouth from behind and tugged her off balance. She grasped at the hand, but hers were still too wet for her to get any traction. Her attacker's hold muffled her scream.

"Where's the file?" a voice growled in her ear. "Where is it?"

Ice flooded her body, freezing her in place.
What file?

"Where is it?"

She tried to shake her head to indicate she didn't know what he was talking about, but the hand clamped over her mouth prevented movement. With his free hand, he grabbed the collar of her shirt and shook her like she weighed no more than a rag doll. Dizziness clouded her vision as her head bounced right and left from the violent jerking.

A hot burst of anger blew up from her soul, took over, and instinct propelled her to fight back. She fisted one hand and swung it backward at hip level, hoping to land a punch in her attacker's genitals. He sidestepped the move and squeezed her face harder. Pain exploded through her flank when something solid hit her above her waist. Black dots rained into her vision.

From the corner of her eye, she caught a quick, blurry glimpse in the wall-wide mirror above the sink station of her attacker. Thinking quick, she slammed her head back, hoping to come in contact with his jaw. The painful, strangled cry told her she had. His grip loosened, and in that second, Lexi had enough space to open her mouth and bite down as hard as she could. He jerked his hand away from her face and spit out an epithet. Freed now, she spun around to face him, bent her arm at a ninety degree angle and shot her elbow upward, connecting with the bottom of his jaw. He stumbled back a few paces, his hand gripping his chin.

"*Bitch.*"

When he lunged toward her again, Lexi let out a blood-curdling scream that had her own ears ringing from the reverberation off the tiled walls. She lifted her leg and aimed her knee for his groin. Unfortunately, he shifted, then quick as lightning, he backhanded her across the face. The blow spun her flat up against the porcelain sink.

He cursed again at the sound of a dog barking, wildly. Grabbing a fistful of her hair, he jerked her head to the side and growled right next to her swelling cheek, "I'll be back, bitch. You'd better have that file," before shoving her forward into the sink again. Her hands reached out to grip the rim as she slammed against it.

In the next moment, he fled through the secondary entrance at the opposite end of the long room.

While still gripping the sink, Lexi sank to her knees.

Brontë, barking riotously, burst through the door, Aiden quick on her heals. The dog reached her first. Whining, she dropped to Lexi's side, her snout running all along her torso, sniffing and licking with fervor while Aiden said her name.

"He went out the other door," she said, through jagged breaths. Aiden pressed her shoulder, then bolted in the direction of her attacker. Shaking, she slid down until she could sit flat on the floor and wound her arms around the dog.

Brontë whimpered and lifted her paws around Lexi's neck in a dog-hug.

"It's okay, girl." Lexi patted her back while the dog cleaved to her. "It's okay."

When Brontë pulled back and stared Lexi straight in the eyes, she swore she read concern in the soulful canine gaze.

And when the dog carefully and gently licked the cheek the attacker had struck, Lexi finally let her frightened tears go.

Chapter 13

"She's in the shower," Aiden told his brothers when he let them into his apartment.

"She wouldn't go to the ER?" Josh asked.

Aiden shook his head, swiped his hands through his temples, and blew out a breath. "The doc who looked her over in the college infirmary encouraged her to, but she refused. He did a thorough exam, from what I could tell. She's got a good-sized bruise on her cheek, and she says there's another on her side. But nothing seems broken."

The past three hours had been filed with filing incident reports with college security and the local police who'd responded to his 911 call. With two incidents in two days logged, the cops who interviewed her were much more thorough with their questioning than the rookie cop had been at her apartment.

Lexi refused hospital attention, claiming she wasn't hurt, just shaken. The security guard on duty had been the one to convince her to go to the infirmary to be checked out.

Aiden had sprinted after Lexi's attacker but had lost him in the throng of students moving about the halls.

"I found the ski mask and jacket tossed in a stairwell," he told his brothers. "Classes were starting up, so the hallway was packed. Apparently, he blended in."

"She able to give any description other than the mask?" Dylan asked.

"Six foot at least. Lean. Brown eyes under the mask. His voice put him in his thirties, maybe older, but not much. Wore musk cologne, he's right-handed and white. She caught a glimpse of his hand in the mirror after she head-butted his jaw," he explained when they both raised their brows.

"She got all that from just a few seconds while she was being attacked?" Josh asked. "And fighting back? She's got incredible observational skills."

"*Oh.*"

The three of them turned to find Lexi, dwarfed in Aiden's robe, her short hair wet and plastered to her head. He hissed in a breath at the swollen, discolored area circling her right cheek.

"I'm sorry," she said, as her fingers swiped at her hair, then squeezed one earlobe. "I didn't know anyone was here."

Dylan crossed to her, and when he pulled her into a hug and asked, "How ya doin' Doc?" Aiden had the uncontrollable urge to punch his brother in the gut.

"I've been better," she mumbled, her gaze centered on his oldest brother.

"Dr. Buckley," he said approaching her, his hand outstretched, "I'm Josh, Aiden's oldest brother."

Of the three of them, four if Rick Bannerman was included, Josh was the tallest and broadest. He also possessed the calmest demeanor, useful in his head-of-the-agency role.

Lexi gaped up at him, her hand dwarfed when she slipped it into his. "Siblings only share 50 percent of the same DNA, on average. Physical characteristics comprise the bulk of that."

Josh smiled warmly down at her, then cocooned the hand he held between both of his and squeezed. "Which is why I'm the boss, since I got the lion's share of smarts."

Lexi blinked a few times at him, then for the first time since Aiden found her battered and bruised in the bathroom, her shoulders relaxed.

"Dude." Dylan shook his head. "You know that's not true. Aiden got a bigger share of brains than the two of us combined."

Her gaze slipped from his older brother to him. The question in her eyes was one he didn't feel like answering right now.

"Let me get you some ice for your cheek." While he went about the simple task, Josh, still holding Lexi's hand, guided her to the couch.

"Please, it's Lexi," she told his brother.

"The description you gave of your attacker is amazing," Josh said once she they were seated. "I'd hire you on the spot as an investigator solely based on your observation skills."

Her hand instantly went to her ear.

"Seriously, from what Aiden's told us, you were blitz attacked. The fact you got a few punches of your own in, and still had the wherewithal to be able to describe him is astonishing."

"It all happened so fast. But thank you. Every fall, the college gives a few free self-defense classes to the incoming freshman females. I usually take the class as a refresher."

"Can you remember anything more about him?"

Josh asked. "Did his voice sound familiar? Or did you get the sense you'd met him or seen him somewhere before? Maybe on campus?"

"I've been thinking about that. The answer is no. He wasn't familiar at all, yet I know if I ever come in contact with him again, I'll know him in an instant. His voice was very distinctive."

"How so?" Aiden asked as he sat next to her. "Here, put this against your cheek. It'll help with the swelling." Instead of letting her do it, he held the icepack against her face.

"Swelling is a predictable inflammatory response to injury and results in increased movement of white blood cells and fluid to the affected area," she said, placing her fingers over his and the ice pack. A crimson flush flew up from her neck to cover her entire face.

Dylan laughed and pointed to his younger brother. "*Finally*. Someone with more smarts than you. It's refreshing."

The thought to hit him again exploded within Aiden. Instead of resorting to violence, he shot his brother what their mother called a *death stare*.

Josh ignored them. Addressing Lexi again, he said, "I'm gonna echo Aiden and ask in what way was the guy's voice so distinctive?"

"When he asked me where the file was, he had a sibilant *s*."

"He lisped?" Dylan asked.

She nodded. "It was slight, but present."

"Again, your observational skills, especially when placed in a highly stressful situation, are exemplary."

"Also, it may not mean anything," she said, "but I bit his hand after his grip loosened a bit. I caught the thenar webspace between his fingers."

When they all gaped at her, she clarified, "The fleshy space between the thumb and index finger."

"Exceptional," Josh said.

"Any idea what he meant about a file?" Aiden asked.

"No. He assumed I knew. Do you think this is what the person who stole my computer and trashed my apartment was looking for? Some kind of file?"

"It makes the most sense," Josh said. "Whoever did this feels you're in possession of something, be it a paper file or a flash drive, but something containing information he wants. And he's not averse to hurting you in order to get it."

Aiden felt her body trembling against him. He pulled her free hand into his and forced her to look at him. "That's not gonna happen," he assured her. "No one is going to get close enough again to you to even try."

"You can't know that for sure."

"We kinda can," Dylan said.

"I've got men posted downstairs twenty-four seven now, and a few surveilling the surrounding buildings," Josh told her. "This place is secure on a normal basis—Aiden wouldn't live anywhere that wasn't—but now it's even better. You'll stay here with him until this situation is resolved. It isn't a good idea to go back to your apartment yet," he added, as she looked ready to protest. "Not unless you want one of my men to move in with you."

Horror widened her eyes to the size of small pancakes. Aiden pressed her hand again. When she looked at him, he said, "It makes sense for you to stay here. Between me, Brontë, and the added security, you'll be safe."

"But I have to go to work tomorrow. My position is already tenuous from all the unscheduled time away."

"You can go to the college"—Aiden nodded—"because I'll be there with you."

"Plus, you'll have protection from our firm. They won't stand out, trust me on that. You won't even know they're there."

She looked skeptical, but kept her concerns—if she had any—to herself. Before leaving, Dylan pulled her in for a hug and whispered something in her ear Aiden would have given anything to hear. His brother managed to pull a small grin from her. She shook Josh's hand again, thanked him, then excused herself to get dressed.

Aiden honed in on his brother and asked, "What did you say to her?"

That shit-eating grin Aiden knew so well danced over his older brother's face. "She'll tell you if she wants to," he said, then clapped him on the shoulder. "We'll be close, so don't worry about anything."

"I'm not." He turned to Josh. "I can feel in my gut this has something to do with her sister's death. Somebody doesn't like that we're poking around."

Josh slid his hands into his trouser pockets and nodded. "Your gut has never failed us yet. You got the trace on her missing laptop?"

"Yeah. Nothing, so far."

"I didn't want to mention this in front of her, but Rick's at her apartment right now, going through her stuff, or her sister's stuff, I should say."

"He's the best at sifting through the minutiae,"

Aiden said.

"Just like you're the best at finding the money. You look into that area yet?"

"I was gonna start on it tonight."

"I'll keep digging around, too," Dylan said. "Any chance we're wrong and this has nothing to do with her sister, but with her? Something college-related, maybe?"

"I can't see it. I did a deep dive on her when I got back from Atlanta and didn't find anything. She's exactly what she says she is."

Dylan grinned again. "A hot librarian with big green eyes and a brain that rivals yours."

This time, Aiden gave in to the urge rifling through him and socked his brother in the abdomen.

"*Ow*. You didn't pull that." Dylan rubbed a hand across the area, pain furrowing his forehead.

"You're lucky it wasn't harder."

"Children, enough." Josh's tone had taken on the pitch of a weary parent's. "Any idea how the attacker knew she was at the college today?"

"Maybe he was watching her apartment," Dylan offered. "Followed her back here, then the two of you?"

"Maybe," Aiden said. "But I didn't feel like we were being watched and followed."

"Well, now we've got eyes on you. I'm heading home." Josh pulled Aiden into a bear hug. "Call if you need anything."

"And you let me know if you or Rick find out anything." Both his brothers left together.

Lexi emerged from the bedroom a few minutes later, dressed in baggy sweat pants and a T-shirt with a cartoon characterization of Shakespeare and the words *I*

Put the LIT in Literature across the bodice. Brontë was at her side.

Aiden glanced up from his seat at the kitchen table where he'd been typing on one of his laptops. He'd expected her cheek to continue bruising but wasn't prepared for the speed with which it had. An angry mix of dark purple and blue branched from below her ear, across her jawline, and up over her cheekbone in a Rorschach blot, the apple of her cheek still swollen.

Anger quivered within him at the thought that any man had put his hands on her in such a violent fashion.

Or at all.

He dug down to his toes for calm.

"They left," he said when her gaze flicked around the room.

She nodded and slid into the chair opposite him at the table. "Your oldest brother is physically intimidating and equally as comforting. That's rare, in my experience."

"Our mom referred to him as the calm in the storm when we were kids. Even back then he could make your legs shake with one look, and yet you felt like he had your back no matter what happened."

With her knees pulled up under her chin, she looked all of ten years old sitting across from him. He wanted to fly across the table, lift her, and place her on his lap where he could kiss all the worry and fears shooting through her eyes away. She didn't deserve any of this. Not being displaced from her home, not being attacked where she worked, not having any answers to her sister's death. If she were weaker willed, he imagined she would have stopped looking for those answers about now and accepted what she'd been told.

But weak willed was something he could never call her, and dammit, he admired her all the more because of it. She'd handled the attack and the queries afterward with calm and grace.

Alexis Buckley awed him, there was no doubt about it.

"Let me get you some more ice." He crossed to the freezer and pulled out a fresh pack.

"You have a lot of those in there."

"Muscle aches, strains, and injuries are an occupational hazard."

When she hissed as she placed the cold pack against her cheek, Brontë whined and licked her bare foot.

"I'm okay, girl." She swiped the dog's head with her hand. "She really is attuned to the emotions of people around her, isn't she?"

"Not really. Until you, she's only been clued into my issues. You seem to have a connection with her."

"Really? Wow." She continued petting his dog. The fact that Brontë felt something for her told him several things, not the least of which was what he'd already discerned for himself: Lexi Buckley was special.

"You're already pretty bruised. Tomorrow it's gonna be worse."

"I can cover it up with makeup. Plus, the ice will help with the swelling."

"How are the ribs?"

"They don't hurt as much as my cheek. The shower helped ease some of the stiffness that started to form."

"You're pretty impressive, you know." Her confused squint had him adding, "You're not exactly tall by anyone's standards. And you said the guy was over six feet. That you were able to fight him off is, like I said, impressive for someone your size."

"Which is why I take the refresher every year with the freshman girls. I've never been attacked before, but the notion it could happen is never far from my mind, especially when I'm walking around campus in the evening."

If he had anything to say about it, she wouldn't be walking anywhere alone for the foreseeable future. Maybe not even forever.

"I'll make dinner," he said a few moments later.

"I'm not really hungry."

"You need to eat, though, whether you are or not," he said, firmly, as he inspected the interior of the refrigerator. "You'll heal quicker if you keep hydrated and fed."

She blew out a huge sigh and closed her eyes for a moment. "I can't argue with that because it's true."

Ten minutes later, he sat back down with the chicken soup Kandy had left for him reheated and the rest of the bread they'd shared cut on a serving board.

"Honestly, how does she make plain soup taste like heaven?" Lexi asked after taking a sample.

He grinned. "Kandy's mother once told my mom that everything Kandy made, she added an extra dash of love to. Sounds corny, but…"

Lexi sighed. "It doesn't sound corny at all."

She grew quiet. When he commented on it, she shrugged. "You'll get peeved with me if I tell you what I've been thinking."

"There's a word you don't hear every day."

Another shrug.

"Well, listen." He laid his spoon next to his empty bowl. "If I promise not to get *peeved,* will you tell me?" The laughter in his voice was unmistakable, and the way he stressed the word had her shaking her head, the corners of her lips lifting a bit. Almost instantly, they flattened again.

"I feel such a tremendous amount of guilt about all this," she confessed after thinking for a few moments.

"All this, meaning..." He flipped his hand in the air.

"Using your and your brother's professional resources to protect me. Involving you all in my mess. Potentially putting you in danger."

Aiden took a beat before replying. "I thought we'd settled this."

"See?" She crossed her arms over her chest as she slumped back in the chair. "Peeved."

"Okay, enough with the peeved crap. It's a stupid word to begin with, and it doesn't describe in any shape or form what I feel right now."

"And yet..." She quirked an eyebrow his way and pointed a finger at him.

Aiden shook his head and dropped his gaze back down to his empty bowl. Arguing was as natural to him as breathing. How couldn't it be with brothers who challenged him at every turn? It looked like he'd need every single debate chip in his wheelhouse to change Lexi's way of thinking.

He took a breath.

"First of all, please remember what my brothers and I do for a living. Protecting people is our business, and to do it well, we have exemplary resources at our disposal we utilize to full effect with every client.

Second…" He stressed the word when she started to open her mouth. She slammed it back shut, and he continued. "It falls under the protection guidelines that there may be some element of danger in every case we take on. Even cases involved strictly with cyber security, so if you're worried we're not prepared for it, don't be. And before you tell me you're not really a client, save it. I don't care if you can't afford to pay us and neither do my brothers. They're doing this as a favor to me. You're a friend, Lexi, and that means we go extra hard at everything we do. So stop worrying. And lose the guilt."

Watching her eyes grow soft and warm told him she was listening. When her shoulders relaxed from where they'd settled below her ears and she uncrossed her arms, he figured she was ready to put the guilt away. And when she sighed and sat forward in the chair again, her attention focused on him, heat shot up from his core.

"I didn't think men like you and your bothers existed," she said.

"Excessively handsome, intelligent, witty, and physically spectacular specimens?" He tried—and failed—to keep a straight face.

Her smile shone like a spotlight. "No ego issues with you, are there?"

"None." His grin widened.

With another shake of her head, she said, "What I meant is you're all genuinely kind. And nice. You barely know me, yet you consider me a friend and are willing to help when you have no clear-cut evidence I'm right about Zoe being murdered."

Aiden's dramatic wince pulled a laugh from her.

"Just what every red-blooded guy wants to hear about himself from a beautiful woman. He's 'nice.' " He shot air quotes around the word.

"You'd be surprised at what being considered nice means to a girl. Most guys appear so at first, especially when they want something. But soon their true personalities break through, and nice isn't what they are at all."

A hard fist drove into his stomach. He swallowed. "Experience talking?"

"Yes, but not mine. My mother's. She fell for guys left and right because they were"—she swiped her fingers as he had—" 'nice' to her. It didn't take long to realize it was because they wanted something. I grew up seeing there was always a price tag for someone being kind to us."

He'd been struggling to keep their relationship from turning personal, especially after that kiss, but with that declaration he knew now he had to work harder. The last thing he wanted Lexi to think was he was helping her because he wanted to sleep with her.

He did. No denying it, and he had since the moment she'd focused those green eyes his way on the plane. And even though she wasn't technically a client, he'd reasoned he still needed to keep his distance until her issues were resolved.

But knowing her past had included a firsthand sexual quid pro quo with regards to her mother made him shore up his resolve even more. He needed to keep his hands off her. No more comfort hugging in his kitchen. That was out. No more sitting so close in the back seats of cars that their knees bumped. And no more touching. Of any kind. Every time he pulled her into his arms, he'd wanted to drown himself in her, carry her to the nearest bed, and let them spend a few hours engaged in his favorite pastime.

He needed to concentrate on what he'd promised to do: help her find out what really happened to her sister and not get distracted by the sweet vanilla scent of her shampoo or the warmth and softness of her skin.

"There are no expectations here, Lexi," he said. "Of any sort," he added to make sure she'd be crystal clear on his meaning.

Her brows knit together under the fringe of her now-dried bangs, and she cocked her head to one side as she regarded him. "I never thought there were."

"Okay. Well." He rose with his bowl in his hand. "Just so you're clear about it."

"What's wrong?"

He didn't turn around from the sink when he said, "Nothing."

When she joined him a moment later, her own bowl in hand, he reminded himself not to breathe so he wouldn't be overwhelmed by her naturally alluring scent. It took every ounce of will he could muster to stay still when she laid a hand across his back, leaned around him, and placed her bowl and spoon next to his.

He tried valiantly to ignore the heat spreading from her fingers through his shirt, scorching his skin and making him…want.

In a move he knew was anything but smooth, he sidestepped her, forcing her to remove her hand.

"I should go check on the clone trace. Make sure it's still running."

"Why wouldn't it be?"

"Because, um…"

Jesus. It shouldn't be this hard to fight an attraction.

"Aiden, what's wrong?"

"I told you. Nothing."

She peered at him so intently he wondered if his nose had grown when he'd spoken.

"It's theorized," she said, "that up to 93 percent of all communication is nonverbal."

He blinked several times. "Okay. So?"

"So-o-o…" She drew the word out and fisted her hands on her slim hips. "You told me you're a good observer because it's part of your job. I am, too. Your words and body language don't match, and when that happens I concentrate on what the body is saying, not the actual words being spoken."

He remained silent, figuring anything he said would only add to the problem.

Lexi took a step closer. Aiden took one backward and banged into the counter, forcing him to stop short. He braced his hands behind, on the tile.

The move caused Lexi to stop short as well. Confusion drifted across her eyes and if he had to admit it, a little hurt as well.

She tugged her finger around her ear and dropped her gaze to her shoes. "Okay, then. I'll let you get to it. I have some…work I can do, too. I…I'll give you some privacy." She turned and nearly sprinted from the room.

Shit.

He'd give anything to run after her and assure her he wasn't brushing her off, because it was obvious from her demeanor she thought he didn't want to touch her.

If she only knew exactly how much he really did. A thick noise from Brontë had him glancing down to where she sat at his feet.

"I know," he muttered, bending to scratch behind her ears. "I'm a moron. You don't have to say it."

He swore she laughed at his back when he went back to his desk.

Chapter 15

Nothing like a man physically backing away from you to let you know how he feels.

Lexi fluffed the pillow behind her as she settled into the spacious bed, the package of correspondence from her office next to her. Her deep sigh wafted around the room.

He'd said he was, in no uncertain terms, attracted to her. And the kiss at the bookstore had been out of the stratosphere. Even when she'd tried to get him to see it was just the adrenaline fueled by the situation making him tell her how much he wanted her, he'd stood his ground.

And she was coming to believe him.

Why, then, had he backed away from her in the kitchen? Shied away from her touch?

She'd like to think he needed to keep his distance to do his job. Her ego, shaky at the best of times, would have been able to accept that reason rather than the one swimming in her head at the moment: he no longer desired her because of all the trouble she'd been causing him and now his brothers. Despite being told they were helping her because they wanted do, Lexi seriously doubted three highly professional private investigators would drop everything for a virtual stranger when, a., it wasn't a certainty Zoe had been killed, and b., they weren't being paid for their services.

She made a promise to herself somehow, someday, she would reimburse them. If it took her until retirement, she was going to do it.

For now, she'd better get ahead of her mail because no matter how apprehensive she felt about it, she had to go back to the college tomorrow. She wouldn't give the provost the satisfaction of censuring her because of another missed day, even if the absence was due to an attack.

At one point, Brontë nosed through the door, ambled over to the side of the bed, and placed her head down on the comforter, her soulful eyes intent on Lexi.

"Hey, girl." She rubbed the dog behind her ears and laughed at the look of abject ecstasy on the dog's face. "Aiden working?"

Brontë snorted, then licked Lexi's hand.

"I wish you could really talk because I'd like to pick your brain about him and I think you'd tell me the truth."

A smile pulled across the dog's mouth. Or at least it looked like a smile. When she sauntered out of the room again, Lexi decided to follow her, figuring she'd be going back to Aiden. The moment her feet hit the floor, she took a beat to ease the stiffness from her legs and upper body. With a quick shoulder shrug and a head bob or two, the muscles in her upper back relaxed.

The living room and kitchen were empty. A quick glance at his open bedroom door showed it unoccupied. The sound of typing brought her to a half-opened door at the far end of the hallway on the other side of the apartment from her room. She peeked in and found the man, seated at a desk, three desktop computers in front of him and Brontë seated at his side. Aiden's left hand gently petted the dog's head as he spoke into a headset.

"Run diagnostics," he said. The screen to his left started scrolling from the bottom, up, thousands of data lines running across it. Aiden typed something into the huge keyboard in front of him, commanded, "Filter encryptions," and random numbers and letters began scrolling on the two other screens.

"Download until end."

He tugged off the headset, turned, and when he spotted her his brows lifted.

"I didn't mean to intrude," she said.

"You're not." He gave the dog a final pat, then rose. Swiping his hand at his desk, he said, "I'm running a few security checks. I like to do it when I've been gone for a few days."

"This is…impressive." Her gaze ran around the room, taking in the filled-to-the-ceiling bookcases lining two walls. "How many laptops do you own?" she asked, spotting three on a table, two more on the floor beneath them. "Or cell phones?" There was a banker's box with at least ten or more she could see.

"Those are prepaids. The lines are secure. We give them to clients for exclusive use to get in touch with us and no one else. My number is preprogrammed into those. Dylan, Josh, and the rest of the guys have their own to hand out."

"Oh." She wondered why he hadn't given her one. *Duh. You're not a client, remember?*

"I haven't given you one because we've been together, nonstop."

"I didn't know you read minds."

His slow grin made her knees turn soft.

"Have you found out anything about my

computer?"

He turned and pointed to the middle desktop screen. "Not yet. That one is your clone. No activity so far."

"Oh. I was hoping…never mind."

"Hey." He moved to her, swiped a hand down her arm, and took her hand in his. Her skin tingled from his touch. "Don't worry. Something'll happen."

She threaded her fingers through his, her gaze magnetized to his face. Aiden glanced down at their joined hands. He swallowed, tugged his hands from hers, and when he flicked his tongue over his bottom lip she did what she'd been fantasying of doing all day: she laid her free hand over his chest and leaned into him.

Aiden swallowed again. "Lex—"

"Can I ask you something?"

He nodded.

"Can we—can we talk about that kiss? In the bookstore? You said we would."

He stared down at her for a beat, opened his mouth, then closed it again.

For some reason, the fact he was anxious served to calm her own nerves.

"We kind of got…sidetracked," he said. "After that."

This time she was the one to lick dry lips. Aiden hissed.

"You know what? I-I don't want to talk about it after all," she said, pulling deep for every ounce of courage she possessed.

He squinted, confusion filling his face.

"I'd rather…do it again."

Lexi held her breath for his response, equal parts

hopeful and wary of what it would be.

"You have no idea how much I want to," he said on a sigh. "No idea at all."

"Why do I hear a but in that sentence?"

One side of his mouth tipped up, revealing that delightful dimple. All too soon it smoothed again as his face grew serious. "I don't make it a habit to kiss, or do anything else, with clients. I never have and never will. It muddies the water, among other things."

She digested that for a moment. "While I applaud your ethical and moral compass, I'll point out several times you've told me I'm not a client. Whether or not you kiss me…or something else, shouldn't be an issue for you, professionally."

His squint deepened, and he cocked his head to one side as he regarded her. A muscle in his jaw tensed.

"It's more than just your professional ethics holding you back, isn't it?"

"Now who's a mind reader?"

Her left brow crept up her forehead.

"I don't want you to feel I'm using you in any way," he said, simply.

Her brain screamed, *Use me, use me whatever way you want.*

Aloud, she said, "Why would I think that?"

"Because of what you shared about how men treated your mother. I don't want you to think I'm helping you in order to get you in my bed, no matter how much I want you there."

Her mouth dropped open as she gaped at him, well and truly surprised. "It never crossed my mind. Honestly. I've never, not for one moment, thought that. Everything you've done and said to me the past three days has shown me you're not the kind of guy who would ever use a woman to his own end. It's simply not…you."

The muscle in his jaw relaxed, his brow cleared, and the tiny lines around his gorgeous eyes went smooth again. "It's not," he said. He circled both hands around her upper arms, then slid them to her back when she burrowed into him, her gaze never straying from his as she tipped her head back to keep him in focus.

She grinned up at him but then grew worried when he didn't return the gesture. "Okay. What else?"

One finger gently swiped across her injured cheek. "You've been through a rough ordeal today. I don't want to hurt you or add to any pain you already have from your injuries."

"Any pain or injury is mostly to my ego for not being quicker during the attack."

"Looked in the mirror lately? That bruise is only gonna get worse."

She winced, forgetting what she must look like. Battered and bruised wasn't a look meant to incite desire, to be sure. But…

Lexi was determined. "I'm not made of glass, Aiden. I won't break."

She got lost in the tiny uptick of his mouth. "Tempered steel can't compete with your backbone. That's the God's truth, and just one of the reasons I want you like I want my next breath."

The compliment pleased her more than if he'd told her she was the most beautiful vision he'd ever seen.

"So." She cleared her throat. "I fail to see a problem."

He stared at her, silent for a few beats. Just when

she thought he was going to say thanks, but no thanks to her offer, he bent and placed the sweetest kiss on her bruised cheek.

"Just so we're clear." He dropped another kiss to one corner of her mouth. Lexi arched against him and closed her eyes. "I want to do way more than kiss you like I did in the bookstore." He moved to the other corner, repeated the move. "Way more. That okay with you?"

She opened her eyes. "The fact you even ask underscores everything I just said."

"Is that a yes, Alexis?"

Instead of answering, she slid her hands up and around his thick neck and clasped them for purchase, then jumped up and wrapped her legs around his waist. A twinge pulled at her side, but she ignored it. Aiden immediately cupped her butt to support her. The undeniable fact he wanted her was evident where their bodies rested against one another.

Her head was higher than his now, so for the first time she looked down at him. "There are over seven thousand languages spoken in the world every day," she said. "In every one of them, my answer is yes."

She leaned down and kissed his grinning mouth.

Holy Christmas.

Kissing him was even better than she remembered. Her toes curled behind his back where her ankles crossed at his waist. As small as she was in stature, she still weighed over a hundred and ten pounds, but Aiden held her without any sign of strain or exertion. His big, meaty hands molded around her ass and kept her secured fully against him.

A low, hot moan bubbled up from deep in the back

of his throat when she shifted, contracted her thighs around his slim hips, and brought all their heat even closer.

Facts danced left and right in her brain about her body's reactions to his. How dopamine and adrenaline and a myriad of endorphins were flooding her system, enhancing her pleasure centers. The physiological changes their bodies were experiencing in preparation for copulation jumped to center stage to explain the long and throbbing mass pressed so intimately against her.

As if she needed an explanation.

As if she wanted one.

No, all she wanted right now was to feel. Not analyze, rationalize, or…think. For the first time in her adult life, Lexi told her brain to, quite simply, shut the hell up.

Relief bounded through her when it paid heed.

Never releasing his mouth from hers, Aiden started walking from the room. With each movement, his considerable erection bumped against her, torturing her with pleasure and promise. A quick eye flick and she knew they were heading toward his bedroom.

Oh, goody.

He kicked the door shut with his foot, spun them, then pressed her up flat against it, all the while his fabulous mouth driving her insane. The fantasy she'd had in the bookstore of him doing just this in the nearby bathroom zoomed back to the front of her mind.

Reality beat fantasy one million percent.

Lexi fisted the ends of his hair between her fingers, marveling at its thickness. While she was busy playing, Aiden had his own agenda. Bracing her against the door on his thighs and using one hand as support, the other snaked down below the dip in her spine, passed the waistband of her sweat pants, then along the back seam of her panties. In one exquisitely tortuous move, he shot lower and around to the front of her, then dragged the tips of his fingers along her wet length. She gasped against his mouth when he pressed two fingers upward against the thin swatch of fabric covering all her heat.

"You're so fucking wet," he said, momentarily abandoning her lips and taking possession of her throat. After sucking the soft undersurface behind her ear, he brought his mouth back to hers and slid his tongue along the seam of her lips, parting them. Twining and suckling her tongue with his, his fingers used the same rhythm against her panty, pushing upward, then withdrawing, only to drive up once again.

Lexi ripped her mouth from his to drag in a huge gulp of needed air and dropped her head back, ramming it against the wood of the door.

She'd think about being embarrassed later. Right now, every thought was concentrated on the movement of Aiden's fingers against the hottest, most sensitive part of her. Like a swollen dam about to overflow, she was right at the brink, waiting to spill. The pain in her face and back were a memory, as every nerve in her body converged on one specific spot.

Never in her entire thirty-three years had she so swiftly come to the breaking point. They were both still fully dressed and hadn't even made it the bed yet, and here she was, one breath away from an orgasm she knew would mimic a volcano erupting.

Aiden nipped his way across her jaw and captured her lobe between his teeth.

"I can feel you tightening around my fingers." His voice was one low, erotic rasp against her ear. "I'm gonna make you come…right now."

The moment he bit down on her neck she came undone. Aiden scraped the panty to the side and dove his bare fingers into her, his thumb taking possession of the swollen and aching mound of flesh he found between her folds. She couldn't have prevented the scream from exploding if she tried. His fingers buried deep, thrumming in and out of her, while his thumb swirled. He rode the waves with her, never stopping his sensual torture until her inner muscles began to go slack.

Logical thinking returned at the same time the realization she was pinned to the door shoved through. She was still balanced in one of Aiden's hands when he gently eased the other out of her, then cupped her ass with both of his again. She pushed against his chest with the flats of her hands, opened her eyes, and stared right into his. Smoldering ash had nothing against the heat bursting from his gaze.

"That was…" She shook her head.

"So fuckin' hot, I almost came, too."

Oh…my.

He pressed his lips against hers, sighed when she touched her tongue to his. She drank from him as he carried her, *finally*, to his king-sized bed and deposited her on the edge. Kneeling in front of her, he pulled her legs around his waist again, then cupped her face between his hands.

"I want to be buried inside you when I do, though," he whispered along her jaw.

She wasn't sure, but she thought she might have

said, "Yes, please," out loud. The movement of his mouth down her neck was too distracting to concentrate.

His low chuckle told her she had. Another item to add to the list of embarrassing things she'd obsess over later.

"But first"—he slid his fingers under her T-shirt and tugged it up—"we have too many clothes on."

Lexi braced when the back of his hand bumped against her lower ribs, but she wasn't quick enough to keep the wince from forming on her face.

Aiden stopped moving, his sexy grin dying as he stared straight at the bruised area. She didn't need a mirror to know how ugly it looked, since she'd already seen it for herself when she'd gotten out of the shower. Her attacker had punched her hard enough to leave knuckle impressions. Four thick, dark purple, and deep bluish-red lines appeared crosswise right above her waist. The hot shower had eased the pain considerably but did nothing to eradicate their horrid appearance.

"Sorry," she said. "It's still a little sensitive. You didn't hurt me."

Anger shifted in his eyes, quickly turning to cold, intense fury. "I could kill him for putting his hands on you."

Her entire body filled with a seductive sense of primal lust as she pictured him garbed in caveman pelts, big and brawny and protecting his mate to the death.

Not exactly the image her feminist brain typically conjured.

She cupped his cheek and sighed when he burrowed into it. "Let's wait until he's found before we plan any executions," she said, hoping to put the laughter back into his eyes.

A heartbeat later, it returned. He skimmed his fingers over the area, then bent and placed a gentle kiss across the bruise. His lips, warm and soft, were a soothing balm to the dull ache.

How was it possible the area that had been sore moments ago, now tingled with expectation?

"My mom was—and is—a big believer in kissing away pains and hurts," he said, pulling back up, the sexy smirk she loved back on his face again as he gazed into her eyes. "She got a lot of practice with me over the years."

The reason why flittered through her mind.

"Now." He gripped the hem of her shirt again. "Where were we? Oh, yeah. Right here."

He had her in just in her thin bra before she could take a full breath. His index finger traced the outline of the swell of her breasts above the satin cup. Lexi shuddered.

"Cold?"

She shook her head.

"Good. Lift up a bit."

Bracing her palms flat on the bed behind her, she boosted her butt up and Aiden tugged her sweats down to her thighs, then over her calves. He tossed them haphazardly over his shoulder, then lifted her legs and eased them onto his shoulders. His mouth and tongue then began torturing her again. First, covering one calf, then the other. When he lifted her leg and sweetly lapped at the back of her knee, Lexi lost the capacity to hold herself upright and fell flat down on the bed with a gasp.

"Like that, huh?"

The laughter in his voice was unmistakable. Lexi clutched the comforter between her fingers, fisting her hands around the material.

"Re-researchers have identified anywhere from thirty-one to for-forty different erogenous zones on the human body, any of which, when touched, can stimulate a sexual re-response. The back of the kn-knee is a particularly sensitive spot on women."

Just when she'd thought she'd gotten a cap on her damn trivia-Tourette's, it bloomed again, this time accompanied by a ridiculous stutter.

Get a grip, Alexis.

"Let's see how many we can find on you," he whispered against her thigh. The warmth of his breath across her skin had her back arching. "Ah, there's another," he said in response to her gasp. "And another," he added when he moved higher.

Even knowing levitation wasn't a real thing, Lexi swore her body rose from the bed with each touch of his mouth on her skin.

"And we already know this is one." He slid his hands under her ass and pressed a kiss on top of her panty, over her labia. Her eyes slammed shut. He nuzzled his nose along the length of her before pushing the fabric out of his way and swiping his tongue across her clitoris.

Oh, sweet baby Jesus.

"You doin' okay, there?"

"Fine," she managed to choke out.

He smiled against her mound, then around her naval, up along her sternum, all the while lapping at her skin as if drawing nourishment from it.

When he rose up from his knees in order to free

one of her nipples from her bra cup and suck it between his lips, Lexi almost lost what little of her mind she could still think with.

"I'm up to fourteen," he said right before he skimmed up the side of her neck. "And we haven't gotten to your back or arms yet."

She didn't think she'd survive him finding the rest, since she was practically immolating as it was. "I-I think we can safely s-say those are givens." She opened her eyes to find him leaning over and staring down at her, his hands pressed into the bed at her sides. In a move so bold she told herself she must be possessed, she let go of the comforter, pulled his face down to hers, and quite thoroughly ravaged his mouth. If she'd intended to divert him from the task of counting all her sensitive spots, she was successful.

With characteristic ease, Aiden shifted her up to the top of the bed so her head rested on one of his massive pillows and then reclaimed her mouth.

Deftly, he unclasped her bra at its front closure and tugged it off.

One of them still had too much clothing on, and when she freed her mouth from his and said as much, she marveled at how quickly he shed his outerwear, tossing both jeans and T-shirt over his shoulder to join hers. He knelt on the bed next to her.

Form-fitting black boxer briefs hugged his thick thighs and clung to his trim hips. The impressive mass bulging against the front of them was nicely outlined for Lexi's viewing pleasure. Like hummingbirds to sugar water, her eyes were drawn to it, her fingers following. Shyly, she skimmed the back of her hand over him, her eyes widening as he pulsed and twitched under her touch.

Oh, my.

"Lexi—" The knot at his neck shifted as he swallowed, while his eyes drifted closed as she grew bolder and traced the length of him with her fingertips.

Power was such an aphrodisiac, and it surged through her at the notion of what she could do to him with just a touch.

"Lie on your back," she commanded, using the voice she reserved for obnoxious students. The one that brokered no argument and told them exactly who was in charge.

Aiden's eyes drifted open as that grin tugged on his mouth again. "Yes, ma'am."

When he was in position, one hand behind his head, cradling it, legs slightly parted, and eyes wide open and watching her, Lexi went up on her knees between his thighs.

She certainly wasn't a stranger to the male body. The few, brief affairs she'd managed to have had taught her what books couldn't. She'd never felt compelled before, though, to do what she was about to do for—and to—Aiden.

As he had to her, Lexi licked her lips and pressed an open-mouthed kiss onto the fabric of his boxers over his penis.

It throbbed beneath her lips.

She did it again, this time gliding along its length and applying just a bit more pressure with her mouth.

It jumped under her touch.

Aiden fisted the comforter with his free hand as she had, his lids dropping to half closed. He hissed.

"The average male erection is just over five point

one six inches," she said as she flattened her hand and rubbed her palm up and down the length of him, still over his underwear. Lifting her gaze to his, she added, "You are so much more than average."

A strangled laugh burst from him, followed by a loud moan as Lexi slipped her hand under his waistband and finally—*finally*—touched him, skin to skin.

His arousal pulsed and grew when she cradled her fingers around the long, solid, hard length of it. A fine sheen of moisture coated the tip, and she rubbed at it with her thumb.

"*Jesus Christ.*"

Aiden's head fell flat against the pillow, both his hands gripping the fabric of the comforter now. Lexi's ears perked when a slight tearing sound came from beneath his fingers. His Adam's apple bobbed as he swallowed.

Power surged through her again. Her hand turned to a fist around his straining shaft as she slowly, so slowly, coated the length of him with his own moisture.

"Want me to count your erogenous zones, too?" she asked.

"I've only got one, and you're holding on to it right now," he said, as a laugh barked from deep down in the back of his throat.

Lexi giggled.

With his eyes open again, Aiden speared her with a look so hot her entire body flushed.

"Sit on top of me," he said, reaching a hand down to her. "I want to be inside you, but I'm so much bigger than you, I don't want to hurt you."

"I told you before, Aiden, I'm not made of glass. I won't break."

But even as the words left her lips, she moved into position, first shoving her panties down and off, and then doing to the same with his shorts. The happy trail of swirling, jet black hair from his naval down past his hips to his thighs was coarse under her fingers as she glided the boxers down.

Aiden reached across the pillow to the bedside table and grabbed a condom strip from the drawer.

"I'm venturing a guess, based on the number of those"—she pointed to the strip—"you're planning on doing this more than once."

The rocket-fast appearance of the grin she loved coupled with the lust in his eyes answered her question for him.

"You really are the smartest person in the room," he said as he tore open a packet.

Lexi felt a furnace of heat erupt in her core as she watched him don it. Her thighs pressed together, letting her know exactly how wet and ready she was for him.

Once he'd rolled it on, she slid her hands up the length of his calves, then thighs, memorizing the feel of his skin. Shifting, she threw one leg over his hip, while he lifted himself upright for her.

"Look at me," he commanded as she poised herself above him. When she did, he gripped her hip with one hand and pulled her down on top of him while he thrust into her.

Both of them went stock still, their gazes locked. The swirling and changing blues in Aiden's eyes mesmerized her. With her hands flat on his chest for support, Lexi swallowed, took a breath, then flashed him a grin. "Told you I wouldn't break."

Gripping her hips with both of his hands now, Aiden said, in a voice filled with stifled mirth, "Let's just make sure." He lifted her up, then slammed her back down again.

For the second time in her memory, a scream shot out from between her lips as she threw her head back and lifted her knees.

Aiden needed no further proof of her strength.

A moment later, they found a rhythm suiting them both. Moaned sighs and the slap of flesh against flesh filled the room. When Aiden reached between their bodies to circle her clit between his fingers, Lexi cried out again, unable to keep quiet.

"I love that I can make you scream," he growled, as he increased the pressure in his fingertips. When he pinched the swollen mound of flesh and said, "Scream for me again," she couldn't have stopped herself from doing so if she summoned up all the will she possessed. Every muscle in the lower half of her body tensed and pulsed and coiled, silently begging for release.

"That's it, baby. Come for me again…scream for me."

"Aiden—"

He lifted up and tugged her head down to his, speared her lips with his tongue, and swallowed her cry. A kaleidoscope of brilliant shards of color and light burst behind her closed eyes as her body went taut, her inner muscles contracting around his driving manhood. Higher and higher she rose until she felt his muscles tense under her hands. All the air in her lungs was stolen from her when he hauled in a colossal, jagged breath. With one final thrust she felt all the way through her body, he emptied into her as he dragged his mouth from hers and moaned, long and deep.

For all her book knowledge about the physiology of sex, Lexi realized she was a mere student when compared to Aiden's mastery of the act.

He fell back on the pillow, taking her with him, still buried and throbbing deep inside her. With her head resting on his heaving chest, his heart hammered like tribal drums against her cheek. A lazy, slightly shaky hand cupped her ass as she closed her eyes and let her body relax.

A long while passed before she had the strength to lift her head. His eyes were closed, those enviable lashes flirting with the tops of his cheeks. A tiny smile graced his lips.

"You were right," he said, slowly opening his eyes and zeroing right in on her. "You didn't break."

He leaned up before she could reply and kissed her sweetly, then nudged her on to her side while he slipped into the adjoining bathroom.

Moments later, he pulled her back into his arms. With her head pressed against his shoulder, she sighed.

"You okay?" he asked, dropping a kiss to her temple.

She wanted to tell him she was better than she'd ever been in her life, but the words, thankfully, stayed silent. It was just sex, she reasoned. This postcoital flood of emotions cascading through her the result of released hormones from a pleasurable physical act and nothing more.

Why, then, did it feel different from any other time she'd had sex?

"I can hear you thinking, you know." He laid his

hand over the one she had on his chest and played with her fingers, the smile in his voice loud and clear.

"My brain never shuts down. Well, almost never. It went silent the moment you kissed me. That's never happened before."

He shifted to stare down at her. "I'm gonna take that as a compliment."

She returned his smile. "It is. A huge one."

"Good to know."

She rubbed her hand across his chest and played with a nipple, delighted to see the sheet beneath his thighs tenting.

Her eyes drifted half closed as she scraped her fingernail down to just below where the sheet lay low across his hips. "You know, the normal refractory period for an eighteen-year-old male is about fifteen minutes. As men age, the time increases."

His sexy smile undid her every time it shined her way. "I'm not eighteen anymore, but I can beat that number easily."

She didn't doubt it one bit, evidenced by the growing bulge between his legs.

"What about you?" he asked.

"Women have a different refractory response. Since orgasm isn't essential for pregnancy to occur, women can perform multiple times without much rest in between."

His shoulders shook with laughter as he kissed the tip of her nose. "While that's good to know, I meant, are you sore at all? I want you again, right now, but I don't want you uncomfortable. We can wait a while if you need to."

She'd called him nice before. Adding that he was a

generous, considerate, and fabulous lover to the description mix was easy. It made her answer a no-brainer.

Rolling to her back, she tugged his arm. Possessed again—and starting to really like the sensation—she told him, "This time I want to be under you," as he settled between her opened legs. "I want to feel your weight on top of me, pressing me down. I want to run my fingers down your back." While she put action behind the words, she kissed him, quick and hard. "And squeeze your ass while you're pushing into me." Reaching down, she did, pulling a deep chuckle from him. His penis jutted against her while she ran her hands up and down his back. "Since we've established I won't break, I don't want you holding back this time."

He squinted down at her. "What makes you think I was?"

"You weren't?" she challenged, widening her legs to make a nesting place for him.

She pierced him with a knowing stare, and then fused her lips to his again. While she kissed him, he slid his hands down her torso and lifted her ass up while he dove into her in one complete move.

Yeah, she was really starting to like this whole being-possessed thing.

Chapter 15

Aiden couldn't remember the last time he actually whistled.

But he figured whistling was warranted after he stepped out of the shower he'd shared with Lexi because not only was he squeaky clean, he was also one satisfied man.

Very satisfied.

Lexi had fallen asleep cuddled in his arms and had stayed in his bed all night. Waking her up with soft kisses and probing fingers had been a delight, especially when he discovered a slumberous Lexi was even more sexy than a wide-awake one. The shared shower had been his idea. Well, in all truth, he hadn't given her the chance to say no, simply lifted her, naked and warm, from his bed and brought her under the hot spray with him.

The bruising over her waist was darker and more pronounced, and he took care when he helped wash her so as not to add to any pain she felt. Although she admitted it was minimal this morning. The swelling on her cheek had him biting back a curse. He swore to himself, when they found her attacker, he was going to mark the man the same way he'd done Lexi. Worse.

Lexi had diverted him from his dark thoughts with her dedication to cleanliness. She'd thoroughly scrubbed all his necessary places and dawdled over a few she felt needed special *attention.* While she spent a few minutes more lingering under the pulsating spray, he'd dried off and tossed on the T-shirt and jeans he'd worn the day before, to go make them breakfast.

Brontë wasn't in her usual spot on his bed when he got out of the shower.

Probably pissed she had to sleep in the hallway.

Aiden's whistling stopped when he reached his kitchen to find an unexpected visitor sitting at his breakfast table patting his dog's head, a dog who had a look on her face that signaled "busted."

Honestly, she got more human every day.

"What are you doing here?"

"What kind of greeting is that for the mother you haven't seen in over two months? You were raised with better manners, young man. I should know because I drilled them into you."

Despite his surprise, his grin came fast and full. Opening his arms, he pulled her up from her chair and into them, lifting her in a hug to rival a grizzly's embrace. "Mom. It's so good to see you."

She patted his back, and he breathed in the familiar and soothing scent of her White Shoulders perfume. Just one whiff of it as a child had brought comfort and solace on days he badly needed both.

"That's better. There's the baby boy I love beyond all measure."

He released her, saying, "I haven't been a baby in a long time, Mom."

"Nonsense. You'll always be my baby."

Knowing arguing was fruitless, he repeated his first question. "Not that I'm not glad to see you, but why the early morning visit?"

"I wanted to make sure for myself you were alive and well. Josh told me your out-of-town case was done and that you were staying put for the foreseeable future."

"I am, but"—he snuck a glance at his bedroom door—"I'm kinda working on a side job right now—"

"I know all about it. The cute librarian with the dead sister."

"How?"

"How do you think? Who in this family can't keep a secret to save their life? Who vomits up every piece of info on you and your brothers there is to know?"

Aiden flexed his hands a few times and sighed. "I'm gonna need to have a few words with Dylan when I see him."

"As long as it's words and not fists."

"I'm not making any promises on that front. If anyone needs a lesson in manners, it's him."

"*Oh.* Excuse me."

Mother and son turned to find Lexi, dressed for work but barefoot, her hair still damp, standing in the living room. She hadn't covered her bruised cheek with makeup yet, and this morning it mimicked the color of a ripe eggplant.

His mother's swift inhale followed her as she made her way across the room and took Lexi's hand. "Dr. Buckley, I'm Aiden's mother, Deborah. Dylan told me about your attack yesterday. How are you feeling this morning?"

Before she could reply, his mother tugged her along to the breakfast table, saying, "I made a pot of coffee and my daughter-in-law, Kandy, sent along some banana muffins she made fresh this morning. They're to die for. But everything she makes is. Let's sit down, and we can get acquainted."

Knowing what he did about her past with her own mother, where she was more the parent than the daughter, Aiden figured the stunned glaze in her eyes and the way her mouth kept falling open and then closing again signaled Lexi didn't know how to handle a mom like his who invented the term *smother-love*.

"Mom, give her a chance to breathe before the inquisition."

Deborah's eyes cut to him, a warning in them he recognized well. When tossed at him and his brothers during their childhood, it usually signaled they should run and hide. Even though he was a grown-ass man, the look still gave him a moment's pause. He swallowed.

"This is twice in the span of five minutes I've had to remind you I raised you better than that, young man."

His entire face heated, and he didn't miss the way Lexi lowered her chin, a grin she was trying to stifle tugging at her mouth.

"Mom—"

Deborah ignored him and, regaining her smile, turned back to Lexi. "Now, dear girl. Tell me all about yourself. And let me say how sorry I am for the loss of your sister."

Aiden released his second sigh in less than a minute.

"Sorry about that," he said a half hour later after kissing his mother goodbye.

"Don't be," Lexi told him. "You're blessed to have a mother like her in your life. It's obvious she loves you beyond all measure."

He cupped the back of his neck and sighed. "Yeah,

well, sometimes her brand of love can be a little exhausting when you're on the receiving end of it."

He was pleased, though, she hadn't been put off by his mother's natural nosiness. Alone again with her now, he crossed from the front door, stopped in front of her, and removed the coffee mug from her hands.

"You never answered her question," he said, tugging her into his arms. "How are you feeling this morning? Any pain?"

"My cheek is a little sore, and when I talk, I feel the skin pulling because it's swollen. Other than that, I'm just anxious about working today. Speaking of which"—she slipped out of his hold—"I need to get ready."

He'd give anything to keep her home with him and not have her go back to the college, especially if they could spend the day in bed.

"You're sure you're up to it?"

"I don't have much of a choice. The provost made it clear what would happen if I missed more time, and today's meeting especially, so…" She shrugged and swiped a hand through her now-dried hair.

Resigned, he nodded. "Go get ready then, and I'll throw some clothes on. I need to check a few things before we go. Plus, Brontë needs to go out. We can leave in about fifteen minutes. Okay?"

After telling him she needed twenty, she left him. While he walked his dog, he spotted two of Josh's guys standing on the street outside his building and nodded to them.

Aiden pondered on everything that had happened in the past seventy-two hours, not the least of which was the amazing night he'd shared with Lexi, while

Brontë went about doing what dogs do.

He wasn't much for morning-after discussions. They were often awkward, mostly unnecessary in his humble opinion, and he did his best to avoid them when he could. He'd never spent a full night in anyone's bed, and before Lexi, no one had in his, either.

And he knew what a jerk that made him. But he wasn't looking to be someone's happy-ever-after, and sleeping next to someone for an entire night gave off a more committing vibe than he was prepared for.

The women he dated were mostly of the same mindset. A few hours of pleasure, a way to relieve some inner stress, and they each went on their merry way.

Why, then, was he so nervous about how Lexi felt about what they'd shared? He wanted to know if she had any regrets, or worries, *hell*, even if he'd made it possible for her to forget about the craziness her life had become these past few days.

And why did having her cuddled next to him when he woke up feel so fucking right?

One thing he didn't need to ask was if he'd made her feel good, because the way she'd responded to him, to his touch, to every little dirty thing he said and told her he wanted to do to her, it was evident he had. She'd enjoyed herself. If the sound of her screaming as she came was any indication, she'd enjoyed herself *immensely*.

As he rode the elevator back to his apartment, he promised himself he was going to ensure she continued enjoying herself for the foreseeable future.

He'd think later about why that sounded so right, too.

****

"Your provost is a moron," Aiden said as he pulled a glass container from his refrigerator.

Lexi snorted as she rubbed Brontë's back. "Succinctly put. He is."

"I admire how you were able to keep your cool today at the meeting. I can think of at least three times I wanted to fly across the table and punch the guy in the face."

"You only got a snapshot today of what he's like. Try dealing with him when the yearly department budgets are due. You'd think he was supporting the college with money from his own account."

Aiden placed the container in the microwave, set it, and then grabbed a wine glass down from the cabinet. After filling it with the Merlot he pulled from his counter rack, he handed it to her.

"I figure you could use this after the day you've had."

"Reading minds again?"

He shrugged.

She couldn't get a bead on his mood. He didn't have a headache, of that she was sure. Brontë, relaxed and seated at his feet instead of nuzzling his thigh like she had in the past when she'd been worried about him, proved it. His quiet mood had started after he'd come back from walking his dog that morning. Had something happened? She wanted to ask, but didn't know if she should. They'd spent so much time together over the past few days, and had shared such an amazing night, but she still knew next to nothing about him and didn't want to seem intrusive.

She was dying to know, for instance, what his mother had meant when she'd whispered in Lexi's ear right before leaving, "You're not his usual type, and thank the Lord for that."

What type of woman did he typically go for? If she were to bet, Aiden typically favored tall, busty, and built blondes in their twenties who were athletic and could discuss sports, not a pixie librarian in her thirties who had trouble throwing a ball with any accuracy and suffered from trivia-Tourette's.

Another thing she longed to ask was had he ever been in a long-term relationship. He hadn't mentioned an ex-wife, so she wasn't sure if he'd been married. Should she ask? Did she have the right after spending one night in his bed, to question him about his past?

And right here was the major reason none of her affairs had made it to more than a few weeks, if that much. She simply didn't know the rules of play. Growing up with a mother who changed men as often as she changed her underwear hadn't taught Lexi the proper way to be a partner in a relationship. Despite her intelligence, she had no real practical experience in being in one. If they were, in fact, *in* a relationship. She could argue it either way, which just left her with more questions and no clear-cut answers.

One topic she knew she could discuss was the case they were currently embroiled in.

"You spent a lot of time on the computer today in my office while I was dealing with issues. Has anything come to light yet?"

"No one has used your computer," he said as he pulled the heated casserole dish from the microwave. While he divided the chicken parmesan Kandy had made onto two plates, he added, "I've been deep diving into the financials of all the major players, though.

Nothing's jumped out yet."

She kept her question of the legality of that silent. Just as she was about to ask something else, a pinging sound came from somewhere in the apartment.

"That's one of my desktops." He darted from the room, Lexi on his heels.

"I set this one up for any media and police alerts." He put on his glasses and glanced down at the screen. "*Holy shit.*"

Lexi followed his gaze, stunned at the message blinking back at her.

Peter Smith was dead.

Chapter 16

"It pays to have a brother with a wide array of law-enforcement connections," Aiden told her after disconnecting his cell call. "Josh knows a guy who's a detective on the Atlanta PD. He pulled in a favor, and this guy gave him the intel on Smith's case."

Lexi, snuggled next to Brontë on the couch, the untouched glass of wine in her hand, said, "From what I heard you talking about, it's apparent Smith's death is considered a suicide."

"Yeah. He left a long, typewritten note where he pretty much laid out a litany of poor financial decisions he'd made that had rendered him penniless and his firm on the brink of bankruptcy."

"Funny how he never gave off any kind of vibe he was in financial ruins and thinking about killing himself when he met with us."

"Sarcasm aside," Aiden said, "you're absolutely right."

"You don't think he did, do you?"

"No, and from the way you worded your statement, you don't either. It's a little too convenient."

"So you don't think by us confronting him about Zoe, he was prompted to take his life?"

"Why would he be? He didn't tell us anything incriminating the day we met him. We only know he was lying because Deveroux told us about referring Zoe to him. As far as proof goes, that's a he said/he said encounter."

"Is there a way to find out if his business truly was going belly up?"

"Of course there is. Like I told you, I've been doing a deep dive on all the major players' financials today."

"And you haven't seen anything to validate what he wrote in his supposed suicide note?"

"Nothing."

"So…what does that mean?"

"I'm pretty sure you think it means the same thing I do."

She nodded. "He was set up. Killed, like Zoe and Shel. But why?"

"Obviously because of something he knew. Something that—"

"The person who killed him doesn't want made known. Again, just like we surmise happened to Zoe and Shel."

They were both silent for a moment. The sound of Aiden's phone pinging again jolted them both.

"Hey, Dyl. What's up?" He flicked his gaze at Lexi. From the way his eyes darkened and a scowl spread across his features, whatever his older brother was calling about was serious.

"We need to go. Come on," he said the moment he disconnected. Rising, he gave a hand signal to Brontë, and she jumped down from the couch.

"Where? Why?"

"Your apartment." He grabbed his keys from the foyer table. "Rick and Dylan found something."

"Oh, my God. What?"

"The guy who broke into it."

She had a million questions while he drove, none of which he could answer to her complete satisfaction.

"All Dylan said was Rick had been searching your apartment, trying to find something we missed, when this guy showed up."

"What? He just rang the doorbell?"

"No. He had a key."

"What? How on earth—"

"You know what I know, Lexi. You can ask him anything you want when we get there. Rick and Dylan have him…secured."

She was afraid to ask what that meant. First the news about Peter Smith, and now this.

What in the name of all that's holy were you into, Zoe?

Dylan stood at the open door of her apartment, waiting for them when they got off the elevator. He gave Lexi a side hug and said, "Doc," before nodding at his brother. He patted Brontë's head. "This one's for the books. Talk about returning to the scene of the crime."

"It's most notably arsonists and killers who do so because they get a weird sense of psycho-sexual pleasure out of reliving the acts where they occurred." She felt the blush all the way to her hair follicles.

Dylan shot a hand over his heart and covered it with its twin. "I think I'm in love," he said, earning at warning glare from his younger brother.

Lexi ignored his statement, asking instead, "You're sure he's the one who broke in here?"

He bobbed his head, once. "Although broke in's a misnomer. He had a key the first time, too, which is why there were no actual signs of a break-in. Rick's got him in your little office. He's been looking forward to meeting you. Rick, not the moron who waltzed in with a key."

Aiden placed a hand at the small of her back and gently pressed in. Just having him, *literally*, at her back, helped chase away her escalating nerves.

Her office, small to begin with, was downright cramped with the two men she found in it. One sat on the floor, a burgeoning black eye gracing his face and zip ties holding his wrists bound behind him; the other loomed over him, mammoth arms crossed over a chest that rivaled Aiden's for girth and muscle. He may not be related to the Keane brothers by blood, but you'd never know it from a cursory glance. Tall like the rest of them and sporting the same midnight hair, the one place he differed from his adopted brothers was in the color of his eyes. While the Keane men all shared various hues of brilliant blue, Rick Bannerman had eyes reminiscent of tempered chocolate, so deeply brown they were almost black. When he trained them on her as she entered, she could feel intense power emanating her way.

The statistic for brown-eyed people died on her tongue as the identity of the man seated shot through her.

"I know you," she said, pointing at him. "I've seen you around the building, doing odd jobs."

Rick held up a wallet. "Damien Castillo," he read. "Your building manager's cousin."

"Is that how you got a key to my apartment?"

When he stayed silent, Rick kicked him in the leg and ordered, "Answer the lady."

"*Ow*. Knock it off, asshole."

Lexi's back went stick straight. "You're the one who attacked me at the college."

"You sure?" Aiden asked from behind her.

"That sibilant *s* is idiosyncratic, remember?"

Aiden pushed past her, squatted in front of the man, and commanded, "Say something else."

"You want my fuckin' life story, asshole?"

"You need a better vocabulary, son," Dylan said. "*Asshole's* getting old."

Aiden looked up at her. "Any doubts?"

"None. It's him."

The sound of his fist connecting with the man's nose reverberated around the room. Castillo screamed as blood spurted from the center of his face.

"You put your hands on her; I put mine on you." Forged iron was softer than Aiden's voice as he rose and stared down at the now-whimpering man. "Understand, *asshole*?"

Shock made her mute. She should have been disgusted or at the very least horrified by the sudden burst of violence from him. But the shock came more from her own reaction to Aiden's actions. That image of him in caveman pelts bounded to the front of her mind again. With it, her nipples pulled and tightened against her bra cups, and if she wasn't mistaken, her panties grew a little wet.

Oh…my.

"Don't hit me again, man," Castillo whimpered as blood continued down his face. "Please, man, please. I'll tell you whatever you want to know, just don't hit my face again."

Rick nodded at Aiden.

"Yes or no?" Aiden addressed Castillo. "You stole a key from the super to get into this apartment."

"Yes."

"Why?"

"I was hired to. Told to grab the laptop, then tear the place up to send a message. I got paid five grand, up front, and I'd get ten more when I delivered the goods."

"Why did you attack me at the college, then?" Lexi asked. "You already had my laptop."

"After I took it to the drop spot, I got another text telling me I needed to find out where some file was from you, direct."

"Who hired you?" Aiden asked.

"I don't know. I got texts with the instructions."

"Where did you deliver the laptop?" Dylan patted Brontë's head as he asked.

"Dumped it in a garbage can over on Forty-ninth and Lex. I never saw the pickup. Just dropped it and bolted."

Rick hauled him up, careful to avoid getting any of the still-dripping blood on him. Holding him in place with one meaty hand, he reached into Castillo's back pocket and retrieved his cell.

"*Hey.*"

"Shut up." Rick shoved him, roughly, then pushed him back down to the floor. "You don't even have it password protected. Talk about assholes." He shook his head. "First rule of business, son, if you don't want to get caught, erase any implicating texts." He turned the phone toward them so they could see the screen.

"Five bucks says it's gonna be a burner," Dylan said.

"You'd win," Rick said after pressing the call icon.

"Out of service."

"Can I get a towel or something?" Castillo asked. "I'm bleeding all over the place here."

All three men simultaneously said *no*.

"How did you know I'd be at the college yesterday?" Lexi asked.

"I think I can answer part of that," Rick said. He showed them Castillo's phone. "Your whole life is in one of these texts. Your address, home phone number, license plate. Moron's even got your work schedule."

"How—"

"Whoever hired him," Aiden said before she could ask her question. "What about yesterday?" he said to Castillo. "How did you know she'd be there? Were you following us?"

When he didn't respond, Aiden lifted his fist. That had the man cowering backward.

"Okay, okay. Just don't touch the face, man." He swallowed, his gaze darting between Aiden and Lexi. "I called the college. Some chick who answered the phone said you weren't due back yet, but you'd come in early to take care of some business. I booked it over to the place and just…waited."

Before Lexi could blink or respond, Aiden's fist connected with the man's nose.

"The first one," he told the now-whimpering man, "was because you put your hands on her. That one was for trashing her apartment."

Aiden flicked his head to his brothers as he laid a hand across Lexi's back. He gave a signal to Brontë who settled down in front of Castillo, her full attention on him.

"Move and she'll rip your throat out," Aiden told

the man.

The requested towel was forgotten as fear covered his now-crying face and his bound body began to shake. Brontë settled down, her paws in front of her, sphinxlike, and stared at him.

Back in her living room Aiden said to Rick, "Call this in since you were here when he showed up."

"You're notifying the police?" Lexi asked.

When he nodded, she said, "Oh, I thought...never mind."

Dylan, with a grin covering most of his lower face, laughed. "What? You thought we'd toss him in the East River or something? Get rid of the body and not let law enforcement know?"

Embarrassment colored her neck and face again. She *had* been thinking along those lines and realized how foolish she'd been. Of course they were going to turn him over to the police. They were the good guys, not some crazed vigilantes.

"I'm Rick Bannerman, by the way, Dr. Buckley. It's nice to finally meet you."

She took his proffered hand and said the first thing that popped into her head. "You're getting married next month."

Good Lord. His smile was...devastating.

"I am."

"How you ever convinced anyone as fine as Abby Laine to marry you is beyond me," Dylan said, shaking his head. "That woman is so outta your league it's ridiculous."

Rick tossed him a speaking glance, then turned his attention back to Lexi. "I've been going through everything in here Castillo tossed, all the books, the furniture, etc."

For the first time since entering the apartment, Lexi glanced around, surprised to see it had been put, mostly, to rights. The books were all neatly stacked in three piles, the tables and chairs had been righted, the counters cleaned, and the cabinets once again closed.

"Did you straighten this up?" she asked him.

"It was a group effort." He nodded toward Dylan. "Josh came by last night and helped a bit—"

Never one comfortable with public displays, Lexi never the less was so overcome with appreciation, she crossed to him and wrapped her arms around his waist. A muffled "Thank you" blew from her lips.

He patted her back and said, "No problem."

"Hey," Dylan said, holding open his arms. "I helped, too."

Sniffling, she grinned and hugged him, as well. When she pulled back, he tossed a cocky smirk at Aiden.

The killer glare the man tossed his older brother was…interesting. She might even venture to say possessive.

"As I was saying," Rick continued, "we found something."

"What?"

From his pants pocket, he pulled out a thin credit-card-sized piece of plastic with a concentric circle of five holes punched into one corner. "We think it's a hotel room key, but there are no identifying marks on it. I'm afraid if we scan it, we'll demagnetize it."

"Where on earth did you find this?" Lexi asked, turning it over in her hand.

"In one of the books. An old kid's book from the

looks of it."

"Kid's book? *The Case Files of Jenny Pertwiddy?*"

"Yeah." He nodded at Dylan, who lifted it from the top of one of the piles. "This thing was taped to a page in the center of the book. There are a bunch of words and letters highlighted, too."

"Oh, my God." Lexi grabbed the book from Dylan's hands and rifled through it. "*Zoe.* You remembered."

"Lexi?" Aiden wrapped a hand around her arm. "What's going on?"

While she flipped to the first page with a letter highlighted, she said, "I used to play a game with Zoe to help her with her spelling words. She had a hard time seeing them in her head, so I'd highlight letters from magazines I'd find in the trash or free books we'd manage to get from old library sales that formed the word she was learning." She ran into the kitchen and pulled a pen and a piece of paper from one of the kitchen drawers. "It helped her see the word in her head better so she could spell it without having to look at it. If this key thing was found in this book, I'm hoping any letters she highlighted can tell us what it is."

"How did you come up with that kind of a teaching tool when you were a kid yourself?" Aiden asked.

"It's how I taught myself to read," she said, simply. For a few minutes, she flipped through the book and wrote all the letters highlighted down. "Okay, here we go." She wrote each letter out on the pad. "It's an address. *Harbor Court Apartments, number five one six, Staten Island.* Why does she have a key card for a place there, when she was based in Atlanta?"

"Only one way to find out," Aiden said. To Rick he

asked, "You'll take care of that?" thrusting his chin toward her office.

"Consider it done."

"I'm coming, too," Dylan told them.

Aiden nodded. "Come on." He took Lexi's free hand and called out for his dog. "We're going on a road trip."

****

"It's almost nine," Lexi said when they'd parked in the empty lot across from the apartment building and crossed the street to the building address. "And this doesn't look like the safest neighborhood."

"Front door's open," Dylan said, pushing through it. Faded and broken black and white tiles in a checkerboard pattern covered the floor, the walls sporting a dull mustard hue. Lightning-bolt-shaped cracks shot from floor to ceiling.

"No name on the mailbox," Dylan said.

An international combination of food aromas and spices wafted from the interior and along the foyer, mixing in a none-too-appetizing scent.

When the elevator door opened, a hint of stale vomit and old urine floated over them.

The brothers looked at one another, nodded, and in unison said, "Stairs."

Aiden and Brontë took the lead, followed by Lexi and Dylan as anchor.

"Here it is," Aiden said. They all stopped outside the apartment door with the number 516 affixed to it.

Lexi pulled the keycard from her pocket and was just about to insert it when Aiden's hand stopped her.

"We don't know who or what's on the other side of this," he said, his voice low and deathly serious.

She nodded. He glanced at his brother, then laid an ear against the door.

"Anything?" Dylan asked.

"It sounds quiet, but…"

Dylan pulled something out his back pocket. "Let me go first."

Lexi blinked. "I didn't know you were carrying a gun."

"Never leave home without it," he told her. "Give me the card." When the lock clicked, he turned the handle and slowly pushed in.

"Do you have a gun?" she whispered to Aiden.

"I've got something better. Brontë." The dog huffed as if agreeing.

"Hello?" Dylan called into the apartment. Silence came back at him.

"There's a light on inside," Lexi said, peeking over his shoulder. "Someone must be living here."

Gingerly, Dylan pushed the door all the way open to reveal a small living room/kitchen combo. An old, rust-colored couch sat in the middle of the room, a frayed braided rug in front of it. The light meeting them came from a standup lamp in front of the room's only window.

The four of them, Dylan leading, then Aiden and Lexi with Brontë, entered the apartment. The entire space could be seen from the entranceway.

An unwashed frying pan sat on the two burner stove, the remnants of something that smelled an awful lot like a greasy hamburger emanating from it. One plate and glass, unwashed, filled the minuscule sink.

Aiden pointed to the other end of the room toward a closed door. Dylan nodded.

"Stay with me," Aiden told her.

"I was planning to," she said as Dylan crossed the room and tried the doorknob. He pushed it open, took a glance inside and said, "Bedroom. Empty." He moved to another door, opened it. "Bathroom."

"Someone has been living here." Aiden opened the refrigerator to find a quart of milk, a half loaf of bread, a jar of jelly, and some eggs.

"Not my sister, that's for sure. Why does Zoe have a key to this place? Where did she get it?"

A low rumble moaned from Brontë, all her attention focused on the front door. Lexi and Aiden turned to the sound.

A reed-thin woman in her thirties dressed in faded jeans and a T-shirt, and holding a paper grocery bag in her arms, stood there, a key card poised in one hand. Toffee-brown hair was pulled back into a ponytail at the base of a long, thin, and pale neck. Café au lait eyes filled with exhaustion and suspicion stared at them across the room. Her angular face was makeup-free and as lacking in color as her neck.

"Because I gave it to her," she said.

Chapter 17

The woman's gaze trained on Lexi. "You're Alexis."

Surprised, Lexi nodded.

"Zoe said if anything happened to her, you'd figure it out and you'd come find me."

"Who are you?" Aiden asked.

"And more importantly, how do you know my sister?"

"Blunt and straight to the point." The woman's lips pulled into the semblance of a small smile. "Zoe said that about you, too. Called you the smartest person in any room, and you don't suffer fools."

Lexi swallowed the ball of emotions choking the back of her throat. "That's not an answer."

With a jagged breath, the woman entered the apartment and kicked the door closed behind her.

"If you found this place, you already know who I am."

It hit her immediately. "Shel Bushman."

She nodded. "Although that's not the name I go by anymore."

"What is?" Aiden asked.

"Marilyn Welch. My mother's two favorite movie stars were Marilyn Monroe and Raquel Welch." She shrugged. "It seemed like it would be easy to remember. You can put the gun away," she said to

Dylan. "I'm unarmed and not in any position to do anything."

He considered her a moment before he returned the gun to his back waistband.

Shel crossed to the kitchen island, placed the grocery bag on the counter. "What happened to your face?"

"I came in contact with a fist," she said simply.

"Been there, done that, bought the T-shirt." Shel shook her head. "I can't offer you anything to drink other than tap water."

"We're fine," Lexi said. "You don't seem upset or concerned or even surprised that we're here."

"Like I said…" She unpacked a generic cereal box and rice from the bag. "Zoe said you'd come."

"You know the world believes you're dead, don't you?" Aiden asked.

She nodded as she put the boxed goods into the cabinets. "That was the plan." She shrugged. "I guess it worked."

"You faked your death?" Lexi asked.

With a sigh, she closed the cabinets and folded the bag. "No. It just kinda turned out that way."

"You need to explain that and what your being here, alive and well, has to do with my sister."

"I'll answer anything you want, just please, let me know first. Is she okay? I haven't heard from her in over a month, and I'm not supposed to reach out. It was one of the conditions."

"Conditions?" Dylan asked.

"Please," she said again. "Where is Zoe?"

Aiden flicked a glance at her. Lexi related the news of her sister's death gently and with a calm she still didn't fully possess. Shel lowered her head, shook it, and fisted her hands on her slim hips. When she lifted her gaze back to them, red-hot fury stoked her eyes. "How?"

"The official report says suicide," Lexi said.

"*Bullshit*. You don't believe that, do you? Your sister was one of the most together people on the planet. She'd never off herself. Never."

"We think that, too," Aiden said, "but why do you?"

Another sigh pulled from deep down insider her. "Listen, I gotta sit down. I been on my feet since six this morning. You mind?"

"Of course not," Lexi said. She moved to the couch with Shel.

"Talk," Aiden said. He rested a hip against the counter while Dylan stood behind them, at the window. Surreptitiously, he pulled back the curtain and peeked outside. Brontë settled next to Lexi and laid her head on her lap. A well of calm drifted through her as she stroked the dog's head.

"First, I gotta tell you how sorry I am about Zoe. She was one of the best people I ever knew."

Swallowing her sadness, Lexi thanked her.

"I met Zoe when I started going to NA meetings to get my life together. I even dragged a friend of mine with me after I'd been going for a few months. Paying it forward, according to Zoe."

"Kim. We've met her," Aiden said. "She's the one who told us you were dead."

Shel winced. "That's still hard to hear, said out loud. Kim doing okay? I left, sudden-like, and I'm not allowed to reach out and tell her I'm alive."

"That's the second time you've alluded to that," Dylan said from behind them. "Who's told you can't have any contact?"

She sighed, long and deep and slipped her shoes off. "Okay, long story short. I was involved with this guy. I thought, well, I thought he was gonna leave his wife. Stupid, but hope...you know? From the moment we met, I thought we clicked. Anyways, we had this big fight cuz he started spending more and more time away from me, giving me a line about work and obligations. I told him I was gonna tell his wife about us. I wasn't, but you say shit you shouldn't when you're mad, you know?"

Another deep breath. "A couple nights later, I was on my way home from a meeting. Kim got stuck working, covering a sick call, and couldn't go with me. Anyways, I got jumped. Two guys dragged me into an alley. Beat the crap outta me, left me for dead. You walk alone in the city late at night, and you always worry something like that's gonna happen."

"Was it a random attack?"

"I thought so at first. But then, after, when I was going over it in my head, I recognized one of them as working for this guy I...knew."

"The man you were seeing?" Lexis asked.

"No. The guy who introduced me to him."

"What was that man's name?" Aiden asked.

She looked across the expanse of the small room at him and folded her hands in her lap. "Peter Smith. He's a hotshot in Atlanta."

"We've met him," Lexi said, sliding a glance at Aiden.

Shel's eyes widened. "Yeah? So you know about

him? His business?"

"That he runs a successful public relations firm? Yes."

They were treated to a loud snort from Shel. "That's his day job," she said. "The face he shows to the world. Nighttime is a different story. He's nothing but a glorified pimp. Introduces his clients to girls for a 'fee.' " She put air quotes around the word. "That's how I met…my guy. Smith introduced us at a private party he had at a downtown Atlanta hotel. It was after one of his speaking engagements." She rolled her eyes with the word. "I'm sure he was paid well for it, too. Fucker."

Lexi looked over at Aiden who gave her a subtle head shake.

"How did you meet Smith?"

She stared at Lexi, her head tilted to one side and her bottom lip caught between her teeth. "You know what I used to do for a living?"

"Yes."

"Smith was a client, first. I picked him up in a bar after another of his conferences. He made me an offer. Specialty work, good pay, and I didn't have to work the bars or streets anymore looking for business. He'd set me up for a finder's fee I'd pay him every month. Sounded like a dream, and I said yes on the spot. I was sick of trolling bars. Worked out good too. Until it didn't."

"What do you mean?"

"When I met my guy, like I said, we clicked. I stopped seeing other clients after that. I really thought this was it. Like in the movie with the redhead pro who meets the billionaire. Smith was pissed. But…my guy was a good client, so he shut up and didn't say anything."

"Shel, I have to tell you, Smith is dead. Just today. The police are treating it as a suicide."

"Well, that would be a lie. Man was his own biggest fan. He'd never off himself, just like your sister wouldn't."

"Continue with your story," Aiden said. "You said you recognized one of the guys who attacked you as someone connected to Smith?"

She took a breath first. "I woke up in the hospital after the beatdown, and that's when I realized I knew the guy. I'd seen him talking to Smith at one of the private parties. A customer got a little too loud and handsy, and Smith had his goon escort him out. Once I made the connection, I knew I had to get outta town. Fast. Those guys had left me for dead, and I was afraid if they knew I was alive, they'd come back to finish the job." She turned her attention to Lexi. "So I called Zoe."

"Why?" Lexi asked.

"Because I knew she could help me."

"Help you how?"

With her head still cocked at an angle, Shel squinted at her. "You don't know about the women's shelter, do you? That she volunteered at a place that helps battered women and girls like me, in the life?"

"I'm finding I didn't know my sister at all," Lexi said, emotion choking her.

Kindness wafted through the tired eyes. "Zoe told me she wanted to make it easier on women who'd had a tough break in life, kinda like your mom had."

Lexi's eyes widened.

"She told us, in group, about your childhood. How your mom was. How you raised her after she died. The shelter took in women and children who'd been abused, abandoned. Stuff like that. You really didn't know?"

She shook her head and bit back tears. *Oh, Zoe. I missed so much in your life.*

"Well, like I said, your sister was one of the best people I ever met. I signed myself outta the hospital, and broken ribs and all, Zoe brought me right to the center. Told the counselors about what happened and that I needed to lie low. They took my bag with all my ID and stuff and got rid of it. I stayed there about two weeks, healing. I wasn't allowed to tell anyone, not even Kim."

"She was the one who reported you to the police as a missing person," Lexi said. "She was worried when you didn't come home."

"Yeah, Zoe told me. We both wanted to let her know I was okay, but the head of the center said we couldn't. Plausible deniability is what she called it, just in case Smith or one of his creeps came looking for me and asking questions."

"You know you were reported dead soon after, right?" Aiden asked. "A body with all your identification was found in an abandoned warehouse used as a junkie hangout."

"Yeah. Again, Zoe told me. She thinks some street addict found my bag in the trash, took it. I had about six hundred in cash in it. She must have gone on a bender with the money and died. Apparently, the body they thought was me was unrecognizable. Lots of decay and animal damage." She shuddered. "I always thought they needed to ID you by teeth records or something."

"They do. I read the coroner's report and didn't see any indication of dental records as confirmation," Aiden said.

Shel shrugged. "Probably didn't want to waste the time or money on a whore junkie." She sniffed, once, then said, "When Kim told her about it, Zoe figured this was like a gift from God or something. She couldn't tell Kim what she knew, and we both felt bad about that. But since I was officially dead, I could get outta town and go someplace, start over. New name. New state."

"And Zoe helped you do that?"

For the first time since coming into the apartment, Shel smiled. It changed her entire face, just as when Kim had smiled at them. Her eyes lit and a tiny dimple popped up on her chin. "Her and the head of the center. They arranged for me to come here, got me this apartment, even the job at the factory. Once she saw me settled, Zoe went back to Atlanta to try and dig up some dirt on Smith and his little operation. I told her to leave it alone, but she was like a dog with a steak bone. Persistent. You know, since you raised her."

It pained her that her sister had been in the same city and hadn't let her know.

"What about the man you were seeing?" Lexi asked. "Did Zoe know who he was?"

"Yeah. I told her. Kim didn't know, though, and Zoe told me she asked her to look into him."

When she didn't elaborate, Aiden pushed. "Tell us."

When she did, Lexi shared they'd already met and spoken to him.

"You did?" Shock colored her face. "Did he…what—what did he say…about me? Anything?"

Lexi stretched a hand across the small sofa and slipped it into Shel's. Telling her the truth was going to hurt because it was evident from her reaction she still felt something for the man.

As kindly as she could, she related how Deveroux had denied knowing either Zoe or Shel.

"Well, I can't say I'm surprised." She rose and crossed to the kitchen. Grabbing a paper towel from its holder, she swiped at her wet eyes. "And I can't believe I was ever dumb enough to think he'd actually want me for me and not just sex."

"The guy's a world class creep," Aiden said. "You're better off without him."

"Do you think he was responsible for your attack and not Smith?" Lexi asked.

She swiped at her eyes again, tossed the paper towel into the garbage. "No. But I can't decide if that's because I just don't want it to be him or he really isn't capable of it."

"He was never rough with you? Showed you a different side of himself when you were alone?"

"Not like you mean. The opposite, in fact. He liked to be taken in hand, if you get my drift."

It took Lexi a moment. The heat rising from her neck to her cheeks was bothersome. To counteract her embarrassment, she said, "He was into BDSM."

Nodding, she said, "Yeah. Not the whips and ball-gag shit some of my clients used to like, but he liked to be dominated. Told what to do, made to be obedient. Called me 'ma'am.' Got punished when he didn't. Mostly vanilla with a little spice, if you get me."

Lexi nodded, thinking it prudent to keep all the statistics and information she could call to mind about the practice to herself.

"So I can't see him hiring someone to beat the crap outta me. Smith, though? He was a real nasty thing at times. Him I could see ordering a beatdown."

"Why?" Lexi asked. "Why would he?"

"I figure cuz he was pissed I stopped the cash flow when I started seeing Richard exclusively."

"Maybe, but I don't think so," Dylan said. "Deveroux asked him to." He addressed Shel. "You were a problem that needed to be dealt with. Smith was his publicist. The deed fell to him."

"We've seen it happen." Aiden nodded. "Some of our well-known clients have publicists who think it's their job to take care of everything they can in order to keep their clients happy, news of their escapades out of the press, and their reps untarnished. They usually pay people off though, not attack them. But it has happened."

"It could have happened like you say." Shel nodded. "Maybe Richard wanted me out of the picture after I got all up in his face about his wife. He was never gonna leave that bitch."

"Did she know about the two of you?"

"I wouldn't be surprised." Once again, her voice gave away the emotions running through her. "She had him on a tight lease with a choker collar." Her lips pulled into a snarl. "But I'm sure she doesn't know I'm here."

"What makes you so certain?" Dylan asked.

She cocked her head, her eyes pulling tight at the corners. "I'm alive, aren't I? They tried to kill me once. I'd think if they knew they didn't, they'd find me and finish the job."

"So no one else knows you're here?" Lexi asked.

"Only your sister and the head of the women's shelter. Well, and now you three."

"So you're safe."

"Let's hope. Look…" She rose from the couch. "If there's nothing else, I gotta get some sleep. I'm back doing another double tomorrow, and I start at six."

"Just one more thing," Aiden said. "Then we'll leave you alone." When she nodded, he asked, "Did Zoe ever mention a file or a flash drive, or give you something and told you to hang on to it?"

"You mean the key? I almost forgot about it. I'll get it."

"Key?" Lexi asked.

"It's to a safe deposit box." She crossed the small room and opened an empty drawer under the kitchen counter, pulled it completely out, then turned it upside down onto the counter. Taped to the underside was a silver key.

"Zoe said if you ever came here, to give you this. Said to make sure it was well hidden until then. She didn't tell me what's in it, and I didn't ask. She'd already done so much for me I would have done anything to repay her. This was easy to do." She handed the key to Lexi. "It belongs to the Bank of Manhattan on—"

"Forty-sixth. Yes," Lexi said. "I know it."

"Okay, well, then."

Before leaving, Lexi caught Aiden giving her one of his business cards and saying something privately to her.

Downstairs, the brothers nodded to one another.

"What did you say to her when we were leaving?"

she asked once they were in his car, Dylan in his jeep.

"If she needed anything, if she noticed anything or anyone suspicious lurking around after tonight, or even at the place where she works, to call us. I'm pretty certain we weren't followed here and the fact she's alive is still a secret, but better safe than sorry."

He flicked a quick glance at her while he entered the ramp for the Verrazano Bridge. Lexi had a dozen or more questions rifling through her head but was prevented from asking any when the car's communication icon flashed. Aiden hit the call icon.

"Dyl?"

"You got a bogey on your six."

Aiden glanced at the rearview mirror, then the side. "Got him. Tag the plates, and send them to Josh."

"On it. I'm gonna circle back to Shel. They picked you up a half mile back, and I want to make sure she's okay."

"Keep safe and in touch."

"Back atcha, baby bro."

"We're being followed?" Lexi asked, swerving around to look out the back window. Blazing headlights directly behind them had her squinting.

"Do me a favor. There's a phone in the glove compartment."

She pulled it out just as they entered onto the bridge.

"There's a preprogrammed number. Hit it. Turn it on speaker for me."

Rick's deep voice shot through a second later. " 'S'up, son?"

"You get Castillo squared away?"

"Delivered him myself to the local precinct. Gave

the watch commander, who happens to be an old academy friend of Josh's, the 411. Last I saw he was being processed. Why?"

"We've got a tail, and I'm wondering if Castillo used his one call to set us up."

"Dylan with you?"

Aiden told him his brother's location.

"Okay," Rick said. "First thing first, you can't go back to your pla—"

The car sprang forward from the impact of the vehicle behind it. The seat belt pulled and locked against Lexi's chest from the hit, and she shot her hands out to the dash to brace herself. Aiden wrestled the steering wheel to keep them from crashing into the car in front of them. A loud yowl blew from Brontë when she slammed into the back of Lexi's seat.

"Aiden?" Rick's voice bellowed into the cab.

"They rammed us. Stay on the line." He checked the rearview again and said, "Brontë's not buckled in. Can you reach around and grab her collar to keep her steady?"

The dog made it easy by moving to the center divider between the seats.

"Hold on."

With that, Aiden floored the gas and guided the car into the left lane, a whisper from hitting the car in front of them. The vehicle following them did the same.

"They're speeding up again," Lexi cried, looking in her side mirror. "Aiden—"

"Just keep hold of Brontë and brace yourself."

Before she could, he increased the car's speed and slid back into the center lane. The car following them clipped their back fender before Aiden moved to the far right lane.

His forearms shook to keep the car from swerving and crashing into the guardrail.

The other car sped up.

"They're almost on us," Lexi said. She was sweating, her arm shaking with the effort to keep the dog contained. Brontë's whimper tore at her heart. "It's okay, girl. Aiden's got this," she said, forcing her voice to stay calm and low.

The vehicle chasing them gunned the engine. The acrid odor of burning rubber filled the cab. Lexi gagged. Just as they were about to be hit again, Aiden veered the steering wheel to the left and flew across two lanes back into the far left one. Traffic on the bridge was its normal heavy pattern despite it being almost eleven at night. But typical of New York drivers, the speed limit was all but ignored, so he was able to weave in and around the other speeding cars easily. The whir of police sirens in the distance echoed around them.

The car following them was several lengths behind. Suddenly, it shot into the center lane.

"They're gaining," Lexi told him, "and he's trying to get back behind us."

"Not gonna happen." With another punch to the pedal, Aiden steered the car back to the center, then the right lane, cutting off the cars in his way. Lexi slammed her shoulder into the door, her fingers loosening their grip on Brontë's collar. She reached for it again. Annoyed horns blared around them.

"You okay?"

"I'll live," she replied. "Just get us away from this."

The following car was boxed in now on all four

sides as Aiden kept his speed up.

They were almost at the first exit off the bridge.

"Rick?"

"Here."

"I've gotta get off. There are too many cars, and now the police are gaining. Where to?"

"Get on the Belt. I'll get you an address."

"Got it."

Glancing back and forth between the stretch of road in front of them and the wake behind them, Aiden lowered his speed as they pulled off the exit ramp and glided onto the Belt Parkway. Traffic was, thankfully, moving at a swift clip. The sound of the sirens dissipated behind them. Lexi allowed herself a full breath as she eased up on Brontë's collar.

"You okay, girl? You slammed into the seat pretty hard." The dog dragged her tongue across Lexi's hand.

"She's tough, aren't you, girl?" Aiden reached over and scratched her behind her ears, all the while keeping his attention focused on driving. "You okay?" he asked Lexi.

"You don't have to keep asking me that," she said. "I've told you several times I'm not made of glass."

"The fact you're not relaying any statistics on car crashes or chases eases my mind a bit, tells me you're not nervous."

That he knew her so well after just a few days was…daunting. He easily realized her trivia-Tourette's was directly related to her nerves and wasn't bothered by it as so many guys in her past had been.

The phone she—miraculously—still gripped in one hand, vibrated.

"That's Rick. Put him on speaker again."

"You guys okay?"

"Doing fine. Where we headed?"

Rick told him the address. Aiden plugged it into the car's GPS with one hand while continuing to steer with the other.

"Papps is gonna meet you there. Talk later."

When he ended the call, Aiden told her, "ETA is fifteen minutes."

"Who's Papps?"

"Josh's brother-in-law. Kyros Pappandreous. He married Kandy's sister, Gemma, and he's a member of the team now. Used to be an FBI agent." He flicked her a side glance, then concentrated back on the road in front of him. "You'll like him."

Of that, she didn't have a doubt.

Chapter 18

Aiden was right. She did like the former FBI agent. Tall, like the rest of them, he was serious, like Josh, but his smile lit his eyes and when he slipped his hand into hers, she felt an instant sense of comfort.

"How are you holding up through all this?" he asked her, all his attention focused on her. "I can't imagine every day you're involved in a car chase."

"It's been an…unusual day, to be sure."

"That's one word for it," Aiden mumbled from behind her.

Kyros had greeted them at the door of a duplex set back from the road on a side street in Fort Hamilton. Lexi took a cursory glance around when they entered through the foyer. Split level, upstairs living area, downstairs bedrooms, sparsely staged with what looked like secondhand furniture.

"Is this a safe house?" she asked.

Ky nodded. "It doesn't get used much. Last time was with that rap star—what's her name, Aiden? The one who was being stalked?"

"Golden V."

"That's the one." Ky grinned at Lexi, and just like she had when Rick tossed a smile her way, she could see women throwing themselves at these guys left and right. "Complained so much about every little thing. Even Josh, who never raises his voice, lost it with her."

While Lexi didn't recognize the performer's name, she imagined she had to be a handful to ruffle the eldest Keane's unflappable feathers.

"We're switching out your car," Ky told Aiden, handing him the keys. "I figured you wanted to go back to your apartment since all your equipment is there, rather than spend the night here."

"Yeah, thanks. I'm running a bunch of programs right now, and I'd hate to have to start over on a new system. Plus"—he nodded at Lexi—"all her stuff is at my place."

Until that moment, Lexi hadn't given a thought to the library, her job responsibilities, or anything else.

"Dylan check in yet?" Aiden asked.

"Yes. No movement on your girl, but he was going to stay put and make sure. We can't figure where you picked up the tail, and he doesn't want to take any chances she's targeted next."

"If they were watching Lexi's apartment, they would have seen my car." He shrugged. "Maybe they followed us to Staten Island. We got any intel on the plates, or the occupants?"

"Josh is working on getting bridge traffic footage."

"That's gonna take forever since he's not law enforcement."

Ky nodded. "I imagine you could do a faster job of it."

He slid Lexi a quick look before saying, "You know I can."

"No doubt. Josh's way won't send up any red flags, though."

"Neither will mine."

"Probably not, but better safe than sorry, legal,

than…not so much. After he spoke to you, Rick told me he figures your moron burglar didn't have time to tip anyone off. The guy also didn't know where you were heading even if he did manage to get word to whoever hired him."

"He could have heard us discussing it when we were in my apartment kitchen," Lexi said. "I've lived there three years. Believe me when I say voices carry. The walls are like cheesecloth. Every sound drips through."

"Maybe," Ky said. "But for now, we're upping security at Aiden's apartment and tomorrow at the college." He addressed Lexi for the last bit. "You won't know there's anyone following you, Dr. Buckley—"

"Lexi, please. After everything you all are doing, I think we can dispense with the formalities."

He smiled at her again. "Rest assured, you'll be safe at the college and at Aiden's apartment tonight."

Brontë leaned against Aiden's thigh and whimpered. He stretched down a hand and rubbed her behind her ears. "I'm okay, girl."

He didn't look tired and none of the outward symptoms he'd exhibited of a headache were visible, but Lexi knew the dog could detect what humans couldn't.

"We should go," she said.

Aiden nodded. Ten minutes later, after giving his partner a back-patting man hug, they were on their way.

"You've had some day," Aiden said after a time.

"I wasn't alone. You've been right there, next to me through it all. Both of you have," she added, rubbing Brontë's head, which rested between them on the seat dividing console.

Aiden

"Yeah, but you're not used to all this. I can't imagine what's running through your head right now. And I don't mean facts and statistics," he added, drawing a tiny chuckle from her. Since her mind had been churning with all the information they'd discovered in the past four hours, Lexi's trivia quirk had gone dormant for the time being.

"Shel's information about Smith is telling," she said.

"Nothing in his online life has popped up that indicates he's the head of a call-girl ring. But that's not surprising. I'm sure the info, if there is any, is buried deep."

"What do mean if there is any? Don't you believe her?"

"One hundred percent. But he might have gone old school and not established a digital presence for his sideline. Or it could be buried in layer after layer of security and dummy corporations. Don't worry, though. If he's got a digital footprint, either Dylan or I will find it. It's what we do."

He shot her a quick glance as he maneuvered them through traffic. "You learned a few things about your sister tonight. Things you weren't aware of."

"And I'm feeling horribly guilty I wasn't."

Aiden sighed. "People keep secrets, Lexi. Even from those they love. It's human nature. We don't want the people closest to us to worry. Otherwise"—he pulled off the highway and onto city streets—"they'll want to protect us."

She turned to him. Even in the darkened cab she could detect sadness crossing his face. "Why does that sound like something you know firsthand?"

He didn't answer right away, concentrated on driving instead. Just when she thought he'd never answer her, he said, "That girl I had a crush on?"

"The one who loved the Brontës?"

At that the dog lifted her head. Lexi scratched behind her ears and was rewarded with a lick to her cheek.

"Her name was Phoebe, and it was more than a crush. I'd known her since second grade, but we never dated until college."

"That's sweet."

With a nod, he continued. "We planned on getting married. She was an English lit major and wanted to be a high school English teacher, while I was premed."

"You wound up not going that route, though. Did she become a teacher?"

He turned to her, and the sadness suffusing his eyes made her heart turn over. "She…died. During senior year of college."

"Oh, I'm so sorry, Aiden." She stretched her hand over and placed it on his thigh. "How?"

"She had mono in high school, and it left her with a compromised immune system. She developed Hodgkin's lymphoma and didn't find out what it was until junior year. She'd get a cold and hang on to it for months, develop fevers that would take her out for days. Her family doc thought they were just layovers from her mono."

"What finally prompted the Hodgkin's diagnosis?"

"I'd been researching ways to strengthen her immune system and found out it was what's called a sequela of mono. I told her about it, and she said she already knew. She'd gotten the diagnosis a month earlier."

"She knew and didn't tell you?"

"She thought, for some ridiculous reason, I wouldn't want to be with her if I knew she was seriously ill. Plus, she said, she didn't want her diagnosis dragging up bad memories for me."

"She was protecting you."

"Yeah." He blew out a breath and stopped at a street signal. "She developed a raging infection during Christmas break in senior year and was in the hospital on reverse isolation for two months. She...died in February."

"I know it means nothing, but again, I'm so sorry." Something clicked in the back of her mind. "This is the reason you didn't go to med school, isn't it?"

He nodded but didn't look at her. "It felt...useless, to even try. All those lofty goals I had and I knew it wouldn't mean a thing. People would still die. Loved ones would be left, devastated and brokenhearted. I knew I wasn't up to it."

She didn't know what to say that wouldn't sound like a clinical response.

"Zoe kept secrets from you for a reason," Aiden said, pulling the car into the underground garage in his building. "You shouldn't feel guilty about her decision to do so. Whatever her motivation, it seemed right to her at the time."

She wanted to ask him if he felt guilty for not knowing about the extent of Phoebe's illness but felt it prudent to keep the query to herself.

In the elevator, Brontë nuzzled against his knee, her soulful eyes focused on him. "I really am okay, girl," he told her, patting her head.

"She's concerned."

"She's probably more hungry than concerned right now, since we never got to eat dinner," he said, with an slight upward tick of his lips. "I know I am. You?"

She shook her head. "I'm just tired. Bone tired."

"Are you having any pain?"

"No. This is one case where I really do look worse than I feel. A hot shower and I'll be fine."

He let them into the apartment, Brontë going straight to the kitchen and to her empty bowl.

"See?" Aiden said.

"I'm gonna hop in the shower," she told him, heading toward the guest bedroom.

"When you come out, you're eating. Don't." He lifted his hand to her when she started to protest. "We've had this conversation before. Even if you don't feel like eating, you need to nourish yourself. If I learned anything when I was sick, it was that."

Her objection died on her lips.

Over the once-again-reheated chicken parm, Aiden asked, "What time do you need to be at work in the morning?"

"Ideally by eight to answer emails and put out any administrative fires. Why?"

"While you were in the shower, I checked on the bank's hours. Lobby opens at eight thirty. I figured you'd want to see what's in the deposit box first thing. Can you be late to work?"

In the shower, she'd thought about how to proceed. Knowing Aiden had as well was…comforting. "I guess I have to be. My name must be on the approved list at the bank since Zoe gave the key to Shel and told her to keep it for me." She forked in some of the chicken, chewed, then swallowed without ever tasting it. "Any ideas what could be in it?"

"It would be great to say a file or something to explain everything that's happened, but I just don't know."

"Well, I guess we'll find out in the morning." Rising, she took her dish to the sink, Brontë following her.

"I'll clean up," Aiden said, joining her.

"I should, since you cooked. It's only fair."

"I reheated," he said. "No work involved. You go get into bed. You look ready to drop."

Because she knew she did, she nodded. Minutes later when she was snuggled down under the comforter in the guest room, the door she'd left ajar slid open.

"Aiden?"

He came in and sat on the edge of the bed. Brontë wasn't with him.

"What's wrong?" She sat up.

He cocked his head at her, his brow folded into a thick line between his eyes. "I was hoping I'd find you cuddled down in my bed, not in here."

Flames ran up her cheeks. "I—I didn't want to...presume."

One corner of his mouth twitched as he stared at her. The other side joined in fairly quick and before she could take a full breath the grin he gave her was part amused, part devilish, and all stupidly sexy.

He leaned his fists on either side of her, his face coming to within inches of hers. "The fact you didn't, makes you even more desirable." Fire and smoke fell from his deep voice. "From your statement, would I be wrong to *presume* you wanted to be in my bed tonight?"

Lexi swallowed. She nodded, her gaze never leaving the warmth of his. When her nerves bubbled to the surface, for once they weren't accompanied by data, but the plain simple truth of her thoughts. "I wasn't sure you wanted me there. I mean, last night was wonderful, it really was. But I didn't know if it was just…a one-time thing. I—I didn't want to"—she shrugged—"assume you'd want me…again."

Aiden shook his head. He tugged the covers from her, then slid one hand under her knees, the other, her back. Effortlessly, he lifted her and said, "I wanted you in my bed five minutes after meeting you. That hasn't changed because of one night together."

"Oh" was all her brain allowed her to say. She laid her head on his shoulder, kissed the sweet spot behind his ear.

He carried her into his room and placed her on the massive bed, which he'd already turned down.

"There," he said, staring down her. "That's better. You look perfect, right there."

Her heart stuttered and swelled inside her breast.

He shut the light and crawled in next to her. She'd assumed—again—he'd brought her here to have sex. His words had certainly intimated it was on the agenda. And she was more than willing, despite how tired she was. When he rolled her to her uninjured side and slid along the back of her, spooning their bodies, surprise drifted through her.

"I thought—"

With one hand tossed over her waist and resting on her tummy, he whispered into her ear, "I know what you thought. And even though I want to be inside you as if my life depended on it, doing every little thing I can to make you scream like you did last night, I know how tired you are. For what I want to do with you, I need you fully rested."

She blushed in the darkness, imagining all those things and how they'd make her come undone.

"Get some sleep, sweetheart." He kissed her temple and pressed along the length of her, his hand holding her in place.

She waited a few beats before asking, "What if I told you I'd gotten a second wind?"

His low chuckle sent all the hair on her body straight to attention.

Shifting, she turned to face him. His eyes were closed, but the utterly sensual grin she longed to press her lips against covered his face. So she gave into the urge and did.

Tentatively, she dragged her tongue along his lips and when he parted them, mated her tongue with his. The kiss started slow and thoughtful, Aiden letting her take the lead. When she cupped the back of his neck and twined her fingers in his hair, clutching and deepening the kiss, he complied.

Every nerve ending in her body exploded when he bit down on her bottom lip.

Second wind be damned.

A month of sleep couldn't have energized her as much as kissing him did. She started to squirm, the lower half of her body turning restless with need.

With gentle care, Aiden shunted her to her back and hungrily ravished her mouth while his hand slid under her T-shirt and pinched her puckered nipple. He smiled against her lips as he captured her staggered gasp.

Pulling back, he stared down at her, and even in the dark, Lexi's body flushed from the heat in his gaze.

"You're sure?" he asked, his voice intense, the need for him to know, profound. The fact he asked, was so concerned for her welfare, had her heart stuttering again. He cared for her, about her. No man ever had before, not like this. Aiden was truly the first man she'd ever made love to, and not simply had sex with. She needed him to know how much that meant to her.

For an answer, she pulled his head down to hers again and kissed him with everything she had, everything she wanted to give.

And, thankfully, he took it all and gave her so much more in return.

Chapter 19

Lexi needed to speak to three people—two bank executives and then the branch manager—before she was allowed access to Zoe's safe deposit box. Luckily, she had Zoe's death certificate copy saved on her phone. After the manager did a quick check to ensure its authenticity and then called up the deposit box agreement Zoe had signed, naming her sister as executrix of the account, he led her and Aiden down to the basement level of the bank.

"After speaking to Shel, I'd wondered why the account hadn't shown up in Zoe's paperwork when I went through everything," she said as she and Aiden waited for the manager to obtain the bank's key. "Now that I know she put the account in our mother's name, it makes sense."

"I'm betting she did it to keep it hidden as much as she could," Aiden said as he absently played with the fingers of the hand he held. He hadn't let go of it once since they'd left his apartment, even driving one-handed so he could keep them joined. A warm feeling of contentment, one she didn't have a memory of ever experiencing before, filled her from head to toes.

He'd been so gentle with her through the night, bringing her pleasure again and again. She'd done the same for him, rewarded when he cried her name as he came. When they'd finally fallen asleep, once again spooned with Aiden's hand possessively circling her waist, Lexi knew, without a doubt, what they shared was unique.

"Here we go," the bank manager said, returning with the key.

Once both were placed into their key slots and turned, the manager pulled the rectangular box out completely from its holder and placed it down on the table.

"I'll give you some privacy."

"You ready?" Aiden asked once they were alone.

Lexi took a breath, nodded, then opened the lid.

A manila envelope with her name written across it stared up at them.

"That's Zoe's handwriting." She lifted it from the box. After opening the clasp, she poured the contents down onto the table. A flash drive in a disc case along with a folded piece of paper fell out.

"I'm gonna assume this is the file Castillo was hired to find. What's the paper say?"

Lexi unfolded it and frowned. She turned it to him, and he read aloud, "Follow the money."

"What the heck does that mean?"

"Only one way to find out." He pulled his laptop from his briefcase and inserted the drive into a USB port. Two keystrokes later and he opened the screen to show two icons. One of them, a video file marked *Lexi.*

"You want to watch it now it?" he asked her. When she nodded, he hit *play.*

Her gasp when Zoe's face appeared on the computer screen had Aiden tugging her hand back into his.

"Hey, sis. If you're watching this, then there's a

good chance I'm dead. That means you found my friend Shel. She wasn't supposed to let you know about the deposit box unless you came looking for me. So. I'm dead. And that sucks."

Tears filled Lexi's eyes.

"You're probably wondering what's going on. I'm gonna try to lay it all out straight for you. Like I said, if you're watching this, you already know a lot. It started a few months ago when Shel got beat up."

Zoe went on to tell them the story much the way the former prostitute had the night before.

"When the dead junkie was found with Shel's stuff, we knew it was a way for her to disappear. I figured the police would find out when they did dental records that it wasn't her, but for the time being, she was considered dead. We put our little plan into action."

She stopped and took a sip from a bottle of water she had at her side.

"I'm gonna guess by now you know about Peter Smith and Richard Deveroux. If not, after you watch this, go into the other file I'm adding to this drive. I can't prove it, but I think Deveroux ordered Smith to get Shel out of his life. The guy is a narcissist. Actually, both of them are. After Shel told me about Smith's business and how she met Deveroux, I started digging to try and get some dirt on him I could leak to the police or the feds. What I've been able to gather is all on the attached file. I could only do so much because my degree isn't in cyber hacking." She gave a tiny laugh. "I wish it was. You should have someone you trust, who's hopefully finance smart, go over the info in the file with you. There are a few companies listed I'm sure are dummy corps used to either launder money or fund Smith's prostitution business, and they were probably set up by Deveroux. He's a finance whiz, and this stuff just reeks of someone with mad finance skills. I kept hitting security walls every time I tried to dig deeper. That alone tells me there's something worth hiding. I hope you can find someone able to unearth the info."

She took another sip of water, and Lexi took the moment to swipe at her wet eyes and glance over at Aiden. If anyone could decipher info from Zoe's work, she was sure he could.

"You okay?" he asked, his hand still gripping hers, worry filling his eyes.

She nodded.

"So, let me get to the elephant in the room," Zoe said. "When I came to New York to get Zoe set up, I didn't let you know. You know that now. No calls, no visits. You're probably hurt by that, but I won't say I'm sorry. I did it to protect you. Smith is a very powerful man, and I have a thought he's not the real brains behind his business. Call it a hunch, but I think he actually answers to someone higher up on the food chain. But even if he's the master of his domain, I didn't want anything to link back to you in any way. Our last names are different, and we live in different cities, so I'm hoping no one's made a connection to you. Now, that only makes sense if I'm still alive and you never see this. I'm gonna go on the presumption making it is just precautionary and nothing is gonna happen to me. But just in case, I want documentation no one can access about all this except for you. Okay." She nodded and took a breath. "Last point. A lot's gone on in my life this past year I haven't clued you in on. It hasn't been because I wanted to avoid you, so get that out of your head right now. I know you, Alexis Elizabeth. You're gonna obsess about all this and try to take the blame for me being closemouthed. Cut it out."

Lexi laughed softly and shook her head. Her sister knew her well.

"You always took care of me, made sure I was safe, and I love you for that. But I'm an adult, and I needed to start doing adult things just for me. Continuing to go to the group meetings was one way to keep my life together. Working at a woman's shelter was something I decided to do to help women like Mom and give back a little. We've never talked about the kind of life she led when we were kids, and I know you tried to protect me from knowing how messed up she was. I understand why you did, and I'm not faulting you for it. You kept our family together even when Mom was alive and God knows after she died. But it was time for me to take total responsibility for my life, my actions, and my decisions. And I'm glad I did since I was able to help Shel, kinda like I wish someone had been there to help Mom. You are the best sister and role model anyone could have, Lex, and I love you with all my heart. I know it wasn't easy on you after Mom…did what she did. But by hook or crook, you kept us together, safe, and fed." She smiled, full face into the camera. "To this day, though, I can't stand mac and cheese."

Lexi laughed.

Zoe's face turned serious again. "If I am dead, the only real regret I have is I didn't tell you more often how much I admire and love you. The people in my group meetings have come to roll their eyes every time

I mention you now, cuz I do it so much. But it's all good-natured. I truly love you, Alexis Elizabeth Buckley, with all my heart and then some."

"I love you, too," Lexi told the screen.

"Now, go find out who killed me and make sure they're brought to justice, because I'd really hate to think I died for nothing. Zoe, out." She saluted, and the recording stopped.

Aiden squeezed her hand and turned her to face him. His face held such an expression of kindness that Lexi's eyes filled again. When he tugged her to him and wrapped his arms around her, a sob finally broke free from deep within her.

"She loved you," he stated, simply, as he rubbed her back.

She burrowed into his chest. Nothing in her life had ever felt as comforting, as peaceful, as being held against this man, his tree-trunk arms folded around her, the sound of his heartbeat steady, calm, and soothing against her ear.

In the span of a few short days, he and his dog had become fixtures in her life and, now, her heart. She couldn't deny it. She loved him. Was in love with him. She'd never felt this way about any man before, and her analytical mind recognized it for what it was.

"Let's wait to open the other file, okay?" he asked.

Back to reality.

Nodding, she pulled back from his embrace and swiped her hands over her wet cheeks. After a quick glance at the wall clock, she grabbed her purse off the table and said, "It's almost nine. We should get going. I don't want the provost saying anything about tardiness when he's already gunning for me."

"Lexi." He wrapped a hand over her arm. When she looked at him after first masking the emotion she knew must be evident in her eyes, he asked, "Are you okay?"

"Fine. Seeing Zoe like that"—she thrust her chin toward the laptop—"was a bit of a shock. But it proved my first instinct was correct and she didn't kill herself. I want to find out who's responsible, who took her from me. Now, more than ever, I want answers."

His expression never wavered or changed as he stared down at her. She couldn't quite read what was floating in his eyes. Concern? Questions? She'd discovered the cocky, double-entendre-speaking, hunky guy she'd met on the plane was a master at keeping his thoughts close to the vest. She envied him that more than she liked admitting to herself.

Finally, with one simple nod, he said, "Me, too. Let's go."

****

He knew the video upset her more than she admitted. There was no way she could hide the sadness floating across her face from him, try though she did. Each moment they spent together he grew more attuned to her emotions, quirks, and coping mechanisms. Lexi Buckley was such a contradiction, that he gave himself a pat on the back for being able to decipher what was running through that uber-intelligent brain of hers.

She was a focused and skilled researcher, evidenced by everything she'd discovered before he came on the scene to help with her investigation into Zoe's death, not to mention how she'd pieced together his medical past. At the same time she gave off an *I'm-not-good-enough* vibe, characterized by her nervous tics and self-deprecating comments.

The woman didn't know what a treasure she was, and that just made him mad. Mad because no one had ever taken the time to tell her how amazing she was, show her her worth, or lift her up on a proverbial pedestal. He considered it an honor to do so and vowed he'd make her see herself for the wonderful woman she was.

When he'd discovered her absent from his bed the night before, he knew without her ever saying a word why she was. And he'd been proven correct. Once he'd made his intentions clear, she'd shown him exactly what he'd hoped she would: a passion matching his own. Free and open, Lexi made love with every ounce of her soul, holding nothing back. As lovers, they were more than compatible. And the more time he spent with her, the realization they were well suited in other, more important ways, became apparent.

He didn't want to insert the flash drive into his laptop for fear it could be traced. It was better to use the encrypted equipment at the office, which is what he told her while they drove to the college. "We'll head there right after you're done here for the day."

If she was disappointed in having to wait, she didn't show it.

"I've got an update on those two idiots who followed us last night," he told her when she finished reading through the day's office memos. This time she was seated at her desk, he relegated to her office couch. Brontë resumed her previous position under the coffee table.

"Tell me."

"Josh spoke to the arresting officer. Seems these

two are hired muscle, low-level enforcers who work freelance for one of the crime families."

"Good golly, that sounds ominous. Which one?"

"The Cassidys. Irish mob based outta Brooklyn, but Josh's source says they've got fingers in all five boroughs. I'm gonna try to find a connection between them and Smith."

"He's not the connection," she said, her spine snapping to attention in her chair, her eyes sharp and gleaming.

"What do you mean?"

She rose and crossed to him. "Shove over." Once he did, she sat on the couch and began typing on his laptop.

The aroma of vanilla drifting from her hair had him leaning closer for a more concentrated whiff. He admired the quick and nimble speed of her long, thin fingers as they sailed across the keyboard. He'd admired them when they'd been wrapped around his favorite body part during the night as well. When the area in question began to twitch, he crossed his legs and asked, "What are you typing?"

"Remember I said Margo grew up in her father's shadow?"

"He was a big-shot stock trader, back in the day. Yeah. So?"

"This is when it really is a blessing to have an eidetic memory." She finished typing and pointed to the screen. "That's her father, Crispin Gallagher. This was taken over thirty years ago at a restaurant in lower Manhattan during a New Year's Eve celebration."

Aiden saw a middle-aged man with a handlebar mustache and a mane of wavy white hair in the grainy black and white photo, seated at a round table of six, two women, three men, and a young girl. They were all dressed to the hilt, the men in tuxes, the women in sparkling gowns. Even the girl sported what looked like a fur stole on her shoulders.

"Okay. Again, so?"

"This man"—she placed her index finger along the man seated to Gallagher's right—"is Eaon Cassidy. Apparently, they were childhood friends."

Aiden gaped at her. "Are you kidding me?"

"Not even a little bit. Get a close look at the girl next to Gallagher."

It hit him the moment he did. "*Holy shit.* That's—"

"A sixteen-year-old Margo Deveroux, née Gallagher."

"So she's the connection to the Cassidys, not Smith?"

"It makes sense. She grew up at her father's knee and, apparently"—she pointed to the screen—"socialized with her father's friends, one of whom was Eaon Cassidy."

"So you think…what? She asked her father's old friend to kill Shel? Or Smith? To what end?"

"Good questions and ones I need to give some consideration to. One question I do have is have you done any kind of a financial investigation on Margo?"

He blinked at her a few times. "No. And I should have. I combined the Deveroux into one search. I realize right now I should have done separate runs."

"Margo was rich in her own right before she ever married Richard. From what I read about her background, she's smarter, quicker, and more willing to take financial risks than her husband. She ruled the trading floor."

Her desk phone rang, and when she rose to answer it, Aiden put his glasses back on and began typing. He should have seen it from the beginning. Margo was a financial player, spoiled rotten, and that cold, calculated gleam in her eye he'd seen at the bookstore told him she was a woman who got her own way. In everything.

He could understand why she would want her husband's prostitute girlfriend dead. But why would she want Smith out of the picture?

"That was the provost. I've been summoned."

Brontë lifted her head from Aiden's feet and gazed up at her.

"Okay, give me a minute to back out of this stuff," he told her.

"You don't have to come with me—"

"The last time you said that, in this very building, you were attacked, Lexi. That's not happening again."

When she pressed her lips into a flat line and squinted across the room at him, he figured she was going to argue the point or give him some statistic about how safe colleges were. He was prepared to argue right back at her all the reasons he wasn't letting her out of his sight.

He never had to, though. With a gentle eye-roll, a headshake, and a quick lifting of her lips, she acquiesced silently. Pleasantly surprised, he followed her from the room, Brontë between them, and stopped while she locked her office door.

"This ought to be fun," she mumbled as they made their way across the campus to his office.

Thirty minutes later she unlocked the door again, and this time she had murder in her eyes. She went immediately to her desk and stabbed in a series of numbers on the phone with the knuckle of her index finger.

"Who are you calling?"

"The president of the college. I want to hear from him, directly, and not just from that two-bit hack we just saw, that I'm suspended."

"He didn't call it a suspension."

"An enforced leave of absence to get my personal affairs in order without pay is a poor euphemism for it, but it's a suspension, never the less."

She held up her hand when he was about to ask something else.

"Priscilla? Hi, it's Dr. Buckley…fine…yes. I need to speak to Dr. Howard…yes, it's urgent. Thank you." She put her hand over the mouthpiece and said, "She's connecting me."

"Think he'll back the moron up?"

"That's what I want to see… hello, Dr. Howard…"

He didn't consider it eavesdropping since she hadn't asked him to leave. While he listened, he settled a hip against her desk and absently rubbed Brontë's head, which she'd leaned against his thigh. From the number of times Lexi was cut off from speaking by the man on the other end of the phone, he figured the leave of absence was a done deal. When she slammed the phone down, he was sure of it.

Turning her back to him, she crossed her arms over her chest and stared out her office window, her back straight as a plank. If he ran a hand down her spine, he wouldn't be surprised it if snapped from the coil of tension she carried there. Her shoulders were rising and falling so quickly he knew she couldn't be getting a full breath with each inhale. The desire to pull her into his arms and kiss away the anger hit him like a brick to the head. Would she accept the comfort?

Throwing caution to the wind, he moved behind her and laid his palms on her shoulders.

Yup. As tight as a drum.

From the subtle tremble under his hands, she was holding in her anger, truly, shaking with it.

Without saying a word, he pressed down, kneading the constricted muscles, his fingertips pressing in, then releasing.

She didn't protest.

After a few moments, the muscles under his grip started to relax. Minutes later, they went slack.

A deep, long sigh blew from her, her shoulders lifting against his hands before dropping back to their natural position. The steel in her spine melted, and she leaned backward, into him. As he wound his hands around her waist and pulled her in even closer, she dropped her head back onto his chest. Never one to miss an opportunity, Aiden did what he'd wanted to do since coming back to her office, and kissed her temple, his lips covering the gentle pulse he felt pounding beneath them.

"You know, from where I'm standing," he said against her skin, "a week off couldn't come at a better time. Without having to be here every day, you can devote more of your time to our investigation. Plus…" He spun her around. The tiny frown line, apparent after her phone call, had flown, her skin smooth and clear again. He cupped her jaw and pressed his lips against hers.

"Plus?" she said on a sigh.

He grinned down at her, then kissed the tip of her nose. "Plus…this." When he kissed her this time, she burrowed into him, winding her arms around his waist.

"I can hear your brain working," he said, as he skimmed her temple with his lips. "What are you thinking about?"

"The fact I've given my life to this college for the past three years, never had a black mark on my record, and this is how I'm treated. I don't even have any legal recourse since I'm, effectively, an employee of the college and not tenured like a professor."

"Again, I don't think it's a bad thing considering all that's happened in the past few days and everything we've discovered. Hell, Lexi, your apartment has been ransacked, you've been attacked *right* here, and we've almost been run off the road where I'm pretty sure the objective was to kill us. Just keeping you safe is a full-time job right now. It'll be a whole lot easier if we don't have to come here every day."

She stayed silent for a bit, then let out another breath, pulled back and said, "Laid out like that, you're right. But I can't stop thinking of what comes next. After the week is up. What if we're no further along?"

"Let's worry about that at the end of next week, okay?"

Her lips flattened, but when she rolled her shoulders and slid out of his grip, asking, "Can we go to your office now and look at the file?" he knew she saw the logic of his words.

****

"Is this room soundproofed?" she asked as he closed the door behind them, her gaze running around the space.

"Yup." He settled down behind one of the desks and booted up a desktop computer. "It's also wired differently. Every computer in here runs through a different router and network."

"Why?"

"So nothing can be easily traced back to us. Some of the information we're commissioned to search for can be considered…classified. While looking for it isn't necessarily illegal, there are channels we're supposed to go through to obtain it. That takes time, and there are days when getting the info we need is a time-sensitive occurrence. This way's easier all around."

A month ago, she would have been appalled at the idea of cutting corners to gather information or of someone hacking into a private system to obtain it. Since Zoe's death, her moral code of indignation at doing anything that could give even a hint of impropriety had shifted.

"Okay, let's see what's on this file." Aiden put his glasses on and plugged the flash drive in.

"It has three subfiles within it," he said after opening it. "Smith, Deveroux, and Bard."

"The owner of the magazine Zoe worked for? Good Lord. He's involved in this, too?"

"Let's see." He clicked on the file with William Bard's name, opened a new window, and typed in a URL listed in one of the three files present. A password screen popped up.

"Dead end," Lexi said.

"For your sister, yes." He tossed her the cocky smirk she loved.

"You can open it, even though you don't know the password?"

"Sweetheart"—he winked at her—"it's what I do."

He typed in a few keystrokes, then opened the two remaining files, each also password protected. "We'll let the program work on deciphering these. Let's see what's in Smith's file."

"A lot of this we already know," she said after they spent a few minutes going over the data.

"Now, this is interesting." Aiden pointed to the screen, then referred back to one of the open windows. "I wonder if your sister made the connection."

"To what?"

"This"—he pointed to the screen—"is the same URL in Bard's file." He switched screens. "See?" Just as he said it, the screen shifted and opened. "We're in. Well, well." He sat back and folded his arms across his chest.

For a moment, Lexi didn't understand what she was looking at. Then it hit her. Reaching out a hand, she grasped his arm, the giddy sensation of dropping downward on a roller coaster pitching through her stomach. "*Aiden.*"

"Zoe said she thought Smith wasn't the brains behind the business. Looks like she was right."

"This must be the file Castillo was talking about. But…wait. That doesn't make sense."

"Yeah, I get it. Why would goons who work for Cassidy try to take us out if Bard is the one this file incriminates in a prostitution ring? Was Castillo working for Bard?"

"There must be a connection between them," she said. "Or…" Her eyes darted back and forth as she tried to connect all the pieces they'd unearthed together.

"I can hear your brain working from here. Or

what?"

"Can you pull up everything you've got concerning Margo Deveroux?"

"Sure." A few keystrokes later, dozens of pages of data appeared. "What are you looking for?"

"The public stock transfers she worked on before she got married."

He stared at her for a moment, his head tilted to one side, his brows tugging together. Focusing back on the screen he did as she asked. "There are thousands."

"I'm only looking for one." She scanned the names as they sped by. "There. That one," she said pointing.

"WAB Publishing." He turned to her. "As in William Anthony Bard?"

Nodding, she said, "Click on the specs. I think she was instrumental in building his portfolio and making him rich."

After reading through the public trading specifications, Aiden leaned back in the chair and said, "You're right. She made him a very wealthy man. So there's another link between all of them. Margo to Bard, and if this"—he tapped the screen—"is to be believed, Bard to Smith with the magazine publisher connected to a prostitution ring."

"And Margo links to Cassidy through her father, Bard to her time as a trader, and Smith, through her husband."

"Shel links to Smith, Bard, and Deveroux, and through him to Margo. Margo's the common denominator in all of this."

Lexi nodded. "It all makes sense."

"What does? You're still thinking the woman-scorned theory?"

"For Shel I am," she told him. "I sincerely believe Margo was the impetus behind Shel's attack, that she set it up. So the question is, did she ask Smith to do it, and if so, is that why he was killed? To keep her involvement a secret? And who killed him?"

"There's still no evidence he was, you know. The police and everyone else are going with suicide."

"They did with my sister, too, Aiden, but we know it isn't true. And if it wasn't Smith, was it Cassidy?"

He nodded. The computer pinged again, the files for Smith and Deveroux finally opening.

"Here's the confirmation for the link from Smith to Bard. These are all payment transactions into numbered accounts."

She leaned in closer, the outer edge of her thigh brushing along his. The simple, haphazard touch had her toes curling inside her shoes and her leg muscles contracting.

"Zoe was able to gather a great deal of information," he said, oblivious to her heightened nerves. "Her investigative skills only got her so far, though."

Lexi swallowed, then took a breath as that horrible guilty wave engulfed her again. If only her sister had come to her with all this. If they'd only been closer, took the time to make time to be together.

If only. Two if the worst words in any language.

Sadness overwhelmed the guilt.

"Hey." Aiden shifted and grasped her hands. Those inquisitive, thoughtful blue eyes bore into hers.

"It's okay. I'm fine."

"Sweetheart, you are way better than fine"—her heart lifted—"but I know you're thinking about your sister right now, and I can guess you're feeling guilty again about being disconnected."

"I'm really beginning to wonder if a side effect of your medical treatment caused an ability to read minds." She shook her head, then let out another breath.

Sliding his chair closer to hers, he kept hold of her hand. "It's not that I can read minds," he told her, bumping into her knees with his own, "it's that I can read you. Your face tells a thousand stories with every expression."

She clicked her tongue and sent her lids to half-mast. "And here I thought I had a great poker face."

"You probably do. Only not to me. It's like your hair and ear tic. The first time I ever saw you do it was in the airport bar, and right away I knew it meant you were nervous. Most people would see it as just a habit."

"But not you?"

His full smile had her toes curling again.

"Trained observer, remember?"

She rolled her eyes. Staring back at the screen she asked, "What are we going to do with all this? Is it enough to take to the authorities? We still don't have a definitive answer to who killed my sister."

"But we've got the why. Or at least think we do. The who should fall out of it if we just keep digging and asking the right questions. Come on." He stood and tugged her up with him. "Let's go get Brontë and fill Josh in."

****

"Your brother is the calmest and most unreadable person I've ever met," she said as they pulled into Aiden's underground garage.

"Which is why I never play poker with him." He

shut the engine and turned to face her, first scratching Brontë behind her ears. "I lost too much of my allowance money to him when we were kids." He pulled her hand into his. "How are you doing?"

"You ask me that a lot. I've told you numerous times, I won't break."

"I know you won't." He kissed her knuckles, the expression in his eyes soft as he held her gaze. "But a few cracks along the way are understandable."

That pulled a grin from her. Just as quick, it died. "I want this all to be over. I want answers."

With a nod, Aiden squeezed her hand. "We're getting them."

They both turned to Brontë when she whined.

"I need to take her for a walk," he said, rubbing the top of her head. "It's been a while."

"You go walk her," Lexi said as they alighted from the car. "I'll head up and start dinner."

"You should stay with us. Just for safety reasons."

"Aiden." She fisted her hands on her hips. "You and your brothers have this building locked down like Fort Knox. Despite saying I wouldn't notice all the security, I have. The guy in the lobby who looks like he eats tanks for lunch, the one stationed at the front door entrance, the two across the street who've been sitting in a parked car. I wouldn't be surprised if he had snipers on the roof."

He pulled her into his arms and kissed her, quick and hard. "I need to have a talk with my brother about hiring less obvious men. They're supposed to be unobtrusive."

"And they *are.* To the average person. But I'm hyperaware right now because of all that's happened.

Don't fault him."

He shook his head. "A brilliant researcher, an unparalleled observer, and beautiful to boot."

Thrilled with the compliment, she stretched up and kissed him on the cheek just as Brontë whimpered again. "Go. Take her. I'll go on up and start dinner. Give me your keys."

She watched him walk the dog out through the exit door, turning once to toss her a smile. Then, she headed for the elevator. When it arrived, she sensed movement behind her and heard her name. She turned, and before she could call out, something heavy and hard struck her from behind and knocked her to the ground. She felt a sharp prick at her neck and then…nothing.

Chapter 20

"I need the security footage from the garage. *Now*," Aiden barked at the building's onsite manager.

Dylan laid a hand on his shoulder. "Easy, bro."

Aiden jerked his arm. "Don't tell me to take it easy, Dylan. She's gone, and it's my fault."

He'd never forget the heart-stopping terror exploding through him after breaking down the door to his apartment when she didn't respond to his knock. A quick search told him she'd never made it from the garage. Dylan had already been on his way over when Aiden called him after first notifying Josh. Questioning the security guys had proven ineffective since none of them had seen anything suspicious.

"It's no one's fault, Aiden, least of all yours." He turned to the manager. "Let's see the disc replay."

"Let me call it up," the fiftyish manger said. The computer screen split into four quadrants. The footage was black, white, and grainy.

"Zoom in on the camera centered on the garage elevator entrance," Aiden commanded. "Roll back thirty minutes."

All three of them watched the monitor as the footage, time stamped, sped backward until movement entered the frame.

"Slow it down," Aiden told the man.

Lexi stood at the elevator, when a woman sidled up

next to her. Lexi turned, her eyes widening and her mouth falling open, when two men entered the frame. One of them knocked her to her knees, the other shoved something into her neck, while the woman turned and spoke to them. Her face was in shadow.

"Is there any sound?"

"Just visual feed, no audio."

"Zoom in on the woman," Aiden told the manager.

A few clicks and the picture grew blurrier. "Any more and it'll really be distorted," the manager said.

Aiden hissed as the two men lifted an unconscious Lexi as if she were a sack of potatoes. A car stopped next to them and they tossed her in the trunk, slamming it shut.

"*Jesus Christ.*" Every hair on Aiden's body stood straight up.

One of the men held the car door open for the woman, and as she slid into it, Aiden was finally able to confirm what he'd suspected.

"That's Margo Deveroux." He pulled his cell phone from his pocket, hit the speed dial, and when the call connected said, "I need you."

"I'll be there in twenty," Rick Bannerman said before the line went dead.

****

"So what do we know?" Josh asked.

The four brothers were in Aiden's apartment, the footage from the security disc copied and opened on his desktop.

"Black, four-door sedan. This year's edition, so I'm thinking a rental," Rick said. He hit a few of the keys, the image increasing in size. "Here's the license from the exit camera."

"Tag it," Josh ordered. Rick began typing.

"I take it we're not notifying the police?" he asked.

"It'll be faster if we run point on this." Josh looked toward his youngest brother. Aiden nodded.

"The Deveroux are in town as part of the husband's book tour," Dylan said, without looking up from his laptop. "They arrived last night and have a suite booked at the Carlisle despite having a penthouse in the city. Wonder why they didn't stay there?"

"Richard's all for show and appearances," Aiden said. "Both of them are. Staying at a pricy hotel makes it seem like they're better than they are."

Josh shook his head. "Rock star behavior."

Aiden nodded. Brontë sidled up to his thigh and pressed against him. He ran an absentminded hand over her head.

"Got it," Rick said. "Rental, like I thought. Agreement's signed M. Gallagher."

"That's Margo's maiden name," Aiden told them. "Which just pounds another nail in her coffin and confirms what Lexi thought. She's the one behind all this."

"It was a pretty bold move to take Lexi like that," Rick said, pointing to the footage running across the screen. "They had to know there would be security film."

"Bold or stupid?" Dylan asked.

He shrugged. "Either way. The two goons with Margo look like hired muscle. I'd bet from Cassidy's crew, based on the car chase."

"Makes sense," Aiden said. "You can't make out their faces, though, to run recognition."

"Why was Lexi taken?" Josh asked. "Why now?

Do you think Deveroux knows she has the flash drive? Or that Shel Bushman is still alive?"

"I'd bet no on that," Dylan said. "There's been no movement on her, and I think if darling Margo knew she was still around, she'd be concentrating on her instead of Lexi."

"I don't care why she was taken," Aiden said, swiping his hands through the hair at his temples. "I just want to know where she is so I can get her back before…" He hated that his voice, filled with fear, cracked.

"She means a lot to you," Josh stated. "More than a client."

He released a breath, feeling as if his entire being escaped with it. "You have no idea."

"Oh, I think I do," his oldest brother said. Thrusting his chin at Rick, he added, "We both do."

Josh's wife, Kandy, had been the victim of a murderous stalker a few years back, which was how the two had met. Josh had been hired to protect her. Along the way, they each realized they couldn't live without the other and had gotten married. Rick's fiancé, Abby, had been attacked by the vengeful husband of one of her clients, in addition to being a target in a murder plot, hatched by a man sent to prison for killing his wife. Rick had insisted on protecting her despite Abby's continued statements she didn't need it. And just like with his older brother, Rick had fallen hard for the tough-as-nails lawyer.

"Yeah," he admitted after a moment. "I guess you do."

"We'll get her back, bro," Dylan said. "It's what we do."

Just knowing his brothers were all in, Papps included, allowed him to take a full breath for the first time since he'd discovered her missing.

"Okay," Josh said, leaning back against Aiden's desk. "Forget about why she was taken. Where they would bring her is more important right now. Any thoughts?"

"I can't see them leaving the city," Dylan said. He tapped the computer screen. "According to this press release, they're attending some gala tonight at the Met. A charity fundraiser. And lookie here." He glanced up at his brothers. "Guess who's also on the guest list?"

"William Bard," Aiden read.

"That could just be coincidence," Rick said. "Although none of us believes in them."

"Your point," Aiden addressed Dylan, "is that Margo's crunched for time if she's gonna put in an appearance at the fundraiser."

He shot his index finger at him.

"So where would she go?" Josh asked.

"I've got an idea." Aiden sat behind his laptop and began typing furiously while his brothers simply waited. Dylan came to stand behind him, Josh next to him. Rick remained seated.

After a few moments he sat back. "These are all the listings I could find under both Deveroux, Margo's maiden name, and Bard, here in the city."

"*Jesus*. There are over, what? Forty properties there." Dylan whistled.

"Why those three?" Rick asked.

"Margo's involved, so it makes sense to search her and her moron of a husband. Bard's connected to both Smith and Zoe, and to a lesser extent Shel Bushman."

"I see what you're thinking." Rick nodded.

"You can rule out the residential properties," Josh said. "I can't see Margo taking her to their penthouse."

"I'd cross off the ones in her name, as well," Rick said. When his brothers all looked at him, he shrugged. "Why draw attention to yourself?" he asked. "You gotta figure she knows we're looking for Lexi. Why would she take a chance and bring her someplace with her name on the lease?"

"That makes incredible sense," Aiden said, his fingers eliminating the properties under her name.

"I'd look for commercial places, warehouses, maybe someplace abandoned," Dylan added. "Easier to hide."

"And secluded," Josh said. "Not a lot of foot traffic."

"Okay. Nothing listed for Deveroux," Aiden said, "but two for Bard. One on the harbor in Manhattan, one in Queens."

"That sounds like just the place you'd take someone you'd kidnapped." Dylan nodded.

"If he's got waterfront property, I wonder if he's got a boat," Rick said.

Aiden typed for a few moments. "This is why they pay you the big bucks, Bannerman. He's got two, actually. A one-hundred-foot yacht and a seventy-foot schooner. The yacht's listed as harbored here, in the city."

"A boat that size is a nice place to hide out."

"Do you think he's involved?" Dylan asked.

"I don't know, and right now I don't care. The objective is to get Lexi back and ask questions after the fact."

All three of his brothers nodded.

"How do you want to do this?" Josh asked.

"You and Rick take the waterfront property. Dylan and I can take the boat."

"I'll call Papps and have him hit the one in Queens." With that, Josh pulled his cell from his pocket.

"I just sent the addresses to your phones, Papps's, too," Aiden said. "Keep them on vibrate and stay in touch. If what we suspect is true, Margo's already killed, or ordered killed, three people. Shel, Zoe, and Smith. I've got a gut feeling Lexi's next."

"Your gut has never steered us wrong," his oldest brother said.

Aiden nodded at him, once, then said, "Okay. Let's roll."

"Hang on." Josh laid an arm on his shoulder. "If you find her, call us and wait for backup. We don't know what kind of muscle Margo's got with her. Or Bard, for that matter, if he's involved. Those two and the driver could be it, or it could be an army, especially if the Cassidys are part of this. Don't go in guns blazing, okay?"

"I'm doing whatever I have to do to get Lexi back," Aiden told him. With steely determination in his narrowed eyes, he added, "And if it means with guns drawn, so be it."

"Aiden—" Josh clenched his fists and took a step toward his brother.

"Josh." Dylan stepped between them and placed his palms on each of their chests, using his body as a barrier. Looking from his oldest brother, to his youngest, and then back again, he said, "Don't worry.

I've got Aiden's six."

Josh's heated gaze matched the glare in Aiden's eyes for fervor. After a tense moment, he retreated. "Make sure you do. Keep in touch."

"Same to you," Aiden said.

****

"There's nothing on her phone or in her purse. No flash drive. No disc or file, either."

The male voice had a smoker's rasp and came from behind her. Lexi kept her eyes closed and tried to orient herself by sound alone. Hands bound at her back, she was seated on a hard chair with something securing her about the waist. Her feet, though, weren't shackled.

"*Shit.* I don't know how much she knows. I need answers. She should be coming around by now. How much did you give her?" a female voice asked.

Margo Deveroux.

Memories flooded through her brain. Saying goodbye to Aiden…waiting for the elevator…Margo calling her name. Then…nothing.

"Enough to knock her out for the ride. It should be wearing off."

They gave me something to knock me out. Okay, that makes sense. You were kidnapped, and now you're tied to a chair. First, don't panic. Remain calm.

An open-palm slap to her already bruised cheek caught her off guard, the force and pain ricocheting her head to the left. Her eyes flew open.

"Good," Margo said, one hand lifted to strike again, a gun in the other. "You're awake."

Lexi had hated Richard Deveroux on sight, recognizing him for the immoral, predatory phony he was. Margo hid her malevolence well behind the façade of a cold, faithful wife and protector. But right now, gazing down at her, her lips pulled back in a grin just shy of psychotic, the full extent of the Margo's evil shone like a beacon in the night.

Stay calm. Don't show any fear. It's like a drug to people like her.

"I must say, for a nobody librarian, you've proven quite annoying," Margo told her. "I've had to devote entirely too much time, effort, and mental energy to you."

Lexi schooled her features not to react but couldn't help the words that leapt from her mouth as her gaze fell to the gun. "Over thirty-eight thousand people are killed every year by handguns in the United States. Thirty-six percent the result of a homicide. Women are more often cited as wanting a gun for protection than for sport."

Margo threw back her head and cackled. Her lids floated to half closed, when she settled on Lexi again, and a glittering, venomous evil winked through them and pierced Lexi right in the gut.

"Aren't you just a fact-filled little mouse." She moved closer and pointed the gun barrel straight at Lexi's forehead. "Which do you think I have it for? Protection or recreation?"

She licked her lips before replying, "Neither. I think you have it because it gives you a sense of power you don't possess without it."

The smirk died, replaced by a snarl. Before she could brace for the attack, Margo backhanded the gun to her uninjured cheek. Black spots danced in front of her eyes as hot liquid Lexi knew was blood, trickled down her face.

"We don't really need to discuss who has the power here, do we, *Dr.* Buckley?"

Prudently, her mouth stayed shut.

"I didn't think so." Margo stepped back and lowered the gun.

"Why am I here?" Lexi asked, once the pain receded and her vision cleared, somewhat. "Why don't you just kill me?"

"It's not time. I need to do this perfectly so it never comes back on me. That's why I brought you here, to William's boat."

"William Bard?"

With a nod she said, "He's going to take the fall for your sudden demise."

"I thought Bard was a friend of yours."

"He was never a friend."

"But you made millions off him. And you made him a very rich man."

"So, you've done your homework I see. What else do you know about dear old Will?"

She debated whether to spill everything she knew, or keep it all hidden. Margo was set to kill her either way, but talking would keep it from happening until help arrived or she could think of some way to get herself out of this situation.

"That he owns the magazine my sister worked for. The one you and your husband denied knowing about."

Margo shook her head. "She was a persistent pest, I'll say that much for her. What else?"

"I know you made him millions when you were a trader, and Bard used some of the money to finance a prostitution enterprise your husband's publicity agent ran."

Her perfectly sculpted eyes rose. "Well, well. You know more than I realized."

"I also know Smith is dead."

A shudder ran down Lexi's back when the smirk morphed to a full-fledged smile.

"It was billed as a suicide, just like my sister's death. I don't believe either of them were, Margo."

At the use of her Christian name, the woman's spine snapped. From the way she looked down her nose at Lexi, Margo's disdain for others she considered *less than worthy* was obvious.

"You killed them. Or had them killed. Either way, you're responsible."

Slowly, Margo ambled around the spacious room. "It seems you've learned a great deal. I underestimated you."

Lexi glanced around her surroundings. She was in a bedroom, a king-sized bed sitting across one wall, twin nightstands bookending it. A moody oil painting depicting a boat caught in a tempest rested above the bed. An arched doorway to the left led to a bathroom, another to the right appeared to be a closet. The room was military precise with nothing on the dresser or end tables she could use as a weapon. One of the lamps would work, but since her hands were secured, she couldn't exactly lift one to throw at the woman.

"Why did you kill Zoe?"

"I didn't," she said, her gaze landing back on Lexi.

"Maybe not personally, but you had her killed."

"I hate repeating myself. I didn't kill, or have your sister, killed."

"I don't believe you."

Margo shrugged. "That's your problem, not mine."

"If you didn't, then who did?"

"Your sister was doing research on my husband," Margo said after a few moments. She leaned against the dresser opposite from Lexi and crossed her wrists in front of her, the gun dangling from her fingers. "She billed it as a profile about his new-author status, but her questions had more to do with his personal life than the book. I realized she'd…discovered…something that would have harmed Richard if it had been made public."

"His affair with Shel Bushman. A prostitute."

Margo's perfect jaw clenched while a vein in her temple visibly pulsed. Her spine shot straight as a rod as her lips curled into another sneer. "That bitch. That dirty, filthy bitch. She actually thought Richard would leave me for her. *Her.* A common whore." She started pacing about the room again, this time her gait was clipped, her free hand fisted at her side. "She thought he was in love with her, wanted to make a life with her. Stupid bitch. Richard will never love anyone but me. He's mine." She stopped short, turned to face Lexi. Hatred oozed from every aspect of her face. "She found out what happens to people who try to take what's mine."

"You killed her."

"No, again. My hands are clean. Smith did."

Just as Shel suspected.

"Did you ask him to?"

Once again, her expression changed. Her eyes narrowed into a cunning, sly squint, and her lips tilted up on one side in malicious sneer. "Let's just say we both understood the benefit of that bitch being gone from the world."

"Did you have him kill my sister, too?"

Margo hesitated just a fraction before answering. "No. That was all his stupid idea."

Lexi gasped. "Why?"

"Because of the article she was doing on Richard. She knew about that woman, knew her for what she was. Smith was afraid your sister would discover the link back to him and to Bard."

"How did he kill her?"

"I don't know the details. Drugged wine or something." Margo's eyes narrowed. "He made it look like a suicide."

The official coroner's report stated Zoe died from barbiturate poisoning, the lethal drug dose found in an opened and almost empty bottle of Merlot on her kitchen counter. Zoe's favorite wine had been Merlot.

"I knew the moment the police informed me of her death she hadn't killed herself."

"How could you possibly?"

She kept silent on their mother's death, and said, instead, "Her laptop was missing, so how had she typed a supposed suicide note and left it, printed out, next to her bed? Her phone was missing too, and Zoe never moved an inch without her cell. Both those things suggested she hadn't taken her own life."

Margo shook her head. "Smith was a moron. He acted on impulse and didn't think anything through. When Richard hired him, I thought it a poor choice. But they'd known one another in college. When you showed up, first in Monroe's office, asking about your sister, Smith panicked. He wanted you out of the picture, like your sister. He called me because he knows I have certain…friends, who specialize in getting rid of pests—"

"The Cassidys."

"Well, well, you have done your homework. Eaon Cassidy was my godfather. His son runs the business now. I called in a favor. Unfortunately, you've proven resourceful, despite all our efforts."

"Who killed Peter Smith, then? And why?"

"Who do you think? Bard, of course. Smith botched it with your sister after Monroe told him she'd been asking questions. Bard realized he was a liability. Taking a page from Smith's book, he fashioned it like a suicide. So far, it's stuck."

"Why are you going to frame Bard for my death then? You have the info he killed Smith. Isn't that enough?"

"No," she spat. "Bard is using Richard's relationship with that whore against me."

"He's blackmailing you."

"He's a son of a bitch. So I'm going to get a little payback, and at the same time, make Richard safe in the public's eyes. Smith may have introduced Richard to that whore, but Bard financed it. William bears just as much responsibility for that. Now that Richard's famous, his reputation has to be pristine. The public doesn't need to know about that conniving whore."

"People have died just so you can keep your cheating husband's peccadillos out of the press? Do you hear how ludicrous that sounds? Why not just divorce him and take every penny he has as payback? Why kill innocent people?"

Fury leapt across her face as she bolted to Lexi, her gun hand raised. "I'll never divorce Richard. He's mine, do you understand? Mine. Forever."

The psychological frameworks for obsessive jealousy and possessive disorders ran through Lexi's head. Thankfully, she was able to curtail giving them a voice.

"Bard values his public reputation as much as his fortune," Margo said. "He's spent his life living a double existence. Consummate businessman by day, and flesh peddler by night. When a dead woman is discovered on his boat, killed with a gun from his private collection, the scandal will shatter him, I'll have my revenge, and nothing he says can hurt Richard."

Saying aloud the woman was insane would be unwise. Still, Lexi couldn't help but throw a wrench into one part of Margo's deranged logic.

"But your fingerprints will be on the gun," she said, thrusting her chin toward it, "not Bard's. How is that going to implicate him? Won't blame point to you, instead?"

Margo's eyes burned with fury. She flew at Lexi and shoved the gun into her temple. "Shut up! Just shut up."

Despite being terrified, Lexi refused to show the woman any fear. She didn't wince from the pain of the hard barrel pushing into such a sensitive area, nor did she flinch at the sound of the gun cocking. Forcing her eyes open, she stared into Margo's ferocious gaze, hoping her own appeared calm and cool.

A harsh pounding came from above them, followed by the unmistakable report of a gun firing.

Margo lifted her head to the noise, and Lexi took advantage of her shift in attention. She snaked one of her unsecured feet around Margo's ankle, then, with a swift swipe of her leg, the woman fell backward, her arms flailing out to her sides for support. She hit the floor, hard, with a *thwack,* her ass taking the brunt. The gun flew from her hand when it banged against the floor. Lexi watched it slide across the room and disappear under the dresser.

Three more shots rang out from above accompanied by male screams, yells, and the sound of running feet. Lexi rocked back and forth in the chair to try and slacken the binding around her waist, while Margo crab walked backward, found the edge of the dresser, then pushed against it to stand.

"How many men do you have with you?" Lexi asked.

Margo ignored her, instead, going down on her knees to search under the dresser. Lexi rocked to a standing position, the chair seat forcing her body into a bent-at-the-waist, ninety-degree angle, her head facing the floor. She might not be able to stand upright, but she could use her head as a battering ram, which is what she did, catching the small of Margo's back with the top of her skull. The woman careened forward and her face slammed into the mirror above the dresser, shattering the glass. Blood spurted from her forehead as she recoiled, screaming.

Lexi used her bound body as a fulcrum, the attached chair swinging from it and pummeling Margo in the hip. The woman stumbled and fell back on her ass again. The movement helped loosen the binding around Lexi's waist, so she shimmied back and forth a few times until it was slack enough for the chair to slip downward. The motion of it dropping to the floor made her stance unsteady, and she stumbled backward, her hands still bound behind her. Unable to reach out to steady herself, she fell at an awkward angle onto her side, banging down hard on the solid floor surface. Pain exploded from her hip. Her vision dimmed, the room turning dark, and she feared she was about to pass out.

Margo frantically searched under the dresser for the gun while shouts and more commotion filtered in from above.

When three rapid and loud barks broke through the haze of her semi-consciousness, Lexi shook her head from side to side and attempted to sit up. The stabbing pain in her hip hampered her movements. She screamed Brontë's name as the barking got closer.

Then, several things happened at once.

Margo retrieved the gun, stood with it cradled in both of her shaking hands, and pointed it straight at Lexi's supine body. Feral hatred sprang from her eyes while blood poured down her cheeks. Her mouth twisted into a sneer as she said, "I should have killed you before you woke up."

Just as her finger began to squeeze the trigger, the cabin door banged open and Brontë charged in, her deep, menacing growl exploding into the space. Startled, Margo turned, the gun now pointed in front of her, aimed at the advancing dog.

Lexi screamed, "No!" and tried again to sit up. The pain blinded her, and her hold on staying conscious faded.

The gun fired, the blast shattering around the cabin.

Through the murky haze of her decreasing vision, Lexi saw the gun drop from Margo's hand. In a slow motion dance, she crumpled to the floor, the sleeve of her dress turning sanguine.

Stunned, Lexi lay, on her side, motionless.

Aiden

The wet warmth of Brontë's tongue, licking her face, and Aiden squatting next to her, finally broke through her shock.

She tried to blink his face into focus but couldn't. He flicked a penknife open and, with one quick swish of the blade, freed her hands. The muscles rebelled against being constrained for so long, and she cried out as the pins-and-needles sensation of disuse flew up her extremities.

Aiden said something, but the gunshot in such close quarters had rendered her momentarily deaf.

"Not protecting your ears when a gun is fired can lead to short-term hearing loss," she stated as she stared up at his concerned face. Her voice was a faint echo inside her head. "If continued, severe and permanent damage occurs, leading to deafness."

She wasn't able to hear his response, but his lips went from flat to crooked, the moisture in his eyes glistening. Her vision tunneled, a high-pitched ring blaring in her ears now. Aiden said something else she couldn't hear, but when he lifted her up in his arms as if she were a rare and delicate piece of spun glass, Lexi closed her eyes and rested her head against his strong shoulder, finally succumbing to the dark.

Chapter 21

"You have a stubborn streak a mile long, Doc," Dylan told her. His mouth pulled into a boyish grin. "A trait I admire in a woman."

"Outta the way." Aiden hip checked him away from the bed, then sat next to a reclining Lexi and placed a cold pack over her bruised hip area. "He's not wrong about your stubborn streak," he told her. "The ER doc said it wouldn't hurt to spend one night in the hospital."

"It's estimated that 3 percent of all inpatients will develop a nosocomial, or hospital-acquired, infection. A significant percentage of those patients will die from their hospital stay and not from the reason they were admitted," she told him, adjusting the pack over the most painful area. "I hate hospitals on a good day, and since neither my hip nor my cheek is broken, it makes sense to recuperate at home. Or in your apartment, as it were."

"Beauty, brains, and common sense." Dylan sighed. "If you can cook, I'm gonna go get a ring tonight."

She had to stifle the giggle that bubbled up when Aiden turned and glared up at his older brother's smirk.

"It's late. Don't you need your beauty sleep?" Aiden asked.

"Nah. I'm a natural since I got all the looks in the

family."

This time, when she laughed, it was followed by an "*Ow.*" Her free hand shot to her injured face.

Both brothers turned serious, but it was Aiden who stroked the back of his hand gently over her bruised skin. Even Brontë, who'd been sitting next to her on Aiden's bed, slid closer, dropped her head onto Lexi's thigh, and whined.

"I'm okay, girl." She stroked the dog's fur.

"Brain is right. It's late," Dylan said. "Since you're in such good hands, Doc, I'm gonna head home." He bent over her, his gaze running around her face. With another grin, he said, "I'd kiss your cheek, but I'm afraid I'd hurt you even more."

Charmed, Lexi pulled his head down and bussed his chin instead. "Thank you. For everything."

"No thanks necessary. It's what we do." He winked, adding, "But you're welcome. Don't forget to fill her in on everything," he told his brother. "And don't forget Sunday."

"I won't. I'll walk you out. Be right back," he told her.

Alone now, except for the dog, Lexi fell back against the pillow and sighed. She could live to be two hundred and she'd never forget the sight of Aiden, gun drawn, shooting Margo before she could shoot Brontë.

"Aiden saved both our lives tonight," she told the dog, patting her head.

Most of the hour after Margo was incapacitated had been a blur as paramedics rushed Lexi to the nearest hospital. But she did remember Aiden in the ambulance, his hand never leaving hers, the look of focused concern crossing his brow, the warmth of his fingers enveloping her cold ones.

After hours of face, head, and hip X-rays, blood work, and more poking and prodding by the emergency room doctors than she cared for, again with Aiden standing watch over her the entire time, she was informed no bones were broken, no muscles were torn. A few days of rest would help.

She spoke, briefly, to the police detectives who came into her cubicle, Aiden and Dylan relaying most of the story. Josh had arrived with Rick in tow and added to the tale. The police left her with a promise to visit for follow up after discharge. She'd been medically cleared into Aiden's willing care, told to ice her bruises, given a prescription for pain meds should she need them, and an order to check in with her private physician when she had the chance.

There had been no discussion on where she was going once she left the hospital. Aiden had simply lifted her from the discharge wheelchair into Dylan's jeep and settled her in the back seat next to Brontë. They'd driven directly back to his apartment, arriving after midnight.

Aiden came back into the room with a new ice pack.

"You really do have a ridiculous number of those things," she said.

"Good thing, too." He sat back on the bed and replaced the one he'd recently brought to her.

"The other one hasn't even had a chance to work, yet."

"Humor me. And you'll thank me tomorrow when the swelling is down. Can I get you anything? Something to drink? Eat? The fridge is still packed with

Kandy's food. I can—"

"Stop. Please." She pulled his hands into her. "You don't need to hover, Aiden. Really." She squeezed his hands to underscore it. "I realize I don't look it right now, but I'm fine."

He dragged in a huge amount of air as his gaze drifted across her face. She knew what she looked like since she'd gotten a view of herself in the bathroom when she changed out of her clothes. Battered, bruised, one eye slightly closed due to her swollen cheek. Not exactly a dream come true at the moment.

"I've told you before," he said after clearing his throat, "you are way more than fine, sweetheart. And before you tell me you're not made of glass and won't break"—she clamped her mouth shut because she had been about to—"you've still been through more than anyone should."

"Granted, but it's over now. It *is* over now, isn't it?"

He nodded. "Your part in it, anyway. You'll need to give an official statement about what went down on the boat, tell the police what Margo said."

"She admitted it was Smith who ordered Shel killed. He took care of my sister, personally."

She explained what Margo had related, while Aiden kept holding her hands. When she told him about the woman's plot to extract revenge on Bard, he said, "She's flat out crazy."

"No, she isn't. Not really. Possessive love forms out of low self-esteem and jealousy," she said. "Her father was a powerful, rich man. I tend to think their relationship wasn't the typical father-daughter one. He never remarried after her mother died, and Margo was always by his side, almost like a surrogate."

"Do you think there was something…sexual, between them?"

"I don't know. Maybe. Maybe not. But she grew up surrounded by powerful men, not only her father. Eaon Cassidy, for one. I'm going to assume she's drawn to a certain type. Rich, powerful, willing to take chances in business."

"Richard Deveroux to a T."

"He has the same type of personality her father did. Margo had a strong possessive hold on Crispen and, apparently, her husband. She wasn't going to allow anyone to take Richard away from her."

"Like I said, she's flat out crazy."

One corner of her mouth tipped up. "We can debate the point, or just agree to disagree on it. Regardless, her jealousy was a contributing factor in all of this. Now…" She shifted and realigned the cold pack over her hip. "Tell me what you know and what happened when I was in the emergency room."

"Are you sure you want to hear it all now? We can talk about it in the morning. You should rest."

"I'm going to crash soon, I can feel it. But I want to know what happened first."

"Okay. You deserve that much, I guess. " He took a deep breath, let it out. "Josh told me before we left the hospital that Margo had the bullet removed in surgery. The surgeons don't know the extent of the damage to her arm yet." His eyes went cold. "I almost wish I'd killed her instead of aiming for her arm."

She squeezed his hand again.

"The police issued a bedside arrest, charging her with your kidnapping and attempted murder after they talked to Dylan and Josh. She isn't leaving the hospital any time soon. We laid out what we know about Smith's death. Josh gave a copy of Zoe's flash drive to detectives, so the investigation's in their hands now. We all have to give official statements, the sooner the better. But for now, you're in no danger."

"Did they arrest Bard?"

"No. That's up to the state's attorney general. I wouldn't be surprised, though, if he isn't pulled in for questioning at least for his business dealings, someday soon."

"And what about the men who were helping Margo? The ones who knocked me out? Were they Cassidy's men?"

"Yes."

"Were they arrested, too?"

"You don't need to be concerned about them—"

"Tell me, Aiden."

He blew out a breath. "That stubborn streak," he mumbled before telling her, "Two of them are dead. The third has been arrested. There was no one else on the boat since it was still docked."

"You and Dylan shot them."

"Lexi—"

"It's okay, Aiden. Really. I know you only did what you had to do to save me."

"Taking a life is never easy, even if it's warranted. It's the reason I don't usually carry a gun." He thrust his chin toward his dog. "Brontë's enough to make most people take heed."

Lexi blew a kiss to the dog. "Shel is okay?"

"Yeah. Dylan's keeping a detail on her for the foreseeable future until Bard is arrested. He isn't taking any chances. Her testimony will help with the prostitution enterprise indictment, so she needs to stay in the shadows for now because we don't know what kind of reach Bard has. The Cassidy guys were Margo's muscle, not his."

"That's good. Shel deserves a second chance."

He sighed again. "Lexi." Moisture turned his lashes to spikes.

The well of emotion in his voice had her insides warming.

"When I saw you with a gun pointed at your head, my heart stopped. Just stopped, dead. The thought I could lose you…" He lowered his gaze to their joined hands, shook his head as his voice broke.

"But I'm alive because of you. You saved me, Aiden. You saved your lovely girl, too. I don't know how I can ever, ever repay you for that."

"By never saying that again." He shifted so he sat back against the headboard with her and wound his arm around her shoulders. After kissing her temple, he cuddled her closer until her head rested on his shoulder. "You don't ever need to thank me or repay me or any other term you can come up with, Lexi. I told you, I wanted to help you get the answers you needed about your sister. The choice was mine to make."

"And now I have them. Thanks to you and your brothers."

"And your persistence."

"Maybe." She shook her head.

"What's wrong?" His fingers gently rubbing up and down her upper arm sent a shiver of desire tripping down her spine.

Ignoring it, she answered, "I thought I'd

feel...relieved, somehow, knowing my instincts were correct about Zoe. But all I feel is a deep well of sadness."

"I think that's understandable, given the circumstances."

"I know you're right, I do."

"To quote you, why do I feel there's a but in that sentence?"

She shifted so she could face him. There was so much she wanted to say to him, confide to him. The need to be honest warred with the need to protect her heart. "I guess I'm feeling sorry for myself, and it's an unusual experience for me."

"Go on."

"For the first time in my life, I'm truly alone. No parents. No relatives. My sister is gone. I'm all alone now." She lifted one shoulder and rolled her eyes closed. "And I can hear how disgustingly pitiful I sound."

"Okay, first of all? You're the furthest thing from pitiful a person can be. The word has no context in regards to you. Second, you're not alone."

"Technically, I am—"

"No. You're not. You've got me." He grinned down at her. "And Brontë." The dog lifted her head from Lexi's thigh and smiled.

"I-I do?"

"You know you do."

Dear God, she wanted to believe him. All the dreams she'd had, now that all the madness was behind them, that he'd still want to be with her, ran though her head. She'd told herself not to get her hopes up, though, as every reason why he wouldn't want to continue seeing her devoured her thoughts.

His brows pulled together, his head cocking to one side. "Or maybe you don't."

"Aiden." She stopped as emotion stole her words. Pulling her thoughts together she said, "You told me there were no expectations here."

"I meant there was no quid pro quo for helping you. I thought you realized that."

She stared down at the comforter.

"Alexis Buckley." She lifted her gaze back up to his. "You are truly the smartest person in any room you occupy, but you have one glaring blind spot in that remarkable brain of yours. You don't know your own worth."

Heat doused her neck and face.

"You are the most amazing, alluring, desirable woman I have ever known. You were a puzzle I wanted to solve when I spotted you across a crowded bar, just to pass the time. Then when we met, I wanted to know everything there was to know about you. You intrigued me, charmed me, and made me so hot I couldn't believe flames weren't shooting out of my ass."

A small laugh had her wincing. "Don't. It hurts to laugh."

"I'm sure if I did some research I could come up with a ream of statistics or a few studies detailing the mechanics of love at first sight. But I don't need the research to back up what I know in my heart and head and every other part of me that matters."

Shifting again, he finger-swiped her jaw, then lazily trailed down the column of her throat.

Her flesh singed everywhere he touched.

"I love you, Lexi. All of you. From that first

moment in the bar to the first time I spotted you do that nervous tic with your ear. I love your brain, your trivia-speak. I love how you love my dog."

Brontë barked.

When she looked back at him, the truth of his words was evident in his eyes. Her heart quite simply grew in her chest.

Taking her hands back in his, he kissed the backs of them. Done, he lifted them to his heart. "But most of all I love how you make me feel, the man I am when I'm around you. I thought I was happy before I met you. I had my family, Brontë. Female companionship when I wanted it."

He chuckled when she pursed her lips and attempted to lift her swollen left eyebrow.

"But I realized the first time I had you in my arms nothing had ever made me as happy as having you right there and in my life." He kissed her hands again. "Now…" He pulled her into the crook of his arm again and kissed her forehead. "You've been uncharacteristically quiet for the past few minutes, which usually means you're not nervous. True?"

She nodded.

"That gives me a lot of hope you believe everything I've said and aren't calling up facts and studies to prove I can't possibly be in love with you after so short a time, or something equally as wrong. Also, true?"

Another nod, this one accompanied by a tiny smile.

Lexi pushed on his shoulders and shifted when he leaned back against the bedpost. Tossing her leg over his lap, she straddled him, only vaguely aware of the pain twinge on her right side. Hands braced on his chest, the steady, smooth, strong beat of his heart beating against her hands, she leaned in and kissed him. Brontë huffed, barked once, then seconds later the sound of her paws hitting the carpet notified them she was giving them some privacy.

As it had the very first time she'd pressed her lips against his, she felt utter warmth engulf her from head to toes, accompanied by a deep and rich sense of *rightness.*

When she pulled back, she said, "Researchers in the Netherlands did a study to try and prove or disprove the love-at-first-sight reaction and found that it's based more on an emotional connection than a chemical one, which is what had previously been believed."

His devilish grin had her thighs contracting.

"They added the phenomenon isn't always mutual when it occurs, and that for some reason, men experience it more often than woman do."

His head tilted to one side while his eyes narrowed and his lips flattened.

"I'm thinking of writing to the researchers of the study to tell them those last two points are based on faulty data."

When her meaning got through, his face cleared and that smile she knew she couldn't live without seeing every day reappeared.

"I love you, too, Aiden. So much it takes my breath away. To know you feel the same way is…" She lowered her eyes, squeezed them shut against the tears threatening, and shook her head. "No man ever has before."

His fingers gently lifted her chin. "Look at me, sweetheart."

Eyes open, her tears made good on their threat and cascaded down her cheeks. Aiden swiped at them when they hit her chin. "I know your life is upside down right now with all that's happened. Your apartment still needs to be seen to, plus your position at the college is in limbo for a bit, but I want you to stay here with me. I know I didn't ask when you were discharged, just brought you straight here, but I need to know what you want, Lexi. I'll honor anything you say. I can bring you back to your space in the morning if it's that. Or you can stay here indefinitely. Hopefully more than indefinitely. But the choice is yours. To plead my own case, though, there are a few perks involved with hunkering down here you should consider."

The seriousness in his tone shot an image of him in her mind that involved a blackboard with him in front of it, prepared to give a lecture, wearing his glasses….and nothing else.

She swallowed, hard, and said, "Such as?"

"Well"—his hands wound around her waist and shifted her closer to him—"breakfast in bed for one. With food courtesy of world-renowned chef-lebrity Kandy Laine. You won't get that back at your place."

"True. Go on."

"Twenty-four-hour nursing care courtesy of yours truly, at your beck and call."

"Tempting, to be sure."

"Seeing Brontë all day long."

"Certainly one of the best perks."

"Plus…"

"Plus?"

"Plus…this."

If she'd had any doubts about what she wanted for

the foreseeable future before his lips found hers, they were eviscerated.

To know this man loved her, wanted her in his life, to care for her and share his life with her, took away all her nerves, all her self-doubts, all her worries.

"Is that a yes, then, to staying?" he asked as his lips skimmed across her jaw.

She pulled his earlobe between her teeth and murmured, "Remember those seven thousand languages spoken every day across the globe?"

He captured her chin in his hands, then his smiling lips with hers.

It didn't take much for them both to get carried away with the kiss. When she flattened herself against him, then unconsciously winced, Aiden pulled back.

"*Jesus*. I'm sorry. Let's just get some sleep. We both need to recharge, and I don't want to do anything to hurt you."

"Saying I'm fine seems redundant," she said, sliding off his lap, "but you're right. I think we both need some sleep."

With the light shut and the bed to themselves, Aiden spooned her against him, keeping his had around her waist.

"I love you," he whispered as she drifted off.

****

One month later…

"Are you sure you're gonna be able to stand being around all this excess testosterone every day?" Dylan asked as Lexi unpacked books from a box.

"Problems associated with surplus testosterone levels include low sperm count, testicular shrinkage, impotence, and an increase in the risk of cardiac issues and prostate enlargement," she said, deadpan.

Four barks of male laughter shot back at her, although Dylan winced a bit.

"I think she's gonna be just fine," Josh said, patting his brother on the back. "Come on. We've got a new case for you, and I need to get you up to speed. Lexi." He nodded at her. "Find me once you're all moved in, and we'll talk." He tugged his brother from the room. "I've got a few ideas."

"Doc." Rick bent and bussed her healed cheek. As she had before, when he smiled, the only word she could think of was devastating. "Your presence certainly elevates the class level around here. It's gonna be a pleasure working with you. And before I forget, Abby wants the both of you to come for dinner Friday night. She'll be in touch with the details."

She thanked him. With a nod for Aiden, he exited the office as his other brothers had, closing the door behind him.

Aiden grabbed her hand, the smile she now knew for certain she couldn't live without seeing every day gracing his chiseled face, and tugged her into a hug.

"I thought we were going to keep it professional at work," she said with a crooked eyebrow lift as she slipped her hands around his waist.

"The only way I'm going to be able to keep my hands off you is if I never come in here," he said, "or if you lock your door. Is that everything?" He thrust his chin toward the empty boxes littering her new office.

"Yes. I can't believe how much bigger this office is than my one at the college. Plus, the view is so different." She pulled out of his arms and walked to the wall-wide windows overlooking the Battery. "I can see the Statue of Liberty from here."

When the provost called, asking to speak privately to her the day before she was due back to work, she wasn't certain what he was going to meet her with. Would she even have a job to come back to? Be censured? He'd taken one look at her still bruised, but healing face, and in no uncertain terms informed her she was being placed on professional probation for unsanctioned used of vacation time over the amount she was granted as an employee of the college. He made a nasty remark about her personal life and cavorting with criminals and flat out stated she was bringing unwanted negative attention to the college. Not to mention setting a horrible example as a department leader to the student body.

She hadn't contested one statement he'd made, knowing anything she did say in her defense would fall on deaf and prejudicial ears. It took her less than one minute to decide to quit. She bid him goodbye, then went back to her office and typed up a resignation letter, effective immediately, and emailed it to him and college president.

Before she could grab her purse to head back to Aiden's apartment, Dr. Howard called, stated his surprise and displeasure at her resignation, and demanded to know why she was taking such an uncharacteristic step with her career.

He'd be receiving an official, typed letter within the week, she informed him, detailing everything. She neglected to mention she was going to send copies to all the department chairs and alumni leaders and maybe even a lawyer.

With that she hung up, went home to Aiden, and

cried for an hour.

Josh and Kandy's arrival that night with their two adorable children in tow had done wonders to elevate her mood. Despite being tongue-tied when Kandy had pulled her in for a full body hug, her Amazonian height dwarfing Lexi, the evening had been wonderful. And the job offer from Josh had been a complete surprise.

When they'd left, Aiden admitted he'd known it was coming, adding that his brother recognized talent when he saw it.

Her new job coincided with her giving up her old apartment and moving in with Aiden when he asked her to make it a permanent situation.

"The view's pretty fantastic from where I'm standing, too."

When she glanced over her shoulder, she found him staring at her ass.

"We've got an appointment with the district attorney in an hour," Aiden said. "You up for this?"

"I am. He's got my deposition, so this is a mere formality just to ensure everything we testified to at Margo's and Bard's grand jury hearings is up to date." She dragged in a huge breath and let it out slowly. At the concern shooting across his face, she said, "I'm fine, Aiden."

With that cocky grin spreading slowly across his face as he crossed to her, he said, "Babe, how many times have I told ya you are way more than fine?" He slid his hands around her waist again, and she cuddled in close.

Never in her wildest fantasies did she ever dream she'd feel this way. To be so loved and so in love with a wonderful man who truly did adore her was something she'd never thought she'd have. For the umpteenth time in the past month, she said a silent prayer of thanks to Zoe. If not for her, she would never have met Aiden. Lexi liked to think her sister was looking down on them, pleased that something so good had come from the horrible Deveroux-Smith-Bard mess.

"Listen," Aiden said. "I've got an idea on what Josh wants to talk to you about, so I'd like to give you a head's-up now. It's okay if you tell him no."

"Okay, well I can't tell him anything unless I know what it is, Aiden."

When he didn't elaborate after several seconds, she pulled back to find his brows furrowed and a sheepish expression crossing his face.

"What?" she asked.

"We've never had a woman work alongside us before," he began, then swallowed. "It raises certain possibilities."

"Possibilities? Like what?"

"Some of the jobs we've been hired to do, like the one Dylan's learning about right now in Josh's office, involve going undercover. Using aliases. Misleading people about who we are."

"Okay. What's that got to do with me?"

"Well, I…I told him about…." He gnawed on a corner of his mouth.

"Oh, for pity's sake, just say it."

His shoulders lifted to his ears when he dragged in a huge breath. "I told him about seeing you in action. In the bar. With Smith."

"You told…" She shook her head. She mustn't have heard him correctly. "You told him I pretended to be something I'm not in order to gather information from Smith?"

His head bobbed up and down. "And about how good an actress you were and the thing with the sleight of hand. Josh thinks it's an advantage to not only utilize your exceptional research skills, but he thinks you may make a good operative, too, and he wants to discuss the possibility with you. Feel you out on it."

"Operative, meaning…?"

"Undercover role playing."

She blinked. Several times.

Licked her lips. Then did it again.

"If you don't want to, it's cool. Josh will understand. Not everyone is comfortable deceiving people. Even if it's for a good reason."

She continued to stare up at him, silent.

That concern in his eyes grew deeper. "Sweetheart? Talk to me. What are you thinking?"

She batted her eyelashes at him and pulled her mouth into a smile she knew could knock him to his knees. It had the effect she wanted because Aiden hissed in a breath.

With her bottom lip tucked between her teeth, she looked up at him from under her lashes, rewarded for her efforts when she saw him swallow and lick his own lips.

"I'm wondering…" She fingered a button on his shirt, then lifted up on her toes to buss his lips. "Where I put that red wig."

Aiden's laugh was loud enough she wouldn't be surprised if it echoed down the hallway of the office.

Dear Reader~

Thank you so much for reading Aiden and Lexi's story. These two people needed to be brought together, and it was a joy for me to give them a platform to find their HEA.

A few insights into one of my favorite characters in the book, Brontë.

I began writing this book at the beginning of 2020, just a few weeks before Covid became a thing. In September of 2020, my husband and I adopted an eight-week-old female chocolate Lab we lovingly named Maple Leaf. Hey, she's a New England girl so she needed a New Englandy name!

Maple proved very smart very quickly, and I began training her before she reached nine weeks with simple commands. I also assigned hand signals to those commands to reinforce the word. The reason I did this is a little convoluted, so bear with me.

I have a condition called PRESBYPHONIA, which, in the simplest form, means I have aging vocal cords. In my case, though, my laryngologist says I have the vocal cords of a one-hundred-year-old woman who smoked for ninety years! I am not close to that age (thankfully) nor have I ever smoked a cigarette, but he predicts that in four to five years, I may be totally aphonic—without a voice.

It made no sense to train Maple in voice commands if I wasn't going to have a voice to command her, so I devised the hand signals. Eighty-five percent of the time now when I give her a command, it is nonverbally, and she responds. At just five and a half months (I'm writing this in January 2021), she already has an extensive vocabulary for words and signs.

When I devised Brontë as a companion for Aiden, I already knew she was going to be his medical support dog, but I wanted to make their relationship even closer, so I gave him my hand signals, reasoning that if the migraines ever got so bad he couldn't speak through the pain, he could at least have a form of communication with the dog.

As for Lexi's trivia-speak, giving her impulse control issues with regards to her eidetic memory was a quirky thing to do and I think made her behavior, insecurity, and thoughts more realistic.

I hope you enjoyed the book and if you did, A PRIDE OF BROTHERS: RICK (Book 1) is out now, with Dylan's story coming soon.

Happy reading!

~ Peg

A word about the author…

Peggy Jaeger writes about strong women, the families who support them, and the men who can't live without them. When she isn't writing, you can find her cooking or reading. She loves to hear from readers on her website

PeggyJaeger.com

and on her Facebook page

https://www.facebook.com/pages/Peggy-Jaeger-Author/825914814095072?ref=bookmarks

Thank you for purchasing
this publication of The Wild Rose Press, Inc.

For questions or more information
contact us at
info@thewildrosepress.com.

The Wild Rose Press, Inc.
www.thewildrosepress.com